Shadows Bane

(Book 2 of the Ruadhán Sidhe Novels)

By Aiki Flinthart

2018

To all the authors out there – both published and aspiring – don't give up.

Thank you to my husband for his unfailing support and willing services as beta-reader. Thanks also to everyone who has encouraged and assisted me along this very challenging journey called authorship. Often, it sucks, and only the kindness of friends and strangers keeps you going.

Shadows Bane

Cover artwork by Harper by Design

A Cataloging-in-Publications entry for this title is available from the National Library of Australia.

ISBN-13: 978-0-6482878-2-7 (Trade Paperback)
ISBN-13: 978-0-6482878-1-0 (e-book)
Computing Advantages & Training P/L
PO Box 3388, Darra
QLD 4076, Australia

NOTE: This book is written with AUSTRALIAN SPELLINGS, not USA spellings.

Discover other titles by Aiki Flinthart at:
www.aikiflinthart.com
Including:

The Ruadhan Sidhe Novels (YA Urban Fantasy)
Shadows Wake (#1)
Shadows Bane (#2)
Shadows Fate (#3)

The 80AD series (YA Adventure/Fantasy)
80AD Book 1: *The Jewel of Asgard*
80AD Book 2: *The Hammer of Thor*
80AD Book 3: *The Tekhen of Anuket*
80AD Book 4: *The Sudarshana*
80AD Book 5: *The Yu Dragon*

The Kalima Chronicles (YA Adventure/Fantasy)
IRON (#1)
FIRE (#2)
STEEL (#3)

Sold! (Contemporary Romance/Adventure)

Short Story Anthologies
Return
Like a Woman

Shadows Bane

Book 2 of the Ruadhán Sidhe Novels

Aiki Flinthart 2018

ONE

Whatever happens, Rowan, keep a lid on it. We're here to observe, only.

Logan's terse instruction whispered in my head as we commando-crawled our way to the tree line.

Will you take your own advice? I returned irony, which he ignored. I needed to remember to close the "window" in my mental shields that let him talk to me whenever he felt like it. It had been comforting, at first. Now it felt more like I had a constant watchdog, ready to put a leash on the minute I even looked like losing control...ah, maybe he had a point.

I settled onto my stomach behind a large eucalyptus tree and eased one eye around the smooth silvery trunk. Beneath me, dead leaves and curls of long-dried bark crackled and poked through the thin cotton of my black shirt. Wet leaves stuck to my elbows. The pungent smell of damp earth and crushed leaves soothed my tight-wound senses. A night bird hooted in the distance. To the north, the city's vast glow lit the sky a dirty orange, dimming the stars and lending a dramatic backdrop to the buildings huddled before us.

From where we lay, only three of the five concrete monoliths making up the MJE Laboratory facility were visible. We needed to know what was in the areas we couldn't see. Almost-automatically, I extended filaments of my mind into the *sianfath*. The taste of ozone tingled in my mouth and my connection to the *sianfath* prickled under my skin like a thousand tiny needles. I tested the immediate area. Lots of eucalypts, a few possums watching us, sleeping birds, a myriad of lizards, snakes, tiny insects and spiders. The usual gamut of Australian scary, bitey things. Nothing else. No people, except myself and Logan.

Pain in my head flared a warning and I pulled back. Whatever else happened, I needed to find a way to get my father's corrupted memories out of my brain. What was the point of having powers if using them could release a monster intent on destroying every human on the Earth?

I caught Logan's eye and slid a thought into his mind.

There's no-one close by. I pointed at the fenced compound twenty metres away, past open ground stripped of cover. *The closest human is that guard doing the perimeter run. I'd rather not push myself out further, though. I'm risking a major brain-fry as it is. Can you check?*

Logan's eyes unfocussed and I left him to it, watching instead for physical threats. The guard continued his slow stroll around the compound. He yawned and adjusted the belt-holster of his gun. The tap-tap of his boots on concrete slapped back a fraction later off the concrete walls around him. Car headlights swept past, illuminating him for a second. He froze, gripping his weapon, until the lights vanished. The swish of tyres on wet road, and burr of the engine dwindled away along the dark street.

An ant bit my arm. I swore, pressing at the sharp burn. That *stung.* Dammit, being half-sidhe and connecting to the *sianfath* was supposed to put me at one with the natural world. Things weren't supposed to bite me, were they? I crushed the brittle exoskeleton, regretting the action as its tiny life faded.

Logan tapped me and pointed at a pair of guards and their dogs, dawdling around one corner of the buildings. They acknowledged the solitary guard, but didn't speak. Apart from the guards, a three-metre mesh fence, topped with rolls of barbed wire, stood between us and the buildings. Security lights and cameras covered every square metre of space between the treeline and the buildings inside the fence. How much of the state electricity grid went into lighting the compound like a prison yard? Clearly Michael Eisen wasn't concerned with his carbon footprint.

If there was a way to get in unobserved, I couldn't see it.

But we needed to get in. Maybe not right now, but soon. In one of those buildings, we believed, my mother was held hostage by Michael Eisen, CEO of MJE Enterprises. No, not hostage, for that implied the possibility of a negotiated release, and communication with someone for that negotiation. As far as Eisen was concerned, I was dead, so he had no one to negotiate with. Anna was his prisoner. To do with as he pleased.

I shuddered, imagining the worst. And I already had a fair idea of what the worst might be.

Logan shot me a warning glare. I sucked a slow breath and calmed my racing heart. I needed to be logical; to come up with some new angle. But I'd been over this a thousand times in the last two weeks. There was no conceivable reason why Michael Eisen should keep Anna this long. He wanted information about the *ocair* from her, but she had no idea what an *ocair* was. Beyond knowing it translated to 'key' in the sidhe language, I had no idea either. Key to what? Eisen wanted it, but why?

Anna wasn't trained to resist torture so why was he keeping her alive – assuming she was still alive – here in his Brisbane lab facility? Not being sidhe, or even half-sidhe like me, she wasn't any use to his genetics research. Could he have real feelings for her? Was it possible their liaison in Cairns hadn't been just a pretence to lure me out of hiding?

There were far more questions than answers. They only served to wind up my fears of losing her, and increase the risk of me ruining the whole exercise. I forced my heart to slow and the dark-chaos in the back of my mind to settle.

Right now, we were scoping out the MJE facility with a view to getting into it. It had taken us two weeks to be sure my mother was still in Brisbane. I could wait a few more minutes so Logan could find out where she was being held and how many people worked here at night.

Finding those out was Logan's job, too. The risk to me – to everyone else – was too great if I tried. I shifted restlessly, resenting the need for anyone else, even Logan. But him I trusted – to a limited extent. Myself, I didn't.

If I lost control, things could end catastrophically.

A deep furrow creased Logan's brow. His dark-rimmed, grey eyes skimmed the compound as he used telepathy to search beyond the visible, into the building interiors. His lean form tensed, fingers whitening where they pressed against the ground. Dark leather strained across his broad shoulders.

I followed his line of sight.

Five figures emerged from a steel door, set into the closest building's blank concrete south wall. Two people were dressed in black, with helmets and night-vision goggles. They carried automatic rifles of some sort. I didn't know enough about guns to be able to tell what kind from a distance. Weren't they illegal in Australia?

A third also wore black, but sans helmet, goggles and weapon. He carried himself relaxed and loose, his arms easy by his sides, dark hair tied back into a low, short ponytail. His face was in shadow as he exchanged words with the guards. He reached behind his waist and metal gleamed dully in his hand. A gun or a knife? Hard to tell.

The final two wore dark business suits, even though the evening air was thick with heat and humidity. The taller had his back to us, his dark head and wide shoulders almost obscuring the last man – who had cropped blond hair and emphatic hand movements. The blond I recognised, even from afar: Michael Eisen.

Adrenalin flashed fire into my blood. I placed my palms flat on the leaf-littered ground. Logan's fingers snapped like steel bands around my upper arm. Flesh pressed against bone as he restrained me.

Don't be stupid, Rowan. There's nothing we can do right now.

I twisted free and glared at him. He was right, though. Physically, I probably couldn't do anything but get myself captured or killed. That wouldn't help Anna.

There was one thing I could do, though: I could end this, here and now. I could drain Eisen's life as I had his men in Cairns. He deserved it even more. There was no reason why I should play the nice guy. Anna always said people were defined by their worst moments. I preferred not to take lives, but killing Eisen would not be my worst moment. It would be my best.

I focussed my newly-acquired psychic skills on the group.

In the depths of my mind, the caged beast rattled its chains. Shadows stirred, hungry. A flash of pain warned me the psychic block holding them back was being tested. I steadied myself, shoving the darkness deep down. I had to control it. But could I, and still use this particular skill?

Gritting my teeth, I ignored both pain and Logan's attempts to get my attention. I reached through the *sianfath,* the connection my people had with all living things, searching for Michael's unique energy signature. The taste of ozone strengthened in my mouth.

There: his scent. His aura was a clean, orange-red non-colour. He tasted…angry; frustrated. Why? No, it didn't matter. A few seconds and he would be dead and all this would be over. Pain flared higher. I pushed through it. Even if this killed me, it would be worth it to rid the world of him and make Anna and Logan safe.

I had him; tasted the sour-sweetness of his life-energy, revelled in his vulnerability. He was defenceless; his life was mine.

TWO

Rowan! What the hell are you doing?
   Back off, Logan. I've got this.
   But one of those men is—

Something intangible slapped at my thoughts, sending me reeling. Hard and uncompromising it sliced at me. Forced me back, behind the safety of my shields. I hid, gasping as the metaphoric sword clanged against the imagined stone walls of my personal mental castle. The stone shuddered under the onslaught.

Logan spoke my name in question. I couldn't answer, couldn't speak through the effort of protecting myself from the assault. I'd never experienced this sort of psychic attack. I had no defences barring the shield I'd recently learned to create. It probably had weaknesses.

I had weaknesses. Stupid impulsiveness was one of them.

At a barked word from the pony-tailed guy, the guards raised their guns in our direction. His head snapped towards us but the hard overhead spotlights highlighted only a long, high-cheekboned face with deep-shadowed eyes; no details. Beside him, the taller, darkhaired man stiffened but didn't turn. He rubbed at the back of his skull then gripped Michael Eisen's shoulder. Together, the two vanished inside the building.

Pony-tail lifted what looked like a radio handset to his mouth. Lights flared, knife-sharp after the comfort of night. A siren wailed. The dogs barked in the distance.

Taking five long strides, pony-tail leapt at the fence and flung himself over, cat-like. He landed softly on the bare earth, rolled and straightened. He stared directly at our hiding place. The other guards raced to a gate nearby. They fumbled with the chain-lock, yelling instructions to each other.

Logan swore. 'Come *on, Rowan!*' He crawled back, away from the ridge, into darkness.

Mesmerised, I studied the man below. He seemed…familiar. He couldn't possibly see me, hidden in the tree's shadow. Could he?

Logan's fingers gripped my ankle, breaking the spell. I squirmed back.

We ran, our feet picking the way unerringly through the forest. Each tree and blade of grass had its own, pale greenish aura of non-light. The path was as clear as daylight, though it would have been dark to a pure human.

From behind came the blundering feet and hoarse calls of guards searching the copse for us. A silenced bullet pierced the thick air and exploded a shower of wood slivers from a tree trunk nearby. Close enough that I ducked. Far enough away to show they weren't sure where we were.

Along with the louder footfalls came the swift, sure steps of someone much more certain. Headed precisely in our direction. I increased speed, pushing to keep pace with Logan. He flew effortlessly through the night ahead of me. Silent, graceful, all but invisible.

A fallen branch caught at my foot. I stumbled, staggered and recovered. Not fast enough. Something slammed into my back and sent me sprawling onto the leaf-strewn ground. I landed hard, forearms in a triangle beneath my chest to catch my weight.

Coughing, I resisted the instinctive, panicky urge to push onto all fours. Instead, I twisted onto my back and lifted my arms to guard my face. A body landed on me, between my raised knees. I clamped them around his ribs and hooked my ankles together, trying to hold him off. Long fingers snaked through my defences, aiming for my throat. His face was in darkness, shadowed by black hair that escaped the ponytail.

I snatched at his arm, yanking it across my chest. His groping other hand I shoved between his body and my knee. One leg went onto his shoulder. He grunted, trying to bring his arm back up from between my legs. I threw my other leg over his neck and hooked a foot around my calf. Pushing onto my shoulders locked on the stranglehold. His movements became more desperate. His nails clawed at my shoulder, tearing at the cotton shirt and skin beneath.

A shout rang out nearby.

He tried to break free. I squeezed tighter, choking. He lifted his free hand. It held a gun now. The muzzle pointed into my thigh.

Releasing him, I kicked. My booted heel connected with his temple and he slumped face-down to the ground, moving feebly. He dropped the gun and it vanished in a pile of leaf-litter.

Footsteps whispered through the leaves.

Blood pounded in my ears. The damp, warm night air held no oxygen as I sucked it into starved lungs. My torn shirt fluttered, my shoulder bare and scratched.

Someone grabbed my wrist and hauled me upright. I struck out with an elbow, only to have it deflected and pinned. Logan released me and checked my attacker. He frowned and made an abortive move towards him.

More footfalls and heavy breathing warned of others approaching. A shot zipped past my shoulder. Too close that time. With a noise of frustration, Logan jerked his thumb at the road and sprinted away. By the time I reached where we'd parked his bike, he was already astride and helmeted. Thrusting a helmet at me, he barely waited for me to throw a leg over the bike before revving the engine and taking off. With one arm around his waist, I checked for pursuit.

My attacker emerged from the shadowed stand of trees and paused. He rubbed at his temple and jaw. His mind – it must be his – brushed mine again. Cold and many-layered but with the lightest of feather-touches, like a kiss. He sent me an ironic salute as we sped away. He wasn't even breathing hard.

'What the *hell* were you thinking?' Logan threw his jacket onto the table and rounded on me. Fury sharpened the line of his jaw. He pointed south, in the direction of the MJE labs. 'We were there for *your* mother and you jumped in like an impatient ten-year-old!' He paced the room's length and back again. 'You almost got us both killed. And now they know someone's watching.'

I glared at him, holding the ripped shirt onto my shoulder. 'I saw an opportunity and I tried to take it. If I'd been able to drain Eisen this whole thing would be over. You'd be patting me on the back like a hero, not yelling at me like I'm an idiot.'

'No,' he said more calmly. He placed his palms on the table and leaned towards me. 'Remember? You said you wouldn't kill anyone again. You're not a killer.' He grimaced. 'I admit killing has its place in the scheme of protecting our people. But I was raised to be a Hunter. You weren't.'

Pursing my lips, I looked away. 'I am, Logan. I lost it in Cairns…those men…'

He waved my objection aside. 'That wasn't you. That was Calain, using you. You have to stop blaming yourself.' Walking around the table, he reached a hand towards me. I retreated. He sighed. 'Not your fault. Don't deliberately turn into exactly what you're afraid of. You're not a monster.'

I hid my face, ashamed of the tears stinging my eyelids. The memory of the power flooding through my mind and body was both terrifying and exhilarating. The thought of letting it free again both tempting and frightening. Becoming a monster wasn't my only fear.

If I let go, I could be invincible and that scared me just as much.

A door opened and Maeve Freyson glided into the kitchen, squinting in the light. Even tousled by sleep and with her rich dark-brown hair plaited over one shoulder, her unearthly, sharp-boned, angular beauty gave me pause. She blinked black-rimmed grey eyes, so like Logan's and even my own, and yawned delicately.

'Hush, you two. You'll awaken Jennifer.' She glanced at her daughter's bedroom door and sank on to one of the uncomfortable steel and timber chairs around the scarred wooden table. 'She's having nightmares again. She just got back to sleep.' Pulling out another chair for me she frowned at us. 'What happened?'

Logan's gaze faded into the abstract as he brought his aunt up to date telepathically. She paled. I debated whether to sit or go straight to bed. If I stayed she would feel the need to lecture me as well. She might be two hundred and eighty, but she wasn't my mother. I was answerable to no-one and responsible for no-one except myself. I liked it that way and I was tired of being told what to do, especially when her good intentions weren't focussed on me. I wasn't family, like Jennifer and Logan. They came first. My presence jeopardised all of them and both of us knew it.

She sent me a frowning look. I folded my arms.

If I had somewhere else to go, and someone else to help me, I'd leave.

I didn't. The only person who meant anything to me was my mother, and to get her back I needed Maeve's help. I swallowed my resentment, though it continued to burn in my stomach.

'So, you found Anna.' Maeve switched back to Logan, possibly sensing my disgruntlement.

He nodded.

I pinned him with another glare. 'You didn't tell me!'

'There wasn't time. Eisen's watchdogs were after us because of your little stunt. All I could tell is that she's alive and in Building Three.' He sent me a sardonic look. 'Though who knows for how long. If they think we're a threat, they'll probably move her.'

I brushed that aside, unwilling to even consider it. 'Was she alright? Could you tell?'

Logan softened. 'I only felt her for a second. She was asleep and not in pain.' He paused. 'And someone's built a shield around her thoughts.'

'What?' Maeve straightened. 'Who? How?'

Logan shook his head. 'I don't know who. It feels...old; well-entrenched. I can't describe it. Maybe Rowan's father did it when he was alive and they were together. Maybe Calain was protecting her. Like he did with Rowan.'

Maeve fiddled with her braid. 'I suppose that makes sense. I never thought to check her mind when we were in Cairns.'

The knowledge my mother still lived seeped past the layer of shock and adrenalin and into my heart. She was my only family and my best friend. Relief diluted the anger and fear that had driven me the last fourteen days. I sank into the chair as my legs gave way and a sob escaped my tight chest. Unbidden, the tears I'd held in since her kidnapping forced their way out. I sniffed and swore, scrubbing the salt off my skin with a dirt-smeared palm.

Logan groaned and dropped into a chair beside me. 'I'm sorry. Sometimes I forget you're only eighteen, and how new all this is to you. It'll be ok. We'll get her back.' He touched the bare, scratched skin on my shoulder. 'You alright? Are you hurt?'

As much as I wanted to believe and to lean on him, I couldn't. I pushed him away, avoiding the flash of hurt in him.

'I'm fine.' I stood and put distance between us. Leaning on the wall I stared out into the humid evening and twisted a curl of my short, auburn hair. I'd give a lot for things to be different.

He stayed where he was. 'Good.' His tone held a hint of regret. 'But we may have a new problem.'

Maeve cleared her throat. 'What?'

I kept my face averted as weeks of frustration and fear coursed down my cheeks and cooled in the damp evening breeze.

'The man who chased us tonight.' Logan paused. 'He was a Daoine Aes sidhe. One of the Fae. One of us.'

THREE

There was someone else there, too, Maeve. A second sidhe, I think. Older, stronger, his mind so well-guarded he was invisible. It was only because I sensed four people but saw five that I knew he was there at all.

<Who?>

No goddamned idea but I don't want to alarm Rowan any more than she already is by mentioning him.

<Yes...you must get her under control, Logan, or she'll kill us all.>

She's stronger than you think.

<That's what I'm worried about.>

'But why?' Maeve stroked the length of her plait where it fell across her breast. 'Why would any of our people assist Michael Eisen? He's Mors Ferrum. The Iron Death's sole purpose for the last thousand years or more has been to find and destroy the sidhe. Why would any of us help them? It makes no sense.'

I wiped my cheeks on the grubby hem of my shirt, poured a glass of cold water from the jug in the fridge and returned to the table. The airconditioner in the old house rattled as it struggled to suck heat and moisture from the summer night. Outside a possum hissed and growled, scrabbling across the tiled roof with a rattle of claws. We all stopped, then relaxed in recognition of the sound.

'I don't know,' I said, leaning my aching forehead against the cold glass, 'but Logan's right. He's young. Or young-looking at least. I suppose he could be any age. I never got a good view of his face, but I did get that sense of familiarity you said is a good indication of meeting a sidhe.' I prodded the sticky scratches on my shoulder. 'He's also really fast and strong. Stronger than Logan. He caught me running flat out, and almost broke out of a leg-choke.'

Maeve's expression shifted to thoughtful. 'Then he's probably full blood. And psychically?'

Logan gazed off into middle distance. 'A strange mind with an odd layering and duality to it. Hidden behind a smooth dome-shield. Calculating and unemotional. Familiar. But maybe only because he's part of the *sianfath* and all the minds linked to it feel somewhat familiar. Although... No, on balance, I'd have to say not a mind I'd ever felt before, so no-one I've met. Well shielded, well trained. And a technician, I'd say.' Maeve raised her brows and he continued. 'Someone's shielded every mind in that compound. Not unbreakably, but enough to stop me reading more than their presence. Including Michael Eisen's.' He glanced at me. 'And his son, Paul's.'

'Paul's there?' My stomach lurched. If Paul was here he must be part of it. He must have flown on the same plane as my drugged, unconscious mother. How could he have ignored that? Or be oblivious to her being held prisoner. Did he think me dead as well?

I'd trusted and liked him. I'd kissed him, for God's sake. Had he been playing me the whole time? Had he been complicit in the attempt on my life and the lives of Logan's family in Cairns? Certain phrases he'd said and the way he'd said them replayed and I almost groaned aloud. He must have been. I'd been too stupid and desperate for acceptance to see it.

When would I learn? People sucked. Every single time I trusted someone it came back to bite me. Even Logan and Maeve. Trusting them had almost got us all killed, and had resulted in my mother's abduction. Actually, that had been my own fault. I'd walked into it. They'd just let me.

'Rowan?' Logan touched my wrist.

I snatched it away out of habit, then muttered an apology. I wasn't yet used to being able to block the precognitive visions that came with a touch of my hand on skin.

'We don't know for sure if Paul was involved,' he said. 'His aura…there's something not right. It feels wrong, like he's not well or…I'm not sure.' He grimaced. 'But, in Cairns, his surface thoughts were nothing incriminating. Now he's shielded as well, so there's no way of knowing.'

'You *read* his mind in Cairns and didn't tell me?' I glared at him. '*That's* how you knew he'd kissed me. And how you knew where I was.' I switched my scorn to Maeve, grateful to have a reason to vent my anger. 'You people have no concept of privacy, do you?'

'We were trying to protect our people, *your* people.' Maeve's voice was low and strained. 'You know that.'

'Ya.' I jerked my chin at her. 'Well, you failed epically and now things are worse. If Michael's got a pet sidhe it's only a short time before he works out a genetic indicator to find every one of you…us. And anyone with any ancestry. He'll start using his network of health clinics to track the sidhe. He wants the powers you have. When he has the DNA, then what are you going to do?'

Logan rose from the table and paced the small dining room. He ran an impatient hand over his short, dark hair, dishevelling it into endearing disorder.

'You're right. But I don't know that finding us is his only goal. He also wants the *ocair* thing he mentioned in Cairns. This "key", whatever that is. But what for?' He addressed Maeve. 'We have to find out and we don't have the resources here to do it. We may have to speak to the Fairchilds.'

Maeve made a gesture as though to fend off an attack. Then she sighed.

'I wish Dante was here.'

When I asked why, she gave a sad half-smile.

'Your half-brother has quite a bit of experience in finding and rescuing abducted sidhe. He also has a gift for welding disparate minds into teams in the *lorntinn* – the unity . But he lives in Italy and we don't have time to waste in getting him here.' She directed a resigned gaze to Logan. 'I suppose, you're right. The Fairchilds are the only ones in this area with the connections we'll need. Logan, you contact them in the morning.' She straightened and stretched her neck. 'I'm sure Rowan will have reservations about this. I'll leave you two to sort it out. I need to get some sleep. Don't stay up too late.' With a nod and a slightly scornful look at me, she swept from the room.

I raised an eyebrow. 'The Fairchilds?'

Logan jerked his head towards the back door. I followed him out to the deck and eased into a creaking slingback canvas chair. It sucked me in like a black hole and, exhausted, I relaxed into it. Logan chose a churchpew-style seat opposite and leaned forward, elbows on his knees.

'They're a family of sidhe, living here in Brisbane. Ian, Erin and Tomas. Father, plus daughter and son in their late twenties. Older than you and I, but young for full-blood sidhe. Their mother died about ten years ago, in Paris. It appeared to be a car accident, but Maeve suspects the Mors Ferrum. The Fairchilds used to live off grid in the mountains on the French-Swiss border. After the accident they changed identities and moved here. They chose the city so Erin and Tom could go to University here. Ian's always complaining about the "press of unaware minds".'

'Sounds like a gem of a guy.' I waited for more, but he said nothing, staring past me, out into the massive backyard. As with every house Maeve Freyson owned – and there were a few – the central feature was a densely-planted back yard. Plants, and the sidhe's connection to them through the *sianfath,* were essential.

Under the *sianfath's* soothing influence, my muscles relaxed and the scratches on my arm healed their own accord. I barely had to think about drawing the tiny amount of energy it needed, now. The ozone taste of the *sianfath's* energy mingled with the scent of orangeblossom and rain. The garden around the building glowed with the *sianfath's* silver-green other-light, and sang with the calls of crickets and frogs. Overhead, between the dark leaves, the dull orange glow of city lights washed pale all but the brightest stars. A measure of peace melted some of my fear.

When it seemed Logan wasn't going to say more, I prompted him. 'The Fairchilds. Why do we need to go to them for help? I'd rather not have anyone else involved.'

Logan sent me an ironic look. 'If you hadn't screwed up tonight, we probably could have avoided it, but now we need them. They're the only ones who might be able to help and they owe me a favour.'

I ground my teeth, knowing he was right and angrier because of it.

He rose and paced the verandah's length twice before facing me. 'Sorry. I just...I don't know if we can work together on this. You should stay put and let me handle it.'

'What? No. Anna is *my* mother. She's Eisen's prisoner because of *me.* She spent most of her life moving all over the world to protect me and I won't sit by and do nothing.' I struggled out of the chair's embrace. Anger, at myself and the circumstances, bubbled into rage.

Pain lanced through my head as darkness hammered at the block holding it in place, trying to use my anger as an avenue of escape. I winced and pressed a thumb to my temple.

Logan's expression turned wary. He backed away a step.

Fury drained into a familiar, empty ache in my chest.

He said nothing, merely regarded me with the cool, detached aloofness that had so intrigued and annoyed me when we met. Now, it hurt.

I smiled bitterly. 'If I become Calain I suspect you'd need to be half a planet away to stop him from draining you. Actually, I have no idea how far away would be safe.'

'Rowan, I—' Contrition knitted his brow.

With a rough laugh I waved him back as he approached.

'No, you're right,' I said, wearily. 'I told you not to trust me, so how can I complain? *I* don't trust me.' I leaned my elbows on the railing and studied the shifting, green-silver non-light auras of the plants below. 'After all, it's obvious the last block in my brain is a token door between my father and the world. It only stops him when things are normal. Well, normal for me, anyway. As soon as things get…interesting he'll come roaring back out. And I can't stop him.'

'That's not true.' Logan's eyes narrowed. 'I've seen you control him, over and over. The only time you lost it was in Cairns, when you were almost killed, and he took over.'

'But he's so strong.' I wrapped my arms around myself. '*I* was so strong when he was free. It was…right. Like I was whole, or doing what I was supposed to do. That scared me more than anything. I killed those men without a second thought.' I examined my palms. 'So easily.'

A quick frown flashed across Logan's brow, but cleared when he caught me watching. 'I'm sure it was Calain's self-interest you were feeling, nothing more.'

I shuddered. 'Who does that? Who installs some psychopathic part of himself into his daughter's head?'

Logan leaned a hip on the railing next to me, crossing one ankle over the other. He looked at me from beneath dark lashes.

'Somehow I doubt he meant it to be that way. From what Maeve says, Calain never had much training as a technician. She taught him what little he knows when they met a hundred and fifty years ago. When he put those mental blocks in and locked your psychic gifts away, he probably thought he was protecting you from discovery by the Mors Ferrum. That bit of his psyche he left behind to act as a sort of last-ditch guardian, though...' He shifted and put his back to the railing.

I curbed my impatient desire to prompt him and, after a short pause, he continued. 'Maeve remembers telling him about it, but she's never done it herself and had no idea he could. It's called a *fartheria* – a sentinel. Normally it acts as a passive observer.' He tilted his head. 'Kind of like a sidhe phone-tracker app for children, watching and alerting parents of trouble. But Calain obviously worked out how to make it tap into and activate your latent gifts. To act as a guardian to help you out of danger.

'Well,' I said acerbically, 'it clearly went pear-shaped when it encountered my *shadow-thought* ability.'

'You were only four when he left.' Logan grimaced. 'He probably didn't know you had the *skath-sheel* gift. After all, the ability to merge with and draw energy from the whole *sianfath* is almost unheard of. And he couldn't have known it might corrupt the sentinel. I don't think, anyway.'

'So.' I tried to wrap my brain around the concept. 'It's not him taking me over? It's some sort of psychic copy, bent on world domination? And psycho-Calain wants to use me as the weapon of mass destruction to achieve it?'

Logan shrugged one shoulder. 'Basically. A shadow of him. The protective instinct, if you like. From everything you and Maeve have said about Calain, he doesn't seem the megalomaniac type, does he? He meddled in British and European politics for a few hundred years but never tried to take the crown or anything.'

'How the heck would I know? Clearly I knew zip about my own father before I met you and Maeve.' I rested a tight forehead on my palms as I leaned on the railing. 'But you said he was half Dark sidhe. That he potentially had the gene for mental instability that defines the Dark sidhe. That they had a historical bent for this sort of stuff. What if I have it too? What if the dark gene is what his ghost-in-my-head is tapping into?'

'Hey.' Logan touched my arm. 'Stop. There's no evidence you're going to become a psychopath any time soon so stop it with the "what-if's".'

I hunched a shoulder. 'What else am I supposed to think? Only a couple of weeks ago I was a high school kid. All I ever wanted was to be normal. Have friends. Stay in one place and have a house I could call home for more than a year. Now...'

His arm encircled my shoulders and pulled me against his side. 'I know. Now you're never going to have any of that. And your mother's being held by a true psycho. Plus, you're forced to rely on people you barely know and don't trust to help you. Sucks, huh?'

I laughed half-heartedly. 'I'm not cut out to be the Chosen One in some stupid story. They're always...' I sighed. 'So *good* and so inevitably-victorious it makes my teeth ache. I'm not like that. Life isn't like that. Especially not mine.'

He kissed the top of my head. 'I wish I could guarantee victory for you, but I can't. I don't know much about what's going on. Or what Michael Eisen's end-game is. That's what scares me – more than who you might be in moments of stress. Calain's influence is worrying but I think you're underestimating your ability to control him. Having said that, I hope you're never again in a position to find out.'

'I sense a 'but',' I muttered.

'But, to get Anna back, your strengths – and your weaknesses – will be tested. Mine too. If you won't stay out of the fight, then we need to work together. And arguing with Maeve doesn't help, either.'

I said nothing. There wasn't anything I could say about Maeve that wouldn't annoy him. After all Maeve was his aunt and his first loyalty had to lie with her and Jennifer. I just wished that weren't true.

I leaned on his shoulder and allowed myself the luxury of feeling close to someone. He held me closer and tucked my head under his chin. We stayed that way a long while, listening to the soft animal sounds of the garden and the occasional swish of cars along the road. The connection to him and the *sianfath* all around lulled me into sleepiness and I yawned.

Holding me away he searched my face. 'You should get some sleep. You haven't slept much the last couple of nights, I know.'

'How?'

His eyes slid from mine. 'Your shields sometimes falter when you're waking from a nightmare. I've seen what you're scared of. What you remember. What you did in Japan two years ago to escape Michael Eisen's men when they caught you; and in Christchurch before that.'

I flinched away, sickened by the recollections.

'No.' He grabbed my wrist. 'Don't run, Rowan. It's not a judgment. I've done worse. I just meant to say I understand how tough it's been for you. Lack of sleep doesn't make it any easier. In fact, it makes it worse because it upsets your brain chemistry and your thinking gets twisty.'

'*That* I know.'

'You're afraid you'll kill indiscriminately; become some dark, horrible thing. But I've *seen* you master it. You can do it again.'

'No.' I broke his hold and moved back. 'You helped me. I couldn't have done it in Cairns without you. Calain would...*I* would have drained everyone in that building if you hadn't helped.'

'Then believe in me,' he said, drawing me close again. He caressed my face. 'I'll be there. On your side.'

I gave him a weary look. 'And if you're not?'

I tried to peel his fingers away, but the world vanished. I'd forgotten to guard against precogs and, evidently, he'd forgotten to shield from me, too.

A needle; a stark room; a hospital bed. Michael Eisen appears, talking to me. Logan's palm strikes my face. His rough laugh. A shove in the back and I stumble into the arms of our pony-tailed attacker, his face still shadowed. Behind him looms a taller, broad-shouldered bear of a man, hidden in half-darkness even though he's standing in the light.

'Rowan!' Logan gripped both my arms. 'What did you see? Let me through your shield. If you've had a precog we need to understand it. What was it?'

Gulping for air I twisted loose and clamped my teeth shut to hold back the words that tried to force their way free. I backed up, heart racing. He stepped closer. I retreated and dropped into a fighting stance.

'No. Stay away from me, Logan.'

'What was it? Calain?' He stayed where he was but there was an edge of tension to his voice.

I got control of the tremor in my stomach and legs. The pricking under my skin faded and the urge to speak the precog went with it. 'Nothing. I'm going to bed.'

'Rowan.'

I left him standing there in the darkness, calling my name.

FOUR

So, will you help, Ian?

[But of course, Logan. We owe you for bringing Tomas back.]

It's not going to be quite so easy, this time. And Anna is a human, not sidhe.

[Well, if it means foiling the Mors Ferrum, I'm quite delighted to be of assistance.]

We'll see you at nine.

[So early? If I must, I suppose. Make sure you bring this Gilmore child. I confess I'm quite agog to meet her. Her father was such a brooding rogue. Did she inherit his charming lack of social graces?]

She's had a...difficult upbringing. She...keeps people at a distance and she doesn't suffer fools gladly.

[Best keep her away from Tomas, then.]

The first hints of dawn brought no easing of my fear. My eyes were gritty and duckfeathers had replaced my brain. I'd slept little, too afraid Logan would read through my shields. There had to be a way to strengthen them, but I could hardly ask Maeve for guidance. She couldn't be trusted not to mess with my thoughts. I'd have to figure it out on my own.

Giving up on sleep, I snuck from the house, into the small dojo nestled amongst trees in the huge backyard. Just as a garden was a feature of every Freyson house so, was a dojo and meditation space.

For that I was grateful. I pushed through a strenuous routine of kata and rolls, and a small measure of peace stole into my soul. Not sleep, but the next best thing. Finished, I settled crosslegged on the centre mat, back straight, and meditated.

After a few deep, cleansing breaths, my pulse settled enough so I could speak.

'Want to try?'

There was a long, tense silence, then a rustle of cloth from a darkened corner. A shadow detached itself and shuffled into the light.

Jennifer Freyson blinked in the slanting, greenish sunlight that slipped in through the eastern window. Her hair was dishevelled, eyes dark-circled. She stood before me, chewing on her lip, poised to flee, holding a blanket around her slim frame.

'Couldn't sleep either?' I patted the mat beside me.

After a moment's hesitation and a half-scared glance at me beneath her lashes, she sat and folded her legs. Tucking the blanket around her bare toes, she traced the tatami floor's criss-cross pattern with one chewed-nail fingertip.

I let the silence stretch. She was a chatterbox so it shouldn't be long before she felt obliged to fill it. Sure enough, a few seconds later her lips parted and her wide-set, dove-grey eyes met mine for a fleeting second.

'Will you teach me?' Her breath fluttered a strand of long, raven-black hair that fell from a centre part to curtain her face. She pointed at the dojo mat.

'Hasn't Logan been teaching you already?'

'Yeah, but he's a guy and he's practically my brother. He's always busy and he snaps at me when I get it wrong.' She shrugged a pettish shoulder. 'And Mother doesn't approve. She thinks fighting's not ladylike. She wants me to do science stuff, like her.

But I want...' Her voice trailed off and her gaze focussed somewhere through me, into her memories.

'You want to be better-prepared after what happened to you in Cairns?' There was no point in sugar-coating it. She'd been drugged and had seen Logan almost killed. That sort of thing scarred a kid, especially one only thirteen. Hell, it haunted me and I was five years older, with more first-hand experience at these things.

She paled and clutched the blanket closer, a hint of tear-shimmer about her lower eyelids.

'Have you talked to Maeve about what happened?'

'No!' She responded with a half-angry, half-frightened glare, as though afraid I'd drag her in to see her mother then and there. When I just waited, she relaxed a fraction, focussed on twisting one corner of the blanket. 'She wouldn't understand.'

I bit my tongue against uttering the obvious retort. Maeve was, after all, her mother, two hundred and eighty years old, and a qualified psychiatrist, psychologist and who knew how many other "ists". She'd also been through the same events – and probably worse at other times in her long life. She was far better placed to deal with treating the aftermath of trauma than me. I was barely holding it together, myself. The last thing I needed was responsibility for Jennifer's mental health. I already felt guilty enough about being partly the cause of her involvement.

Jennifer scrubbed a fist under her nose and gave a defiant sniff. 'All she talks about these days is the stupid Mors Ferrum and protecting the sidhe.'

She warmed to her theme, so I kept shutting up. Maybe talking about it would help her, even if I didn't want to hear. I owed her that much, at least.

She straightened and tossed back her hair. 'I mean, we've chased *all* over the world for this guy who's taking our people. Which I get.

I do. He took Jonathan, my half-brother. I never met Jon, but I know we have to stop people disappearing and everything.' She went back to twisting the blanket. 'But what about me? I just wanna have a *life*. And I want to *do* more than study science. I want to learn cool stuff like you – fighting and picking locks and things. When does what *I* want get to be important?'

Ah. Yep. After "she doesn't understand", the second age-old cry of youth: "It's not fair. What about me?". I kept cynicism hidden. After all, I'd not long ago made the same plaintive cry to Logan and received an answer I hated: never. At least Jen had known her sidhe heritage her whole life. At least she knew *why* she couldn't live a normal life. At her age, all I'd known was that I had to pretend to be normal and run if anyone found out I wasn't. So my mother and I had run.

A lot.

Logan had been patient with me when I was coming to terms with who I was, so I should pay it forward and be patient with Jennifer. He was a better man than I, though. Patience had never been my forte. I thrust aside the urge to tell her to suck it up and stop being a baby.

Jennifer grimaced. 'I'm so *sick* of being bossed around and dragged around. If Mother hadn't made me go to Cairns I'd never've…' She fell silent, the horror displacing petulance.

Nope. I'd had enough of her wallowing. It was an unpleasant mirror to my own conflict that I wasn't in the mood to see right now. I jumped to my feet, ignoring her frightened start.

'C'mon.' I held out a hand. 'Let's do some training. I'll teach you a few quick and dirty escape and disables. And we should be able to invent some kick-ass ways to use your telekinesis if we're smart. I wonder if you can use it to increase the power of a strike? Interesting thought.'

Jennifer blinked at me in astonishment. 'But Mum says I should never use it in front of humans. She says it's too dangerous and singles me out.'

'Sure.' I raised a cynical brow. 'But I think you can be trusted not to dance cutlery on the table at restaurants. You want to be better prepared next time something happens?'

She nodded.

'Well, you have a big advantage, if you use it right. You'd be stupid not to train it.' I considered the still-quiet main house. 'I think, though, for the sake of family peace, you should keep what we work on to yourself. Deal?'

As I expected, the lure of rebellion against her mother was too strong to resist. Colour flooded her cheek and her happy sparkle returned. She threw the blanket into a corner. Her pink, Hello Kitty pyjamas were a little incongruous, but I managed not to laugh.

'Do you really think I can do it?'

'Sure, why not?'

Her eagerness faded a little. 'Mother says girls are better suited to intellectual pursuits. That we should leave the fighting to men.'

I snorted. 'I can hear her saying it. I call BS. It's your life, Jen. Even at thirteen you're already stronger and faster than most humans. By all means, talk your way out of anything you can. But there will come a point where you can't. Then what will you do? You have huge potential, Jen. Don't let Maeve's insecurities or your own stop you from fulfilling it.' Wise words. If only I could heed them myself.

Jennifer lifted her chin. 'What do we do?'

'Right.' I raised my hands. 'First thing you're going to learn is a set of escapes against various grabs. And I warn you, I'm not going to go easy. You have to be able to do them against full-strength attacks. Ready?'

She smiled for the first time in two weeks.

An hour later we were both hot and flushed. I called a halt, not wanting either of us to be injured. Jen glanced at the house, her moue of disappointment segueing into a resentful frown.

'Mother says breakfast is in ten minutes,' she said. 'I'd better shower.'

'You did good,' I said. 'We'll do some more tomorrow.'

She grinned and dashed inside.

'You're good with her. More patient than I am.' Logan appeared from nowhere.

I jumped. 'Don't *do* that ninja-thing on me.'

'Sorry. Just came to tell you, we're going to meet the Fairchilds after breakfast. They live close by. They're all home at the moment and willing to hear us out. Will you come?'

'Do I have a choice?'

'You always have choices, Rowan.'

I gave him a wry smile. 'I know – "but sometimes we don't like them" – according to Maeve.'

'She's not wrong.'

'Do you trust these Fairchilds?' I studied him, sensing ambivalence when he thought about them.

'Trust, yes. Like, not always.' He grimaced. 'Ian's over four hundred years old, so he's pretty good at hiding his true thoughts. Very…charming. Tom is…difficult. He's one of the sidhe I helped your half-brother, Dante, rescue from a lab a couple of years ago.' Logan shuddered and made a dismissive gesture. 'I've known him a long time, but he's very cagey. I'm pretty sure he's still struggling psychologically with his capture by the Mors. As for Erin, his older sister, well… don't make the mistake of taking her at face value. She comes across as an airhead, but she's one of the smartest people I know. She likes to…encourage people to do what she wants.'

There was a lot he hadn't said and wasn't letting slip through his shields, either. Protecting her or me? Or himself?

'Ah!' A tall man, lean to the point of thin-ness, tossed aside a newspaper and unfolded himself from a dark leather chair. He tugged on the hem of a burgundy velvet jacket. 'I'm so glad you're here to relieve the tedium. The newspaper is so depressing. Nothing but stories about seven people disappearing in Brisbane in the last two weeks. Mass-shootings in America, economic disasters, and global warming. Humans don't understand how much they need us, do they my dear Maeve?'

He appeared to be about fifty, his dark hair showing a gleam of silver. Like Maeve his face was all unusual angles, latte-skinned and with wide-set eyes. But where Maeve had dark-rimmed eyes of a soft grey, his were ice blue. The dark borders and black irises made them startling against his skin. His mesmerising gaze held mine for a fraction too long.

He greeted Maeve with a cheek-kiss that seemed to carry genuine affection. Then he shook Logan's hand, holding it between both of his and asking earnestly after his health. Jennifer tugged on his sleeve and Ian raised her fingers to his lips in oldfashioned courtesy. She giggled and blushed.

When he came to me he paused. 'You must be Rowan Gilmore,' he said, a hint of amusement in his tone. 'Ian Fairchild. At your service.' He bowed but didn't offer to shake. The aloof expression on Maeve's face told me why. She'd forewarned him about my ability to "read" a possible future through skin contact.

What was he afraid I'd see? I tucked my hands into the pockets of my baggy shorts and let him see my ironic understanding. He smiled, inclined his head and waved gracefully at the lounges.

'Please, be seated all of you. Harry? Do serve the refreshments now, please?'

The upright, white-haired older man who'd let us in the front door reappeared with the practiced silence of a long-time invisible servant. He vanished into what I assumed was the kitchen. I couldn't shake the feeling I ought to be wearing long skirts and curtseying as I inspected what was visible of the two-storey Victorian house.

Although only minutes from the centre of Brisbane, Ian had secured the closest thing to isolation possible. The massive house was set in acreage, near the river, and surrounded by paddocks and patches of eucalypt forest. We'd entered via a short path through a spectacular rose garden. To either side of the carved front door, with its ornate stained glass inset, two bay windows protruded, their drapes closed against the morning sun.

Inside, Harry had led us along a narrow, high-ceilinged hall of white-painted timber, and hardwood floors. We'd found Ian in an airconditioned back room crammed with bookcases overflowing with gilded, leatherbound books, and lit by two wide, arched windows. Soft classical music drifted from an old-fashioned timber radio cabinet. The smell of leather, dust and coffee lingered in the still air.

In one corner, a large, roll-top desk bore the only jarring note to an otherwise beautifully-staged room: a laptop with its screen undimmed and still showing a search engine result, the text too small to read at this distance.

I eyed Ian again as he ushered us into various seats. The notion that he had, indeed, staged the room stuck with me. Why though? Was he trying to impress us with his age and wisdom? To what end?

FIVE

['Sblood, Maeve, she looks so much like him!]

   <I know. And is just as headstrong, arrogant and untrusting.>

   [But will she do what we need her to?]

   <To be honest, Ian, I'm...not sure. Logan is fighting me; protecting her. And she's closed the back door I built into her shield, so I can't get into her mind anymore to plant suggestions.>

   [So we need to win her trust?]

   <If we're going to use her ability in the way it was meant, yes.>

   [Hmmm – let me consider the problem.]

I waved away Harry's offer of tea and biscuits. Maeve and Jennifer accepted. Logan declined, leaning back in his chair. His eyes flicked to the door as a footstep fell somewhere overhead.

Ian chuckled and sipped his tea. 'She's coming, lad, be easy.'

Logan stilled, his cheeks flushing dark.

'Father, are they here—oh!' A young woman appeared in the doorway, fingertips artlessly on her generous cleavage. She widened her eyes – the same ice-blue as Ian's – and laughed lightly. 'Silly question. Logan. How lovely to see you again.' She drew Logan to his feet and kissed him on the mouth. When she withdrew she bit her bottom lip with a saucy, sexy little smile. I dug my nails into the leather armrests. She whispered something into his ear.

Logan chuckled but leaned away. He indicated Maeve, who offered her fingers like she was expecting them to be kissed.

'Erin, dear,' she said, 'how are you? It hardly seems like two years. We must chat about your research paper later, too. One or two little things you overlooked in your mitochondrial DNA analysis that might help. I see you're making progress on the work around how DNA folding affects gene expression, though. That could be most helpful.'

Erin pursed her lips then flashed a determined smile and shook Maeve's hand. 'I'd be glad to have your advice, of course. After all, you have *years* more experience than me! I've finished my *first* doctorate and you've got, what, six is it? Of course some are a little out of date, aren't they? Have you done one in genetics too? I can't remember.'

Maeve's smile thinned.

I suppressed a laugh. Insult-tennis. Score: one all.

'Erin.' A bored masculine voice sounded from outside the door. 'Stop being such a prat. Get out of my way.'

'Oh Tommy. You're such a child.' Erin sashayed into the room. She stopped at the space on the couch-end, putting her between Jennifer and me. There she ran her hands down her slender shape and tucked the flowing scarlet folds of her strappy sundress under her legs before sitting. She gave Jennifer a conspiratorial little smile and a quick hug, whispering something into her ear. Jennifer blushed and gazed worshipfully at her.

Before Erin could turn her attention to me, not that I wanted it, the final Fairchild edged into the room. Tomas was, like his sister and father, tall and slender. His eyes, too, were icy and striking against dark gold skin. Where Erin's glossy dark hair was cut into a funky, asymmetric bob, Tom wore his long and tied back into a low ponytail. His gaze fell on me, his bored expression twitched into a frown. Then he smoothed it away and went back to looking like he'd rather be anywhere but here.

He dropped into a chair and the soft light from a desk lamp lit his face. What I initially took to be a shadow was a pinkish scar on his left temple – a recently-healed cut.

I sent a swift thought to Logan on our private connection. He sent Tom a sideways look. His frown deepened then cleared.

No, not the same mind as at the MJE compound last night. I've known Tom since I was a kid. Besides, Maeve trusts the Fairchilds. She's known Ian for two hundred years. They've been allies against the Mors Ferrum that whole time.

Who are you trying to convince: me or you? I cut the connection and strengthened my shields. Logan might be certain Tom wasn't our attacker from last night, but I wasn't.

Leather creaked as Tom sank back into his chair. He wore a black t-shirt, black cargo pants with black calf-high military boots. All he needed was eyeliner and a nose piercing to go with the surly attitude and he'd make an excellent goth. He tilted his head back, his eyelids drooping to the point where it became difficult to see what he watched. I had the distinct impression it was me.

'So.' Ian slapped his trouser-clad knees. 'What can I do for you lovely folk?' Maeve opened her mouth but he tapped his temple. 'Wouldn't this be simpler if we drop into the *lorntinn*?'

"Unity" I silently translated the word from the sidhe language, *Henath*. Maeve had mentioned it last night in reference to my half-brother, Dante. I hadn't really paid attention. Some sort of telepathic group-think? *Henath* I'd inherited from my father, made it sound like the *lorntinn* required me to let others into my deepest self and I wasn't prepared to do that – with anyone. I also doubted Maeve would be comfortable with me that far into her head.

I sent her a strait look.

'Perhaps.' She shifted on her seat, crossing her legs elegantly at the ankles. 'But out of deference to Rowan's newness to all this, we can speak aloud for now. She's still learning the skills needed to be deft with telepathy and finds it rather tiring.'

Her words were an unexpectedly-polite way of letting me off the hook.

Ian regarded me as an entomologist would a new bug. 'Very well. And I understand you're Calain Gilmore's daughter?'

I straightened. 'Yes, why?'

'Fascinating. Apart from the blonde hair I guess I can see the resemblance. I'm astonished someone managed to convince him to have a child. He was so adamantly against it.'

I quashed a flare of hurt and flicked hair off my shoulder. 'It's a wig. Mine's auburn.'

'Can't blend in the *lorntinn* or create a glamour to change your appearance in the minds of humans?' Erin smiled sweetly. 'That's a shame.'

She chuckled when I didn't deign to reply. I'd learned to create a glamour a week or so before, but it took more concentration than I was used to and I had a bad habit of letting it drop at the wrong moment. Wigs were easier; what I was comfortable with after a lifetime of running and hiding.

Ian continued to reminisce as though Erin hadn't spoken. 'Yes, I recall Calain had auburn hair. He had the most unfashionable habit of leaving it unpowdered.' He waved dismissively when I looked askance at him. 'I knew him, in France. Around 1760 or so. Not long before the revolution. We moved in the same circles for a time. He was Earl of Lothien and I was Comte de Cholet. We were never friends as such. He was always so…inscrutable. And he did prefer the company of humans. Or perhaps he enjoyed meddling in their affairs. He was forever doing so.' Ian chuckled. 'One day, at the Duc d'Orlean's soirée, we found ourselves at odds over…a woman? No, that was a few weeks before. Oh yes – a game of cards, I believe. He accused me of cheating so I was obliged to call him out.'

I gaped at him. 'You challenged my father to a *duel*?'

'Yes. They were such different times.' He surveyed the luxurious room. 'So much less clean and civilised. We take so much for granted these days. Don't you agree, Maeve?'

She smiled tolerantly. 'I don't miss much about the seventeen and eighteen hundreds, I must admit. Except perhaps the Mors Ferrum's inefficiency. It was undoubtedly easier to go undetected then.'

'Ah.' Ian inclined his head. 'And so you deftly remind me we are not here to wander down memory lane.'

'But,' I couldn't help asking, 'what happened – at the duel?'

'Oh.' He shrugged. 'Calain didn't attend. But the king's guard did. I suspect someone informed on us and he got wind of it. Of course, he wasn't known for his skill with a sword, so probably just as well.' His lip curled in the faintest sneer for an instant before being replaced with a sweet, genuine-appearing smile. 'If he had, you may not be here today, my dear girl.'

I caught Logan's warning glance and quashed the instinct to defend my father. We were here for information. Insulting our host wouldn't help my cause – even if he was a class-A jerk who deserved it.

Erin patted her lips in an exaggerated yawn. 'Father, I'm sure it's a fascinating story, but can we get on with this?' She checked her watch. 'I do have to get to the lab *sometime* today. I'm close to working out how to reverse gene suppression and you know how important that is to your precious cause.'

'Yes, yes. Of course.' Ian patted her arm then sharpened his gaze onto me once more. 'You said these Mors Ferrum who've abducted your mother are after something called an *ocair*, a "key", is that correct?' When I agreed he rubbed his jaw. 'I'm sure I've heard the word before. Erin have you come across it in our library anywhere?'

Tom stiffened. His mouth pressed into a thin line.

Erin waved aside his words with a scornful laugh. 'Father, you know it's not me who reads these dusty old things. If it were up to me I'd hire someone to digitise them and get rid of them. Computers are one of those things about this century that makes it so much better, remember?' She wrinkled her nose and touched Logan on the knee. 'Should see how much trouble I had even getting him to *email*. I bought him the laptop and he hardly uses it at all. So stone age. I think—'

'I've heard of it,' Tom said, still appearing half-asleep and slumped in his chair.

Ian rolled his eyes. 'Well, why didn't you say so? Sit up boy and tell us.'

The scathing look Tom sent his father spoke volumes, but he didn't move. Instead his eyelids closed and he spoke in a bored voice.

'It's in the *"Fisana"* – the "Visions" – by Mairi Silverblade. 1405. Top shelf of the humidity-controlled cabinet, fourth from the left. The last page. On the left side of the page about halfway down.' He cracked an eye as Logan rose and strode over to the bookshelf. 'You'll need to use the gloves and I hope your *Henath* is good.'

'Tom has an eidetic memory.' Erin grimaced. 'He likes to show off but forgets a good memory isn't necessarily a sign of intelligence.'

'Nor is sleeping with your professor,' Tom drawled.

'How *dare*—'

'Children!' Ian said. Erin flushed, eyes glittering.

Mockery flitted across Tom's thin lips.

Score: one-love to Tom.

The rest of us sat in uncomfortable silence.

Logan found the book and a pair of white cotton gloves and brought both to the coffee table. He pushed them across the polished timber to Tom. With a sigh, Tom drew the gloves on and gently flipped the age-spotted pages.

'Oh, do hurry, boy,' Ian said. 'They haven't got all day and nor do I.'

Tom ignored him, if anything turning the pages even slower. Finally he stopped, tracing the spidery, flowing script.

'It says: *"And in the year of the Lord 1403 an* ocair" – a key – *"shall be created in the realm of the three crowns. In the..."* There's a word here I can't read *"...of the* sianfath *and the* lorntinn" – the unity – *"that key shall be the downfall of those that persecute the Ruadhán Daoine Aes sidhe."* That's all.'

I jumped at the sound of my own name, the Celtic pronunciation of Rowan. Of course he was using Ruadhán in the way the Daoine described themselves, with its meaning as "Light", to distinguish from the Dark Elves who carried the gene for mental instability. The gene my father, and possibly I, carried.

Tom perused a few more lines then slid the book away. He tossed the gloves onto it and resumed his reclining position.

There followed a long silence as everyone stared at the book.

I pulled on the gloves and dragged the tome closer.

'Maeve.' I traced over the gilded decorations on the spine and cover – a stylised Celtic tree. 'Mairi Silverblade. Didn't you mention an Aeona Silverblade?'

Maeve shot me a frowning look, but she needn't have worried. I was hardly going to tell them the reason she'd mentioned Aeona was because I carried the same psychic gift – the ability to draw energy from all living things, not just plants as was normal for the sidhe. I'd been an outcast amongst humans my whole life. The last thing I wanted was for my ability as a life-energy vampire to make me a pariah amongst my own species.

'Yes,' she replied, her tone cautious. 'Mairi Silverblade was her sister. Mairi was a renowned precognitive. Her visions were always true, and often many years in advance. Though they were limited to events that happened during her lifetime.'

'What happened to Mairi?' I inspected the traces of dust and gold glittering on the glove. 'I mean after Aeona disappeared?'

'I believe Mairi went into hiding. Rumour was her final vision was of her own death, in 1415. She was burned as a witch in some remote Irish village.'

Ian swiped a hand over a face aged by grief. 'Yes. Mairi was my grandmother. The book came to me a few years ago when my father passed away. Tomas has been translating it. My *Henath* is limited as my father was determined we should blend in so as not to suffer my grandmother's fate.'

I touched the book. 'I can probably help.'

Tom cracked an eyelid and sneered. 'Really? You think you can do better? It took me two years to teach myself enough *Henath* to translate that book. Good luck.'

Maeve oozed smugness. She gave me a little nod. As much as it irritated me to be the pawn in whatever little game of sidhe politics she was playing, I did want to read that vision. I opened the book and found the page.

Tapping into the section of my mind holding the entire Henath language I released English as my default language and let Henath take over. The words fell into place with perfect clarity, even allowing for the difficulty in deciphering the faded, curling text. What looked like age spots resolved into indications for telepathic colouring of the words and changed the meanings of some completely.

'It says: *"And in the year of our lord 1403 a key shall be"* – not created – *"born in the realm of the three crowns. In the* embrace *of the* sianfath *and the* lorntinn, *that key may be the deliverance of those that dispossess the Ruadhán Daoine Aes sidhe."*

Tom's mouth fell open. 'You can read it *that* easily?' His whisper held hope and disbelief.

'My father Gifted the whole language to me before he died,' I said diffidently.

He leaned forward, eager and excited for the first time. 'Will you Gift it to me?' He pointed at the bookshelves. 'There are a dozen more books I'd like to read. On healing and how to use other psychic skills that are lost now because we're all so scattered and unpracticed. It would be incredible if you could.'

I flushed beneath his amazement. 'Sure. I don't see why not.'

'Well.' Erin lifted a shoulder. 'You can count me out. I don't see the point in learning a dead language. I'm perfectly capable of using my healing and telepathy when I need it. Otherwise, there's nothing in these roach-infested books that's useful in this day and age. You'd be better off finding a way to get the Mors Ferrum off our backs and helping me hide our genetic code from the humans than burying yourself in the past.'

'Actually,' Logan put in, staring at me, 'I think giving us a way to get the Mors Ferrum off our backs may be precisely what Rowan's done.' He waved aside our questions. 'You translated that passage as *"the key will be* born *in the realm of three crowns"*. During the middle ages, the heraldic symbol for Ireland was three crowns on a blue background. So it refers to a person, or perhaps an animal,' he conceded, 'born in Ireland in 1403.'

We all nodded in agreement.

'Then it said the key *may* be the deliverance of those that dispossess us, right? So it's obvious. The whole thing is moot: there *is* no key anymore.' He spread his palms.

Maeve paled. 'You mean you think *Calain* was the key?' She glanced at Ian, who shook his head a fraction. Catching me watching, Maeve's usual, unruffled cool returned. What was that about?

She frowned. 'He said he thought he was born sometime in the early 1400's but he didn't know when. He grew up in rural Ireland. His parents had abandoned him – given him to a peasant couple to raise as their own. He didn't remember much of his parents or, at least, he never spoke of them. But he did remember being left in a barn.'

I twisted my father's heavy gold signet ring on my middle finger, studying the emerald and crest. I'd dreamt of that exact scene: a child abandoned and frightened. It must have been one of my father's memories, leaking from behind the block that held both them and my gift/curse locked away in my head.

'But Calain's dead,' I said, unable to keep the bitterness from my voice.

'Exactly,' Logan responded. 'You said Michael was desperate for the *ocair*. I'm thinking that a garbled version of Mairi Silverblade's vision has reached the Mors Ferrum. They must think the *ocair* is something that will help them...I don't know... destroy us, maybe? And if we can convince Michael Eisen the key is gone then we might be able to negotiate your mother's release.'

'But it said: *"may be the deliverance of those who dis...dispossess the sidhe"*,' Jennifer piped up. 'Doesn't that mean the humans? What does it mean by "deliverance"?'

'Salvation, perhaps?' Ian shrugged. 'Though from what I'm not certain. ' *"Those who dispossess"* could mean the humans. They are certainly the cause of deforestation and the destruction of our habitats.' He gestured languidly as he leaned back in his chair. 'But it could also mean the Dark sidhe. Interpretation of visions is always difficult. Made more so when – as we've seen – the Henath is easily mistranslated by someone who lacks the skill in understanding the telepathic nuances accompanying the text.'

Tom shot up from his chair. Snatching the book, he stalked from the room and slammed the thick timber door behind him.

Erin sighed into the silence. 'Honestly, brothers!' She rose and brushed at her skirt. 'I have to get to work. Walk me out, Logan?' She drew him to his feet.

'There is one more thing you could help us with, Erin,' he said, glancing at Maeve, who gave a small nod. Erin left and he followed.

Why was it always so cloak-and-dagger with Maeve? She must have some ingrained prejudice against honesty and open communication.

'Jennifer. Rowan.' Maeve smiled on us. 'Would you be so kind as to give Ian and I a moment? Perhaps, Jennifer, you can take the tea things back to Harry in the kitchen.'

I stood. 'I'll go talk to Tom.' It would give me a chance to decide for myself if he was my attacker from last night.

'My dear girl,' Ian said. 'If you can talk him out of these dreadfully childish sullen turns I'd be grateful. He's twenty-four and he's been acting like a human teenager – staying out late with the most vulgar people. And he can't take well-meant criticism at all. It makes him quite impossible to live with.'

He made me almost glad my father wasn't around during my teen years. How did someone live for four hundred years and still be so clueless about dealing with people; family especially?

SIX

[Once Tom has the language, perhaps, he'll actually be of some use to me. I'll put him to work finding out what we can about this ocair thing and perhaps he'll cease his constant complaining. Honestly, Maeve, I've despaired of him since Logan brought him back to us.]

<I know, but be patient, Ian. He's still a boy, and it wasn't an easy time. I wish he'd let me into his mind to see what damage was done.>

[It's nothing time won't fix. I should know, after all. We've all experienced... unpleasantness and we've all managed to put it aside, eventually. So will he.]

<Perhaps.>

After opening several doors on the ground floor I tiptoed up the creaking, narrow staircase and found Tom lurking in a more modern living room that must be for his and Erin's use. With clean white couches and a large plasma TV on the wall, it didn't seem to suit Ian's taste for the antique. Tom sprawled on a couch, a gothic horror novel on his lap. Jennifer sat next to him, barefoot and nibbling a biscuit. She giggled at something he said as he stared moodily out the window. The Visions book lay closed on the smoked glass coffee table behind them.

I paused in the doorway, reluctant to intrude.

'She'll steal him from you if she can, you know, Rowan,' he muttered, still facing the window.

Jennifer jumped from the couch like a child caught in wrongdoing. Did she think I was going to scold her for talking with someone she'd known for much of her life?

I smiled at her but responded to Tom. 'Who'll take who from me?'

'Erin. She'll take Logan. She's never wanted him before, of course.' He swung around, tossing the novel aside and grimacing at me. 'But she's a dog in the manger.'

'Oh.' I blushed and waved his words away. 'Logan and I aren't...' I trailed off in the face of his irony and Jennifer's wide-eyed interest. 'Anyway. It doesn't matter. Here.' I strode over to him, hand raised.

He reared back.

'I'm just going to Gift the *Henath* to you.' I paused.

His apprehension segued conflict and then into wary acceptance. He held still, lips drawn back in a grimace of distaste as I touched his forehead. The *sianfath's* connection prickled under my skin. The warm taste of ozone teased my tongue and I slid into Tom's thoughts.

Logan was right: Tom's mind wasn't the same as the one that had attacked me last night at the MJE compound. Similar in a lot of ways, as all sidhe were, I assumed, but not the same. His was a lot more complex, darker, and in a great deal of pain. More than he probably wanted me to see. The man at MJE had felt...black-and-white in his thinking. Like a drone taking orders without wondering about implications; cold.

It took me a moment to refocus and remember Maeve's instruction on how to do the Gifting. I struggled with it until I pictured the process as a version of copy-and-paste on my computer. Then it seemed simple enough. I searched for somewhere to transfer the information. His thought-shield image took the form of – not surprisingly – a gothic mansion, dripping in gargoyles and pointed arches. Part of one wing appeared half-ruined, with broken windows and gaping holes in the stonework. Symbolic of something, or just artistic?

He'd opened a door in the intact wing. It led into a dark room already half-full of shadowed, hazy objects I couldn't quite bring into focus. His own thoughts and beliefs, presumably. There wasn't enough space to fit the *Henath's* entire complexity, so I constructed a room extension, suited to the architectural style, and deposited the information inside.

Tom jerked away when I was done. 'Holy shit! That's…incredible.'

'What, the language?' I sat on the couch, relieved. Using the skill hadn't resulted in killer headaches, as it had before Maeve removed most of the blocks.

Jennifer asked if she could have the *Haneth* as well and I complied, adding a room to her gingerbread house and feeling guilty. I'd promised Maeve I'd Gift the language to Jen and Logan two weeks before. Then it annoyed me that I felt guilty; that I felt I still owed Maeve something, even after the way she'd used me to flush out Michael in Cairns. But the fault wasn't Jennifer's. She ought to have a language that was part of her heritage. I needed to remember to Gift it to Logan as well.

Afterward, Jennifer seemed to feel she was in the way. She thanked me and then Tom, for what I didn't know, collected her shoes and muttered something about finding her mother.

Tom waved as she left and regathered the thread of our conversation. 'The *Henath* is amazing – way more interesting and complex than I realised – but what I meant was the way you did the Gifting. It was…odd. Where'd you learn that?'

I fiddled with the button on the cuff of my shorts. 'It felt rude to dump a whole lot of new data inside your shield. I figured adding an extension would make it less intrusive. Did I do something wrong?'

He touched his forehead 'No. You're right. Normally Gifting is…almost painful.' His mouth twisted. 'My father could never understand why I hated his Giftings. I've always felt it was the mental equivalent of physical assault.'

I stood and put distance between myself and his words under the pretext of inspecting his collection of novels. His take on Gifting sickened me, as much because of its truth as the realisation I was now capable of doing such a thing. I could force thoughts onto an unwilling receiver.

I'd been sexually assaulted as a sixteen-year-old, but I'd been able to defend myself. What was the defence against a mental assault, other than shields? Because, if last night was any indication, I was going to need something better.

'Is there…' Could I trust him any more than Maeve? Was I just comfortable with him because he, like me, was rebellious against the adults in this situation? Well, I had no-one else to ask. 'Is there some way – other than putting up shields – of defending against a mental attack?'

Tom strolled over. We stood together at the shelves, not looking at them, or at each other.

'What sort of attack are you talking about?'

'Last night at the MJE complex we were chased by another sidhe,' I admitted. 'He hit at my shields so hard I was scared he would break through. I'm new to this. My shields could probably do with some reinforcing and I'd be grateful for any advice.'

'This Eisen character has a sidhe working for him?' Tom fingers fluttered over his mouth and chin.

I nodded.

'That's bizarre. Any idea who? Light or Dark?'

When I shook my head, he was silent awhile.

Then he slid me a sideways look. 'You are staying with one of the best psychic technicians and teachers in existence. Why not ask Maeve, or even Logan?'

I walked to the window, rubbing my palms on my thighs. In the garden below, Erin twirled a rose, sniffed it and laughed at Logan. He smiled back at her.

'Let's just say, even though I'm staying with the Freysons, I'm not exactly on the same page.' I folded my arms and turned from the window. 'We have common goals at the moment. Once my mother's safe we'll take different paths.'

Tom raised a brow at me. 'You're not on Maeve and my father's crusade to rid the world of the Mors Ferrum?'

I laughed bitterly. 'I'll happily rid the world of Michael Eisen and all his damned minions, if I can. But after that Anna and I are *so* gone. I'm not going after the dragon's head – the guy who runs the Mors. What's his name? Alexander Dyson? I'm not St George – I have no faith.'

'In what, the crusade or Maeve and Logan?'

'Either. Both.'

Tom's thin, Byronesque face lit into a smile much more charming than his father's by virtue of being more real.

'I get you.' His mouth twisted into irony. 'Probably more than you know. I envy you, too. At least your mother loves you, and you have the option to leave once this is over. My father has never, even once, said a word of praise to me. Nothing I do even raises a smile, and believe me, I've tried.'

There wasn't much I could say. Ian favoured Erin and to say differently would be a blatant lie. I tried a new tack. In my view, Tom would be vastly improved if he got out from under Ian's thumb and found out for himself who he was and what he was good at. Waiting for Ian to approve of him was a fool's game.

'There's nothing stopping you, is there? I mean, if you want to go, then go.'

He snorted a short laugh. 'We're the first children my father's had for over a century. He's kept us tied very close and he's a little out of touch with modern parenting. You learned useful survival skills. I learned ballroom dancing, fencing, languages, politics and how to invest money.' He spread his arms. 'But, of course, I have no money of my own to invest and he won't trust me with his to learn.'

'They're useful skills, though,' I pointed out. 'Well, maybe not ballroom dancing, but the rest. And your eidetic memory is pretty useful. Maybe card-counting?'

'Good idea, but I don't think I could count on it – pun intended,' he said wryly.

'What? Your memory? I'm confused.' I smiled at the interplay. 'Isn't the point of an eidetic memory that you *can* count on it and remember everything?'

He paused, hunching a shoulder. 'In that case, I'm in trouble because I've forgotten important things.' He said it in the awkwardly lighthearted manner of one who knows they've used a clumsy segue to introduce a topic weighing on their mind. 'You...you won't say anything to the others?'

'Of course not,' I lied. I'd learned long ago to only keep secrets that helped me survive. 'You're serious about forgetting things?'

'Yes.' He pushed a fingertip into the centre of his forehead. 'And that's what's worrying me. I assume Logan told you he'd got me out of a Mors Ferrum lab?'

'Not the details. He said he thought it still bothered you.'

Tom laughed. 'That's an understatement, but it's easier to keep it to myself. It upsets Father when I mention it. Erin doesn't give a damn. Maeve wants to poke around in my brain like I'm a lab-rat.'

'I know how *that* feels.'

He hesitated. 'It's just…ever since then, I have gaps in my memories I can't explain. It scares me. I feel like…I'm not quite in control any more.'

I shoved my hands into my pockets. 'I'm not a psych, but I do understand. I've been taken by the Mors myself. Not for very long,' I added when hope and curiosity sparked in him. 'I'm pretty sure I have repressed memories. I gather memory loss is a common side effect of trauma. Look.' I hesitated, feeling gauche. 'We don't really know each other, Tom, but if you need someone to talk to, I'll listen. I can't guarantee I'll give good advice, but it might help.'

'It's not just…' Tom tugged on his pony-tail, glancing at me and away again. He uttered an uncomfortable half-chuckle. 'Anyway. You've got more important things to do than listen to me whinge. Your mother, for one.'

It was my turn to laugh derisively. 'I'm pretty sure she's only important to me and I'm just a footsoldier in this war. People like Ian and Maeve are the generals. They have the long view. As Maeve likes to remind me: individuals aren't important; it's the survival of the sidhe species we need to focus on. But I hate being a pawn. I won't sacrifice my mother to Maeve's chessgame against the Mors Ferrum.'

'That's how I feel, too, like a pawn.' Tom narrowed his eyes thoughtfully. 'But in chess, y'know, sometimes the pawn can get to the back of the board and become a queen.' His smile widened. 'I can help you reinforce your shields, but I don't know much about psychic weapons. Maybe there's something in the library. I'll do some Henath reading. See if I can find a weapon fit for a queen.'

I already had a weapon. The ultimate one that could kill everyone around me with a thought. But it came with a couple of drawbacks – head-exploding migraines and a tendency towards psychotic megalomania and world domination.

SEVEN

[So we're agreed?]

   <Yes. We need proof, one way or the other. I've wasted enough time coddling her.>

   [Indeed. But Erin's not to know, beforehand.]

   <Of course. Her reactions must be genuine.>

'Ah.' Maeve's gentle voice greeted me as I descended the stairs ten minutes later. 'There you are. Ready? Is Tomas comfortable again?'

'He's fine,' I replied. Ian emerged from the library behind Maeve. His narrow scrutiny of me was followed by a swift, secretive smile.

Jennifer appeared from the kitchen, brushing chocolate cake crumbs off her tshirt. Maeve regarded her with that age-old expression of resigned parenthood, but said nothing more than 'Really, Jennifer'. Then she swept out the front and we traipsed along like obedient ducklings in her wake. Jennifer poked her tongue out at her mother's back. I kept my expression bland, but with an effort.

Outside, Maeve donned a pair of black sunglasses and said an affectionate farewell to Ian.

'You will remember to send me those plans, won't you?'

He bowed and spread his arms flamboyantly. 'Even though it entails using that damnable laptop, I shall, indeed. By tomorrow morning at the latest. I'll get in touch with my contact at City Hall this instant.'

'Thankyou. You're too kind. Can we count on all three of you, should we need more...physical assistance?'

He bowed lower. 'Of course. It would be an honour and, indeed, a pleasure.'

Maeve smiled, called Jennifer away from smelling the roses and headed for the car, parked in the dappled shade of a jacaranda and already strewn with its blossoms.

I gave Ian a polite thank you and glanced at the window overhead. Tom saluted but withdrew from the window when Erin glared at him. Logan cocked his head in question. I looked pointedly back at him and at Erin, still glued to his side.

He put space between them and said to her, 'We'll meet you there.'

She waved an airy, flirty farewell to him and a cooler one to me before disappearing in the direction of the garage. A second later, a bright red, convertible sports car roared out from behind the house. She swung into the long driveway and planted her foot, vanishing with another wave and a spray of gravel and purple petals.

I walked in silence next to Logan until we arrived at Maeve's much more sedate, dark sedan. Logan took the driver's seat, with Maeve beside him, which suited me fine. I climbed into the back with Jen and stared out the window, thinking.

'We're going to follow Erin to her lab,' Logan said, when Jennifer questioned him, a few minutes later, on where we were going.

'But why?' she said guilelessly.

'We can't do much about finding Anna until Ian sends us the blueprints for the MJE buildings.' His eyes met mine in the rear view, though he spoke to Jennifer. 'But Erin's lab has a DNA testing machine. She's going to test Rowan's blood.'

'Oh, really?' I said. 'I don't recall you asking me if that's what I wanted.'

'You already said you did – back in Cairns. It's part of the reason I thought contacting the Fairchilds would be helpful.' He kept his calm before my irritation. 'She works as a geneticist at the University of Queensland. She has cutting edge tech at her disposal and she's keeps an eye on the latest research results from around the world. She's been invaluable in hiding results and arranging for samples to be switched in labs everywhere. The DNA sequencing of our kind would be further along if it weren't for her work over the last eight years or so.'

'Is this your way of telling me I can trust her?'

'Pretty much.'

I turned back to the window, seething. 'Well, I don't.'

'Well, that's no surprise, is it?' he replied, 'since you don't trust anyone. Even when they're genuinely trying to help.'

I kept my face averted, disliking both him and myself.

An uncomfortable silence filled the car for the entire drive to the University. Even the campus's pretty, tree-lined grounds, with its hodgepodge of graceful, sandstone buildings and clunky brick block monstrosities, wasn't enough to interest me at this point.

I followed the others through long, white corridors towards Erin's lab, but my feet dragged, heavy with reluctance. The smell of chemicals and cleaning fluids caught in my throat and stung my eyes. Maybe someone would stop us and demand an explanation for our unsanctioned presence. No-one did. Muffled laughter and the clink of cutlery on plates down the hall indicated where some people were in the building. It seemed thinly populated for a Friday, though.

The lab contained more computers and fewer bubbling flasks than I expected. It was well lit, spacious and modern, with vast expanses of benchtop and a number of computer screens showing incomprehensible images. Several paper-strewn desks and workstations attested to other scientists working there, but none were around. The faintest hint of coffee hung in the air, competing with the scent of antiseptic.

Erin in her lab was a different person. Complete with labcoat and gloves, she dropped away the flirty airhead persona; replacing it with a professional scientist. She produced a cotton bud and gestured imperiously to me. I hung back.

'Logan?' Maeve waved both of us forward. 'We've never done yours. Why don't you go first and show her there's nothing to worry about?'

Logan swabbed the inside of his cheek as Erin instructed. At Erin's challenging look I did the same and, after a moment of reluctance, handed it over. She prepared the samples and took them into another room, reappearing after a few minutes and stripping off her gloves and mask.

'It's an Ion Torrent Semiconductor unit so it'll only take about two hours.'

'That fast?' Maeve's brows rose.

'The modern age is an amazing thing,' Erin retorted, her expression bland and tone even. 'The problem is we have a backlog of other tests and I can't bump them because they're for the Professor. Come back this time tomorrow.'

'Tomorrow!' I protested. 'I don't have time for this.'

'Very Millennial of you. Tough.' She curled a lip. 'Go into the city and do some clothes shopping.'

'I don't need clothes.' I took a step closer, glaring at her. 'What I need is a way to get my mother back from the Mors Ferrum. And it's pretty obvious you're useless in that regard.'

She snorted in derision. 'You don't have a clue what I can do. And if your mother's been taken by the Mors then you can kiss her goodbye. She's dead, or as good as. I should know.'

'Erin!' Logan jumped in and grabbed my shoulder as I took a half-step forward. 'Back off, Rowan,' he said in an undertone. 'Leave this to me.'

Unable to bear the mixture of scorn and deep, old pain in Erin's expression, I spun away and strode to the window. There, I surveyed the treetops and buildings, the scattering of white clouds streaking across a vivid blue sky. Part of me wanted to slap Erin, to force her to recant her words, to wring a belief in my mother's safety from her pouty lips. Another part shivered deep inside and feared facing the probability she told the truth; that my mother was already dead; that my efforts were in vain and could get others killed as well.

I snuck a glance over my shoulder at Maeve, Jennifer and Logan. What right did I have to risk their lives when they had no care or interest in my mother's life? But I had to try; had to know her fate for certain. And how could I get into a place as secure as the MJE complex without help?

Frustrated, I gritted my teeth. Up until now I'd never needed anyone except Anna. It had been only the two of us, surviving, running and hiding my secrets, for fourteen years. We'd coped. Until I'd screwed up in Cairns. Now I was forced to rely on Maeve and her family and it grated. They had their own agendas and I didn't know what those were.

I just wanted someone to trust.

'Hey.' Logan touched my arm. I jerked away then muttered an apology.

'Let's go,' he said, jerking his chin at the door. 'We'll come back tomorrow. For now we do have shopping to do – not for clothing. There's a decent martial arts supply shop in Fortitude

Valley. We'll drop Maeve and Jennifer home and go there. Then we'll hit an army surplus store I know and grab a few things.'

'At least that's something. They might have a practice dummy I can hit. I can't stand all this waiting and doing nothing.'

He grinned. 'I had noticed.'

Several hours later, considerably more relaxed, I followed Logan into Maeve's house and dumped a bag onto the kitchen table. There was nothing like a good weapons-buying spree to lift a girl's heart. For a short while, I'd been able to put aside fear and just enjoy myself – and Logan's company. We'd laughed over some of the impractical cosplay-type weapons on display in the shop and drooled over a genuine Japanese katana from the seventeen hundreds.

Logan placed a life-sized silicone head-and-torso dummy on the table and gave it an experimental throat-jab. He grinned in satisfaction.

'Always wanted one of these.'

'Me too.' I spun it towards me and lashed out with an elbow to the jaw, followed by a series of hand-strikes to throat and jaw critical points. The head jiggled and maintained its stoic scowl.

'Be interesting to see how long it will stand up to our full-strength strikes,' Logan said. 'You were pulling those.'

I grimaced. 'Ya. Bad habit, I know. You were right in Cairns. I'll have to learn how to strike at full-strength. Humans in a dojo are always so breakable.'

He smiled at me, grey eyes wondering. 'Have I told you how much—'

Jennifer bounced in and reached for the shopping bag, only to have her wrist slapped by Logan.

'Not for you, kiddo.'

She poked a tongue at him. I winked at her and opened a thought-window.

Later, Jen. I found you a couple of useful little things. We can try them out when the others are in bed.

Sweet! Thanks.

She gave Logan an angelic smile and skipped over to the stove. A large pot of something bubbled on the heat. She lifted the lid, sniffed, stirred the concoction with a wooden spoon, then tasted it. Smacking her lips, she added coriander to the mix.

Catching me watching in surprise, she grinned. 'I like cooking, but Mother doesn't like Thai food, so I don't get to make it much.'

'Isn't Maeve here?'

She shook her head. 'She had to go meet someone.' I waited and she shrugged. 'We need new passports, in case we have to get out fast. She's getting you one as well.'

I opened my mouth to protest, caught Logan's warning look, and closed it again. Maeve was right. I had one set of papers but I always liked to have two. I hadn't had time to search the dark-web internet sites to find anyone since we'd left Cairns. Having someone else arrange things left me unsettled, vulnerable and exposed.

We spent lunch pleasantly enough, just the three of us. Jennifer's laksa was delicious. After it settled, I convinced Jen to let Logan help me train her and he agreed not to tell Maeve. Jen hugged him ruthlessly then we trained for an hour in the dojo, teaching her how to deal with multiple attackers. She picked it up fast, gaining confidence and power with every successful takedown. Grinning, sweating and bouncing with energy even after the sparring was finished, she hugged me, then dashed off to shower and change. Logan left as well, heading to the kitchen for a drink. I followed more slowly, running a handtowel over my neck. I flapped my tshirt to cool myself and leaned against the dojo's outside wall.

The sun reflected off the house next door's red, corrugated iron roof. The sound of traffic drowned out the twitter and chirp of suburban birds. I touched the rough bark of the massive jacaranda tree that dominated the yard. Its eyewateringly-purple blossoms carpeted the ground at my feet and clashed beautifully with the sharp blue sky. The scent of warm earth and water rose as sprinklers came on and misted the garden in sparkling drops.

The *sianfath* called to me; its soothing nothing-everythingness tempting me to leave the solid cares of my body behind. I rested my cheek against the trunk and closed my eyes. Slowly, with infinite care, I let tiny portions of my self slide into unity with it, then stepped free of my body so as not to disturb the ever-watchful presence in the back of my mind. Pain flared as I worked around the block to use this *shadow-thought* skill. I stilled for a moment, and it subsided, leaving only the needle-prickles under my skin.

Tendrils of me intertwined with the lives of each tree, each fern, each ant, each bird in the garden, tasting and understanding, drawing energy, holding onto a sense of belonging I couldn't find elsewhere. Mindful of past experience, I anchored one core part of me into my body, fixing it with metaphoric ties so my body wouldn't be left lifeless, no matter how thin I stretched.

A brilliant red, green and blue parrot fluttered by and landed on my shoulder. I bonded with it and felt/saw myself through its curious eyes: short auburn hair; grey, dark-rimmed, abstracted eyes. A nose too sharp and mouth too wide for beauty. Dark-gold skin warm in the sunlight. The bird walked close to my ear and nibbled gently on the lobe, rubbing its head against mine. The *sianfath's* bright, silver-green energy filled me, healed my tired body and helped to soothe my fears, a little. They weren't gone, but at least I didn't feel quite so alone. I was one with the world, its life-force entwined with mine, one mind, one entity.

Behind the block in my mind, the thing that was Calain stirred. The block shuddered and sent muddy ripples through the connection's purity. He tasted the power. Wanted me to suck the world dry, to lay waste, to wipe the planet clean of humanity.

And the worst thing was: I could do it. It would only take one moment of weakness. Or for someone to remove the last block standing between me and Calain's ghost. One bad choice and I could be the instrument of death for the people I cared about, and more.

The connection trembled again as someone else's presence in the garden created a disturbance and wrecked my concentration. I wasn't practiced enough to control all the tiny filaments of me under such circumstances. My body-anchor could snap and I'd lose myself. My body would die and I'd dissipate to merge entirely with the world's life-force.

Slowly, I pulled myself back into my heavy, corporeal form; smaller, alone and disorientated.

Someone gripped my elbow as I sagged against the tree. I opened my eyes.

'You ok?' Logan inspected me.

I twisted free of his grip, too open to connection to handle the tumult of emotion flooding through his touch. Worry, fear, distrust, longing, desire, admiration. All of them shuttled through his thoughts and under my skin.

'Do me a favour?' I reinforced my shields against him. 'Don't touch me when I'm stretched out in the *sianfath?*'

He paused. 'Why?'

'Your shields are non-existent when I'm in it. I can read everything you're thinking and, right now, I'm hanging on by the teeth. I can't deal with how you feel about me.'

Stepping back a pace he paled and swallowed. Understandable. He'd been reared in the belief his shields were inviolable. The sidhe respected each other's privacy and wouldn't dream of even trying to penetrate a raised shield. To be told they were useless against me must be frightening.

I sighed and re-entered the dojo. I was tired, but even the *sianfath* hadn't quelled the unrest bubbling deep in my mind and body. I had to *do* something towards freeing my mother. And I knew what, I just wasn't sure what the result would be.

'Logan?' I leaned on the wooden doorframe. 'Can I ask you a favour?'

He shifted closer, an arm around my waist, fitting himself against me. He kissed my temple. 'Anything. You know that.'

'I need to find something out about Calain. Then I might be able to use that information to negotiate for Anna's release.'

He frowned. 'I know I suggested it, but I'm having second thoughts. We might be overestimating the Mors Ferrum's humanity. I hate to admit it, but Erin's right: they aren't known for releasing captives.'

A soft breeze swept through the room and sweat cooled on my skin. I shivered. 'I know, but I can't do nothing. If we get those plans for the buildings tomorrow, then we can think about strategies. For now I won't sleep if I don't try something.'

Logan sighed against my hair. 'What do you want to do?'

'I'm going to go behind that block and see if I can sift through Calain's memories. See if there's a stand out moment when he realised who he was and what it meant. Whether he really was the *ocair.*'

He stiffened. 'Is that wise? This memory-dump thing is new. We don't know what might happen. You might get trapped in there. He could break free and take over again.'

'I know.' I moved away, colder without his arm around me, and sank crosslegged to the tatami mats. 'That's why I want you to keep watch. If it goes wrong, do whatever you have to.' I produced my new karambit blade from its sheath in the underwire of my bra and laid it on the mat before me. 'I mean it and you promised me.'

He swore, staring at the knife with open loathing. I straightened my back and raised my chin in challenge. He sagged, nodding, and sat across from me, knife within reach but untouched.

'Don't lose control, Rowan.'

'Believe me, I'll do my best.' I smiled bleakly. 'Besides, imagine how hard it would be to get the blood out of these tatami mats if you had to use that knife.'

Logan didn't laugh.

I focussed inward.

Since creating the mental reproduction of my family estate home in Ireland under Maeve's guidance two weeks before, I hadn't really taken the time to explore it fully. As instructed, I'd built the image to represent security and safety. It hid and protected my thoughts from other sidhe. Each major room held a part of my mind. I'd been in the real building only a year ago, on a holiday, so it was fresh and clear as I walked the empty corridors.

The front entrance and grand hall, with its medieval stone walls, huge oak beams and massive fireplace was for the superficial thoughts uppermost on my mind. The place I let people into when I wanted telepathic communication. Off that, in the Elizabethan wing, with its leaded windows, hardwood floors and patterned ceiling, were various rooms holding the six or seven languages I'd rediscovered, including *Henath*.

The opposite wing, built sometime in the Baroque period, held far too much gilding, cherubs and painted ceilings. I found the whole thing uncomfortable and revolting. Which could be why I'd relegated my precognitive ability to its tastelessness.

Beneath it all were the dungeons – accessed only through the cellars under the original medieval kitchen with its vast fireplaces and heavy oaken worktables. There, in the deepest cellar, behind stone and a thick, iron-strapped doorway, I held "me". The core of who I was. What that meant, I wasn't sure, but it needed to be protected.

And in the furthest dungeon chamber, deep behind more oak and steel, lay Calain's memories.

I ducked through the first, low timber door and paused. When I'd visited in the real world, the dungeons had been open to tours and re-stocked with instruments of torture. My father had been gifted the estate by Queen Elizabeth the First, early in her reign, so he hadn't been responsible for building them. Had he ever used them, though? Had he put his enemies into these tiny, lightless cells? Had he tortured them?

I hesitated before the final door, the one representing the last block in my mind, and tried to calm the thrum of adrenalin in my blood.

'You don't have to do this,' Logan whispered.

'Shut up. I do. I have to know for sure if he was the *ocair*.' I refocussed and phased through the oak as though it were insubstantial.

EIGHT

Maeve, how far away are you?

<About half an hour. I'm waiting on the last pieces of paperwork. Why, Logan?>

I have a feeling Rowan's going to do something stupid.

<Well, stop her. You're the only one she's likely to listen to. What is it? Show me.>

This…

<Ah. I expected she'd try soon. Let her make the attempt. It may prove useful.>

What? It's more likely to go completely wrong and you know it.

<We need the information and she needs to know she can control it. Let her try. That's an order.>

Dammit, Maeve. What aren't you telling me?

Calain studied his hands. They were dirty, and covered in calluses, but long-fingered and slender. Womanish his stepfather called them. His right held the leather grip wrapped around the smooth shaft of a fine yew bow he'd finished making last week. His second-year apprentice piece. Approved by his stepfather, grudgingly. Its pale cream and gold tones gleamed in the half-light and it thrummed when he plucked the string to test the tautness.

What had he been doing? Oh yes. He'd come to the woods to hunt for mushrooms and herbs, and to see if he could take down a hare or maybe a bird for dinner for his mother. But he'd been distracted by the forest's beautiful heartbeat, the rush of pure joy that always filled his body when he came here.

A rustle in the nearby undergrowth brought his bow up, arrow nocked and drawn. He held his breath, left thumb anchored beneath his ear, arrow tip aimed. His back muscles trembled for the new bow was a heavier draw than his old one and he wasn't yet used to it.

'Prithee, Cal, hold!' A quavering, girlish voice floated from inside the shrubbery.

He uttered an oath and relaxed, letting the string down without firing. 'Grace Williamson th'art a rogue of a child. Show thyself.'

Grace squirmed out, squeaking as a branch caught in her long red hair and another plucked at her woollen tunic. Calain slid the arrow into the cloth quiver behind his hips and slung the bow across his shoulder. He bade her stand still while he untangled her. When she was free, and the leaves plucked from her wild hair, he bent down. Though he was small for his twelve years, she was yet smaller at just six. Her defiance and energy always made her seem larger.

'Thou dost know thy mother forbade thee to follow me into the forest.'

She put her hands akimbo and thrust her pointed little chin at him. ''Tis thy mother too and she bade thee care for me whilst she's at market. Yet thou didst leave me alone!'

Calain straightened, shifting his shoulders to ease the pain of the willow stripes across his back. 'Not my mother, step-sister. Nor my father, as he reminded me, most strongly, this morn when he found fault again with my work.' He stalked away.

Grace walked beside him for a moment, skipping occasionally to keep up with his longer strides. She tucked small, cold fingers into his.

'Born thus or not, I still cleave to thee as my brother,' she said meekly.

Calain sighed. 'Forgive me, sister. I shouldst not take mine ill humour out on thee. Now speak truth. Why didst thou follow? Th'art too old to be afeard of an empty house.'

'Oh!' She did a little skipping turn and tugged free, clutching at her skirt. 'The crier came past calling news. There's to be a witch-burning in the village. All art commanded to attend. Tarry not for 'tis to start anon.' Without waiting, she dashed away, her bare feet flashing their dirty soles, long red hair flapping behind her.

Calain followed more slowly, reluctant to attend. Public trials and executions made him sick and those of folk accused of witchcraft chilled his blood. There but for the grace of God went he. But his stepfather would notice if he didn't attend. As would Father Mallory. Callain crossed himself and muttered a prayer.

Around him, the forest voices whispered sweet temptations, calls to join them, offers of succour and health. Resolutely he shut them out. Not even Grace knew of the allure the green places had for him. To speak of it would result in his being cast out or earn him a place of his own on the pyre. His step-parents and Grace would be shunned by association. Little though he liked the stern discipline of his step-parents, their house had sheltered him for the last ten years and he owed them thanks, if not respect, for his place at their hearth.

He was not ready to leave yet. But in three more years; once his apprenticeship was over and before he was bound to a new master. Then he would let his feet take him whither they wished.

He emerged from the woods and paused at the edge of a green pasture, staring across the valley at the scattering of small, thatched houses. Through it snaked a stream and the road he meant to follow one day. To the west, high above the village on a ridge overlooking the road and the deep, cold lough, loomed the Earl of Lothien's great stone fortress. Beyond that, who knew?

Grace called out from afar and he jogged along the stone field boundary to catch her. They slipped into the village unremarked and found a spot near the smithy, soaking in forge-warmth as the spring afternoon turned chill. Calain lifted Grace to sit atop a wall while he contented himself with glimpses of the pile of faggots stacked in the town square.

A woman stood, bound to a post, in the middle. Her plain shift was torn and bloodied, her long hair uncovered, lips and cheek bruised. Yet she waited with her chin lifted, showing nothing but sadness and resignation. No fear. Not young, but not old, still pretty in spite of the bruising, with glossy dark hair and pale, dark-rimmed eyes, startling against skin the colour of old oak.

'She looks like thee, boy.' A rough, sneering voice startled him out of his study. 'Mayhap th'art a witch too. Ha ha!'

Calain didn't look and didn't reply. Nothing he could say would prevent the teasing, anyway. He hunched his shoulders and stared fixedly at the shifting crowd before him.

'Didst hear me, boy?' William Smith's thick fingers grabbed at Calain's jaw and forced him to look at the pile of timber. 'An she's a witch, mayhap thou art, for thou hast the same eyes and skin. Too fae by half.' His expression shifted, crafty. 'Or mayhap she ist thy mother! Shall I call the curate and have him add thee to the pile? For all he deigns to teach thee thy letters, he'll burn thee fast enow an he knows the truth of thee.'

Burning torches were thrust into the base. Flames caught and flickered in the dry tinder. Agonising hope leapt with them. His mother? Was it possible? A shudder of excitement and fear wracked Calain's body. Could it be her? Had she come for him only to die?

'Afeard art thou?' Smith leaned closer, his breath rank with ale and rotten teeth. 'So thou shouldst be. Thou art not worthy of a place in a house as Godly as the Williamson's. They shouldst have cast thy skinny rump out into the woods to be eaten by wolves the night thine whorish mother left thee.'

Inside his belly, long-repressed anger mounted, burning in Calain's wiry body until he trembled, not with hope but with rage. Calain kept his attention fixed on the leaping flames, holding himself in stone. His fingers flexed into claws. It would be so easy to break the other boy's arms, to snap bone and tear hair from his head in great clumps. Calain was stronger and faster than any village boy, even the ones near to being full men. He could—

The woman on the stake uttered a low, sobbing moan. She cried out in a strange language, not Gaelic, English, Latin, or French, for he knew those well from the curate's teachings. Flames licked at her shift and smoke billowed around her in strange seemings: shapes of animals and the majestic forms of ancient oaks. The crowd muttered, most crossing themselves as they backed away. Smith released Calain and scurried off to join his hulking father, the blacksmith, who cuffed him aside.

The woman spoke again, pleading. Her uncanny eyes searched the crowd. Was she seeking a saviour? None in this God-fearing community would dare step forward. Two days of prayer and fasting had spared it the ravages of the plague fifty years before. Now none dared question the power of God and his representative on Earth. The curate's word was law. If he said she was a witch, she was so condemned.

Father Mallory, pale and clutching at his bible, ordered her to repent her sins and to be taken unto the Lord. He was not a strongwilled man – forever scraping and bowing to the Earl, the parish priest, and the Bishop. Calain watched every word he spoke in the man's presence, both disliking and respecting him equally. For the curate's obsession was to rid the world of evil in all its forms. He considered witchcraft to be the worst.

Grace, perched on her wall, spoke Calain's name in fearful tones. He ignored her, sickened by the scene but unable to avert his eyes.

The woman cried out as her clothing caught alight. But the cry was not one of pain, but of joy and relief. Her gaze fixed on Calain. He took an involuntary half-step forward, drawn by the happiness, the welcome, the outright love that softened her pain into acceptance. Sparks swirled high into the air around her.

Calain. I ha' found thee at last. Praise be the Mother!

-*Ma...mamai?*- He whispered the word in his mind. To hear her there seemed perfectly right.

Tears fell from her pale eyes. *Nay child, thou'rt not my bairn. I am but a messenger from thy mamai.*

-*Where...where is she? How canst I be of help to thee?*- Calain moved forward another step, half-intending to throw himself into the flames and tear at the bonds.

Nay! Hold, little one. Thou'lt be in dire peril an thou dost try to help. My time is come, as 'twas foreseen. I ha' but one task to complete and I may go in peace. Let me release thy gifts before I leave thee. I'm sorry. This will pain thee greatly. Remember me. Remember them. Know thy heritage. Know thy path.

Her face vanished in flame. Pain destroyed thought. Hers, his...he didn't know. Inside his head something burst. His mind burned as her flesh blackened. His muscles twitched as hers contorted. His mouth opened and his scream echoed hers as she sucked superheated air into her lungs. He clawed at his skull, dragging at his hair and scratching at his scalp as the agony blossomed. Desperate to escape it, and the babble of words and thoughts pounding at him from all sides, Calain ran.

Hands clutched at him but he twisted free and slapped them aside with ease long-hidden. Voices called his name, outside and inside. Footsteps pounded after him, but he outdistanced them on feet as fleet and sure as those of a young buck. He left the village behind, with its stench of burning flesh, chorus of fearful cries and crackle of burning wood. He plunged into the cool forest without stopping, driven by the need to find solace from the agony.

Calain ran until a stitch in his side stole breath and the pain in his head became such he couldn't see clearly. Deep in the old forest's trackless ways and far past the extent of usual foraging expeditions, he kept on, forcing himself, stumbling over roots and stones, the world shimmering through tears. Clinging to a tree he drew strength from it and the pain in his mind subsided a little; enough to stagger onward, deeper, further away from home and hearth.

The sun sank behind the western mountains and the temperature dropped. Darkness ate at the impetus driving Calain's flight, leaving him cold and shivering. The forest closed in, looming, fearful. Calain stopped still, listening, sure something watched him. Had he been pursued? Would he be dragged back to bear the same punishment? Condemned as a witch because of his connection to the woman who'd burned today?

The last feeble rays of sunlight faded and he shivered in his thin woollen tunic and hosen. He'd never been out at night in the forest. There were wolves and wild dogs in these hills. He hesitated, glancing back over his shoulder. Should he return? An image of fire and pain flickered and he groaned, pressing at his forehead. No. Not after that scene. There was no going back and no-one but Grace would care or notice anyway.

His head throbbed, sharp stabs of pain occasionally knifing through his thoughts. Was he going mad? Had the demon possessing the witch jumped into his body? Perhaps he should seek the curate? He remembered the man's fanatical, excited expression as he watched the woman burn, and shuddered. There would be no cure and no comfort from him.

No. He'd left now and done was done. He could survive. He had his bow, knife and waterskin. He needed to find shelter; to sleep until the headache wore off. Then he would make his way over the hills to another village; one in need of a bowyer-fletcher, or a hunter.

Calain opened his eyes and straightened, throwing his shoulders back. He gaped, blinking. Darkness no longer shrouded the forest. Neither moon nor sun rode in the sky. Yet he saw clearly. Every plant, every leaf, every vine, glowed with a strange, greenish non-light. Not bright, but etching everything in perfect detail. He touched a leaf wonderingly, then snatched his fingers back and stared at them. His whole body shimmered with the same aura. But it was comforting rather than frightening.

He stroked the gleaming trunk of a huge old ash. Something tingled along his arm, warming him from the inside out, tasting of fresh-cut hay. He snatched his hand away. The feeling stopped. He touched the tree and let it happen, revelling in the sense of wellbeing and strength. When he felt full – for want of a better word – he withdrew and rearranged the bow and quiver on his back. He sucked a quick breath. The raw willow-switch scores from that morning were painless. He felt his skin beneath the tunic. The welts were gone.

'Mayhap I am a witch,' he said aloud. 'But if this be witchcraft, then I'm not afeard. Nay.' He flung his arms wide. 'I embrace it for I ha' never felt so hale. God could not ha' meant this to be evil.' No one replied, and he might have imagined the rush of welcome emanating from the trees themselves.

NINE

<Logan? What's happening?>

Nothing. She's still in there. She seems physically ok, thanks for asking.

<Don't speak to me in such a disrespectful tone, young man.>

Then stop treating her like she's nothing more than a tool in your damned game of politics, Maeve. For all her bravado, she's scared.

<She's not just a tool, Logan. If we do this right she's a weapon. The weapon that could mean the end of this war for all time and save millions of lives. Surely that's worth the risk?>

Oh yes, because weapons are great at saving lives. Ask the people of Hiroshima.

Agony tore into Calain's mind again and he clutched at his skull, groaning. He staggered a few steps but fell over a root and collapsed into a pile of leaves, damp and half-rotted after winter. Shivering and aching to the core, he burrowed deeper and piled them over himself. There, he spent the night. Not sleeping, for that was impossible in the cold and damp, yet not awake either; drifting in and out of pain. Voices swelled and faded; faces appeared, lecturing, teaching, begging for forgiveness.

When the first hints of grey light leavened the green-dark shadows into morning, he awoke. He brushed the blanket of leaves aside, staring blindly into the half-light. The bitter, sharp edges of him had hardened into steel overnight. He was more than the boy he had been yester-e'en. Much more.

Not a witch. He was something else. He raised his face to the silver-lit treetops and laughed. He belonged here. He, and his people, the *Ruadhán Daoine Aes sidhe*. He knew who he was, now. Why he was different. Why the humans hated him so. He and his kind represented everything they feared – the dangerous, the untameable, the powerful. Everything they attributed to gods, be it one or many. Everything inexplicable and frightening. That was where the sidhe existed.

But where the *Ruadhán Daoine Aes sidhe* had spent tens of thousands of years living in harmony with all things natural, humans were bent on destruction, on domination, on crushing what they feared most. Left to their own devices, humans would obliterate his kind and their habitat. All the Earth's wild places would wither under their ignorance and greed.

But, then, why had his parents abandoned him then to human care? He searched the newly opened sections of his mind that held the parts of their stories he could so far reach and read. His heritage. Ahhh. They feared his destruction by the Dark ones, or his use as a pawn in the great wars into which his parents had been drawn – because of who he was and who he might be in the future. Yet they had chosen poorly in their desperation. Humans were weak and selfish. The Williamsons had tried to mould their changeling babe into a human but had produced only a sidhe with a dislike of their kind that ran bone-deep.

But there was little to choose between humans and the Dark ones, as far as he could tell. Both were bent on destruction of one sort or another. And both needed to be stopped. The Mother Earth deserved not such ungrateful, wretched, hard-handed children.

Yet, a seed of doubt flowered: he was flawed, too. He was half-Dark and doomed to self-destruction before he even began this journey. Had his father succumbed to the alteration of mind that was the fate of those cursed by Darkness? His mother's memories were too much to understand. It would take years to tease through all that had been left by her. Years to understand what it all meant and who he was supposed to be.

One thing was certain: he was the *ocair*. He accepted that, though his task seemed impossibly huge. And how was he to achieve his destiny if he was also fated to become what he despised? Would his just cause be corrupted by the forces of Darkness waiting deep within? How would he know if his mind had become clouded by ambition and greed? Who would be his guiding light without parents or friends to ensure his sanity?

He stared out into the brightening forest, debating, soaking in the strength and certainty of the *sianfath*.

Suspended in nothing, visible across the centuries, a pair of grey eyes stared back. There was his solution. 'Daughter. I come. Together we'll succeed where I cannot, alone. But bide whilst I grow to deserve thee.'

I opened my eyes to what would be darkness for a human, but for me was still illuminated by the *sianfath's* glow outside the dojo. Logan's silver-green aura was tinged brown with worry. Beyond the sliding doors, the thick garden pulsed with the same non-light that had awed my father six hundred years before in that long-gone Irish forest.

A breeze whispered in the leaves and blew cold on my skin. I sucked a long, shuddering breath and touched my cheeks. They were wet with tears. Scrubbing them dry, I rested my elbows on my knees.

'Rowan?' Logan's touch on my shoulder carried the undercurrent of fear, as though he wasn't sure if I was the person whose name he'd spoken.

'Yes, it's me.' Part of me wished it wasn't; wished this was all happening to someone else. Would that I could give over responsibility for my mother, the sidhe, the whole damned world, to someone more qualified.

'You were crying.' He was quiet, hesitant. 'What happened?'

I cleared my throat, trying to sound and feel businesslike. But the memory of Calain's horror and pain ached in my chest and strangled my voice.

'You were right. He is...was the *ocair*.' I avoided Logan's sympathy, staring out the door, soaking in the *sianfath's* soothing influence. 'And his mother did the same thing he did to me. She dumped memories of her life and who he was behind a block in his mind. I didn't catch the details of who she was, but when the block came down it almost sent him mad. He was only twelve. The release was triggered by the burning of Mairi Silverblade. He watched her die.' I shuddered.

Logan shifted closer and put an arm around my shoulders, drawing me close. I clamped down on my emotions and gritted my teeth. I wanted nothing more than to sob into his shoulder and, for once in my life, give in to the terrible uncertainty that had always haunted me. But I couldn't, because he had no more idea of how to move forward with all this than I did. In fact, probably less, given I now knew what Calain's role was supposed to be.

'He was supposed to stop the humans destroying the world,' I murmured, fresh tears stinging my eyes. 'That's the *ocair's* role. Calain spent his whole life trying to stop wars, slow development. He pushed for environmental protection long before it was even a thing.'

Logan frowned. 'That's a good thing, isn't it? What's wrong?

I wiped away the tears, anger displacing lingering remnants of his pain. 'He gave up. He somehow saw me in his future and thought I could help him. But once I came along, he just…quit.'

Logan rubbed my back. 'Why?'

'I don't know, do I?' I snapped. 'Maybe he decided global warming was inevitable and his life's work was a waste. So he jumped off the cross-Channel ferry and drowned himself.' I bit down on hurt. 'More likely he realised I wasn't what he expected and it was hopeless after all.'

'Hey.' Logan lifted my chin. 'That's not fair. You were a kid. His choice wasn't anything to do with you.'

I said nothing. Logan was wrong. Calain had worked tirelessly for six hundred years or more. Only to quit when I came on the scene. There must have been something wrong with me. It was the only explanation that made sense.

'Enough,' Logan said. 'It's late and you're tired and worried. Sleep on it. Now we know Calain was the *ocair* we'll do our best to convince Eisen to let Anna go and give up on the idea of finding it.'

He rose. I struggled upright, knees stiff. My watch showed two hours had passed while I sifted through Calain's memories.

'Do you think…' I pondered my father's emerald and gold signet ring. Anna had worn it for ten years, then given it to me on my eighteenth birthday. It had been my father's for five hundred years. I didn't remember him ever wearing it, but it held his coat of arms and was the only thing of his I owned outright. I wasn't even sure I wanted it any more. 'D'you think,' I repeated, gathering my thoughts, 'he passed me his memories in the hopes I'd continue his work? Maybe he meant for me to carry on?'

Logan grabbed me by the shoulders, his expression fierce. 'Don't even *suggest* that to either Maeve or Ian. Don't even *think* it around them. If you do, they could twist it to mean *you're* the *ocair* and use you as some sort of bargaining chip with Eisen. Keep that to yourself. Deal?'

He paused, made a noise of frustration and kissed me. As always, the spark between us flared. Even as I revelled in the taste of him, I fought the desire to turn this brief moment of passion into something lasting. But this was the wrong time to start anything, no matter how tempting. He broke the kiss first and lowered his head. When he raised it again, there was such hunger and confusion in his expression, I almost relented. But he let me go.

'Sorry,' I murmured.

'Why?'

'Well, still bad timing and…well, you and Erin seemed…um…'

He gave a wry laugh. 'No, there's never been anything between us. I'd be blind not to notice her sudden fascination with me coincided with your existence.' Regret and amusement flickered in him as he leaned in and kissed me again, sweetly but far too quickly. 'To be honest, I sort of thought she might go after you.' He grinned.

'She's bi?'

He nodded.

'Useful to know,' I said.

When he grinned wickedly at me I shrugged. 'Not my thing. Just a "know your enemy" moment.'

Logan sighed. 'She's not your enemy. None of us are, Rowan. Get that through your stubborn skull and we might be able to work together a lot more smoothly. Try to get along with Maeve.'

I looked away.

'Please, Rowan?' He ran stiff fingers through his hair. 'I'm struggling to keep this whole alliance between you and Maeve working. Bear with me. I promise I'll work out some way of getting

Anna out. Then we can leave this behind and get the hell out of this whole war if you want.'

I smiled and followed him into the house. My heart warmed under the strength of his protectiveness. He'd shown himself truly on my side. Against his aunt and everything she stood for. Normally he tried to tread a diplomatic line between us. Tried to smooth relations and keep us working together without taking sides.

What had changed?

I woke early the next morning, too anxious about the DNA results to sleep. I dragged a grumpy Jennifer out of bed before the sun cleared the horizon. She yawned and protested, but came alive when we entered the dojo and started warmups. Her enthusiasm for combining my martial arts skills with her telekinesis apparently outweighed her love of sleeping in. I passed her a set of slender throwing knife-darts and a belt to hold them. She caressed them like an ordinary girl would a new dress. I grinned. Maeve would be annoyed. That made me even happier.

We practiced throwing knives and darts until she got the basics down pat. Then we switched to hand-to-hand combat and experimenting with her telekinesis. By the time the sun balanced on the neighbour's roof, we were both panting and sweating in the humid morning warmth.

As Jennifer bowed and turned to leave, I lunged at her, intending one last surprise attack. She shrieked and thrust both hands out, one behind and one at me. Something invisible punched me in the stomach. I flew a metre backward, let my knees fold and collapsed to the mat. My momentum carried me through a backward roll. I came to my feet laughing and fighting for breath with a frozen diaphragm.

Jennifer inspected her hands in astonishment. Her face split with a grin as wide as a door. 'That was *so cool*. I didn't even *think* about it.'

'Awesome, Jen.' I grinned and thumped her on the shoulder. '*That's* your go-to instinct move. Keep it. Practice it. Now let's go get breakfast.'

Inside the house our euphoria vanished under Maeve's blatant disapproval. She didn't say anything aloud, but her pursed mouth and glittering eyes spoke for her. She'd never learned self-defence, having been born in an era where women simply didn't. Jennifer's chin came up. There followed what was obviously a rapid-fire telepathic argument. Jennifer's expression hardened into tearful anger and she stormed out, slamming her bedroom door.

I gave Maeve cool disdain. 'You may not think it's ladylike, Maeve, but what I teach her is way more useful than degrees in biochemistry or psychology.'

Maeve thumped a plate onto the dining table. Her pale eyes flashed and she tossed her long braid back over a shoulder.

'Martial arts may kill individual enemies, but education will kill hatred and misunderstanding.' She pointed at me. 'You are too quick to act and too slow to think. We need to find a way to work *with* humans if we're all going to survive.'

'So why the hell are you trying so hard to destroy Michael Eisen and the Mors Ferrum?' I held back my instinctive urge to yell hot defence back at her.

She busied herself with cooking eggs. 'Because they're an archaic hold-over from another time. They're so entrenched in their hatred of us that there's no way forward. We tried, once upon a time, to reason with them, to show them how vital the sidhe are to the whole world's health. They wouldn't listen then and they won't now. So we work on two fronts.' She cast a quick look under her long lashes at me. 'The Hunters kill the extremists, like Eisen. People like me, Ian, Calain, and one day Jennifer, teach and educate and try to *show* the humans how wrong they are; how self-destructive.'

I stopped a snide reply about the pointlessness of such an effort and considered her words, with Calain in mind.

'What do you mean "vital to the world's health"?'

She folded her arms. 'I mean the sidhe are a keystone species. We play a critical role in ecosystems. All over the world, in the last wild places, the remaining dedicated sidhe are doing what they can to keep things working. Just by our existence we unconsciously regulate the flow of energy in the *sianfath*. If that flow stops…if we're all wiped out…then the ecosystems across the world collapse and everything dies. Everything.' The flat, unemotional way she delivered the line convinced me of her belief more than anything.

I glanced out at the garden. My connection to the *sianfath* was a fundamental part of me now. 'What about the Dark sidhe. They must have the same abilities, so they know that, too. Why are they so destructive?'

'Of course they have them. In fact, even humans have the gene that lets them sense the flow of the *sianfath*. Only, in humans, the gene isn't expressed any more, so they can't feel the damage they're doing. That's part of what Erin's studying.' Maeve's mouth twisted. 'But in the Dark sidhe…well, the nature of mental ill-health is to be self-destructive in some way. But part of the problem is, those with an active Dark gene can sense and take energy from the *sianfath*, but they can't tell when they've passed the point of no return for the ecosystem.' She looked directly at me. 'A truly powerful Dark sidhe is a destructive force capable of laying waste to both human and sidhe worlds without thought of consequence. Luckily, there haven't been too many over the years, and we've been able to…remove…most of them before they got too out of hand.'

Something in my stomach froze as the implications of her words sank in.

That was the real reason she was so keen to have my DNA tested. With the Dark gene and the *shadow-thought* gift, *I* could be the most destructive thing to ever exist.

I'd known it since Cairns, when I'd sucked the life from three men and felt the ability within me to do worse. Clearly Maeve also understood the extent of my powers.

If I had the Dark gene, what would her next move be?

TEN

[Is everything in readiness?]
   <Yes.>
[Are you sure this is the best way?]
   <I know him, Ian. I know what I'm doing.>

The drive back to the University a couple of hours later was silent, though I half-sensed a rapid conversation going on between Maeve and Logan. It had tense overtones and I stayed out. If Logan was starting to question Maeve's motivations and tactics that could only be a good thing – for him and me. He'd been reluctant to throw me to the wolves in Cairns, but he'd still gone along with it. Probably out of habit and trust in Maeve. Hopefully he was coming to see the negatives of blind faith. She was arrogant and too uncaring about the…well…pawns, for want of a better word.

I wasn't willing to sacrifice Anna or myself to Maeve's long-term big strategies. And I'd prefer to have Logan on my side if it came to a face-off.

Back in Erin's building, I stopped outside the lab, in the quiet, white corridor. My breath froze in my chest. Logan paused and waved the others ahead. He waited until they were out of sight and drew me into an empty office.

'Hey.' He raised my chin so I was forced to meet his gaze. 'It's ok. I know you're scared you might carry the same gene that drove your father to suicide, but I promise it'll be ok.'

'Logan, I don't know…' I pushed him away and paced the tiny, cluttered space. 'I mean – who wants to be told they're going to become mentally unstable? You said the Dark sidhe have a nasty rep – Genghis Khan and Hitler and all those – but none of *them* had more than the speed and strength, and telepathy of a normal sidhe. As Maeve reminded me this morning. none of *them* was capable of true world domination. I am and it scares the crap out of me.'

'I don't blame you. But there's a lot modern medicine can do now to correct brain chemistry imbalance and Maeve has done a huge amount of research into this. If anyone can help, she can.'

What could I say? Nothing that wouldn't offend him and right now I needed to hear what he was saying, regardless of the truth. With my mother gone my one pillar of support in this world had been cut from beneath me. As much as I hated to admit it, I couldn't do this alone.

I allowed myself to lean into Logan's strength. Buried my face in his shoulder and fitted myself against his body. He hesitated then wrapped his arms around me, his lips pressed to my neck.

The idyllic illusion of security lasted only a minute before the physical closeness and the scent of his skin stirred feelings in me best left untouched for the moment. I let go and retreated, unable to suppress a rising blush.

He stroked my hot cheeks. 'Come on. I'll be right there with you, I promise.'

We left the little office but, outside the lab doors Logan stopped me. He hesitated, then smiled, unshadowed by any sort of hidden fear. His habitual wariness softened. Gently, he traced the line of my jaw and lips. I shivered, my skin warming under his touch.

'Before we go in, I want you to know I've done a lot of thinking lately.' He watched me carefully.

'About?'

'About us.' His mouth twisted into wry humour. 'And I've come to the conclusion that I've been an idiot.'

I chuckled. 'Tell me something I don't know.'

'No, I mean: no matter what the results for you are today, once all this is over, I'd still like to give us a shot.'

'But what about your parents? I figured me having the Dark gene would make it too hard for you. Didn't you say your mother was killed by a Dark sidhe and your father by the Mors Ferrum? How could you be with me, feeling as you do about the Dark sidhe?'

'We'll work it out. You can't be held responsible for your genes.' He grinned. 'Besides, I've got a therapist for an aunt. I have no excuses for carrying baggage around.'

I laughed, lighter than I had been for days. I opened a thought-window and sent him a blown kiss. He responded in kind, and with a real kiss as well. The brief interaction, intimate and uplifting, left me warm and almost happy.

Let's go, shall we? He crooked an elbow like he was escorting me to a ball. I dropped a little curtsey and tucked my hand into it, letting him lead me to my fate, be it good or bad.

Still smiling, still entwined in thought as well, we straight-armed open the swinging double-doors and re-entered Erin's lab.

Maeve, Erin and Jennifer faced the door, their expressions variations on horrified anticipation. Erin held two innocuous-looking pieces of paper. My heart dropped. I tried to tug free of Logan's arm, but he held tightly. It didn't help. The results of my test were written in their dismayed expressions.

'Oh.' Maeve came forward, brushing a tear away from one cheek. 'I'm so sorry Logan. I didn't know!'

I ground my teeth. Apologising to Logan because I was defective was pretty cold, even for her. But her attention was fixed on Logan, and more tears spilled.

'*You* have the gene.'

Logan stopped dead, his cheeks ashen. He released me and took a step back.

'No, that's impossible.'

Erin came forward, holding the paper. 'I'm sorry, Logan. I ran both of your tests, so I could show Rowan a comparative. Hers came back negative. Yours is positive. She doesn't have it, you do. Here.' She thrust the paper at him but he pushed it away, shaking his head.

A tall, swarthy man strikes out at a tiny, blonde woman. His face twists into a satisfied snarl as she tumbles down a set of stairs and lies motionless at the bottom.

My knees buckled beneath the image's power.

Logan backed away, half-bent over, staggering, thrusting blindly at tables and chairs. Ignoring our calls, he lurched to the door and shouldered through it, vanishing with only the sound of uneven footsteps marking his passage.

The four of us were left in silence and uncertainty.

'What was that image?' I looked at my hands. 'I wasn't touching him so it can't have been a precog.'

'What image?' Maeve said.

'We still had a *barul dorus*...' I'd slipped into Henath so I translated for Erin. 'A thought-window, open. I saw a man who looked like Logan. He hit a blonde woman so hard she fell down the stairs. I'm sure she was dead.'

Maeve paled and leaned on a desk, exchanging an appalled look with Erin. 'The repression is failing. He knows.'

'If that's true, we have to go after him.'

'What the hell are you talking about?' I glared at Maeve. 'What repression? Are you saying that was some sort of repressed memory of Logan's?'

'Yes.' She sank onto a lab stool and holding the bench until her fingertips whitened. 'Logan's mother wasn't killed by any random Dark sidhe. She was murdered by her husband, Finn. Logan's father.'

Jennifer clutched at my arm. I froze, gaping at Maeve in wide-mouthed disbelief. Erin showed no reaction. She folded her arms over her chest and lifted her chin at me.

'You knew about this, too, didn't you?' I scowled at her.

Her jaw muscles jumped. 'I was there. In France, twelve years ago. I was fourteen. My father asked me to collect Logan and bring him to our place, so his parents could have an evening out. Logan was eight.' She shuddered and wrapped her arms around herself. 'We were in the kitchen and heard Finn and Helen arguing on the stair landing. Finn was...crazy-jealous about some man she'd met. Helen denied everything. Finn wouldn't believe her. He hit her. She fell and died. The expression on his face... All I could think was to get Logan in the cab and out of there.' Erin pressed thin her scarlet lips and swallowed hard. Tears fell.

'So why on earth would you tell Logan his results this way if you knew there was potential for him to have the gene when he did the swab?' I took a half-step towards her, fists clenched. Jennifer dragged at my arm, holding me back.

'I *didn't* know!' Erin snapped. 'No-one did. Not until just now. I knew about the murder, but not that Finn was a Dark sidhe.

Maeve was cool and blank as she stroked Erin's shoulder. 'Ian called me and I flew in to take Logan. Finn wasn't arrested. He was taken by the Mors Ferrum. Helen's body disappeared and the whole thing never even made the news.'

'So, what?' I growled. 'You decided repressing the memory was the best option? What about letting Logan work though it; come to terms with it?'

Maeve lifted her chin, cool. 'We've agreed to differ on methods. I fear this is one of those times. I've been training Hunters for over two hundred years. They perform best if given good incentive to pursue their targets. By telling Logan his mother was killed by a Dark sidhe and his father by the Mors Ferrum – both truths, as it turns out – he's had extremely good motivations.'

I gave a horrified laugh. 'I can't believe you said that. You...wow. And I've been worried about *me* being a monster. You take the cake, Maeve.'

'Is that what you're doing with me? Have you been lying to me, too?' Jennifer's question was shaky and plaintive. She clung to my arm with a grip that ground the bones together. 'Did you have me so you could make another Hunter? Someone to kill people?'

Maeve put on a small, brave smile that probably fooled Jennifer as little as it did me. 'Of course not, sweetheart. I fell in love with your father and wanted you more than anything. You're not going to be a Hunter, remember?' She stroked her daughter's shining dark hair. 'Can we talk about this later, Jennifer? We must find Logan.' Jennifer jerked away.

'Give me the keys,' I said. 'He can't have gone far.'

Maeve felt in her pocket. 'He has them.'

Erin stripped off her labcoat and tossed it aside. 'Maeve, you and Jennifer catch a cab home, in case he goes there. We'll take my car and find him.'

'But *I* want to go!' Jennifer said. 'He's *my* cousin. I want to help find him.'

'Be still, Jennifer!' Maeve snapped. 'This is not about you. Leave this to the adults.'

Jennifer blanched. She let out a wordless cry of frustration and stalked from the room. Maeve groaned and hurried after her, pausing only to extract a promise from me that we'd keep her informed.

Erin and I eyed each other with mutual distaste. She collected a shiny black handbag that matched her high heeled sandals and jerked her chin at the door.

As we dropped into her car, her jaw clenched and her fingertips whitened on the steering wheel.

'Have you two done it yet?'

'What?' Thrown off-balance by her abruptness, I left off scanning the road and blinked at her.

She pursed her lips. 'You *know* what I mean.'

'What the hell business is that of yours?' I flushed and glared at her.

'No, then.' She thumped the wheel. 'Dammit. That will make it more difficult.'

'What?' Clearly I'd missed something vital along the way in this conversation.

She rolled her eyes. 'You've got a lot to learn about sidhe. Once you've had…satisfying sex with another sidhe, there's an unconscious bond. Like a green thread that ties you together through the *sianfath*. The connection means you can *always* find each other. If you only have sex once or twice then it fades over time, but it takes a year or two. It's part of the reason we find it so difficult to find mates and why sidhe rarely have casual sex or fake orgasms – with each other, anyway.' Her smile was bleakly amused. 'Who wants their one night stand to know exactly where they are when they leave the next morning without saying goodbye.'

My jaw dropped and I seemed to be incapable of putting a sentence together.

'And if the tie breaks, it hurts you – psychically. There were cases where the death of one lifelong partner lead to the other's death, it was that painful.' Erin waved vaguely out the window. 'Needless to say, back in prehistoric times, there were endless rituals around a marriage and a lot of angst went into choosing a partner. Whole families got consulted because any new member would be irrevocably tied to their child so they wanted to be certain it was a good match.'

'Holy shit.' I found my tongue. 'Is it any wonder we're practically extinct? It's astonishing we managed to survive this long, between that and the damned Dark gene.'

Erin snorted. 'Preaching to the converted, sweetheart. If I could find a way to switch off the genes responsible for those two things, I'd bloody well make a fortune from the sidhe trying to find partners. Now, since you two haven't done the nasty yet, where would you suggest we look for Logan?'

I sought inspiration out the window. 'Where's the nearest big parkland with a lot of trees? One with a drive through bottle shop or a pub on the way to it would be perfect.'

She scowled out the window. 'That'd be the Mount Coot-tha Botanic gardens. Logan never struck me as the drinking type, though.'

'I agree, but I think this could be one of those exceptions.'

'You might be right. You tell Maeve where we're going and I'll tell my father.'

When I looked at her askance she shrugged pettishly. 'He wanted to know your results and he gets very snarky when I don't keep him in the loop about where I'm going. The one thing I *hate* about living with him. That and his incessant whining about the pace of modern living. But genetics research pays shit and he has a lot of money, so I have to keep being Daddy's good little girl.' She pressed the ignition and squealed onto the road, her mouth set in a mulish grimace. 'Believe me, if I had a choice I'd be gone. I only did genetics because he insisted.'

'What did you want to do?' I couldn't help but be curious.

She wrinkled her nose and checked her blind spot as she changed lanes too fast. 'What does it matter? It's not like I'll ever get to do it while he's alive, and that'll be at least another five hundred bloody years. Stop sticking your nose in.'

I shut up. Her privileged life didn't seem quite so attractive now.

ELEVEN

<It has gone to plan, Ian.>

[I'll notify our man.]

<Yes. Send him to the Gardens. That's the most likely place.>

[Very well. Are you sure, though, Maeve? I'll send a message through their spy but there's still a chance our man could be found out and this could all turn very nasty.]

<It's a risk we have to take. We need her sufficiently motivated against the Mors Ferrum to use her full gift without hesitation. We need to see what she can do. I suspect it won't take much. A threat to Logan now should do it.>

[Indeed. She's a very angry young woman. I certainly don't want to be her target.]

<You won't. She won't find out.>

It took only a few minutes and, before we even got near I felt the connection with the *sianfath* expand to fill the empty depths of me. This garden was the strongest source I'd felt since being in the little stand of rainforest behind the Freysons house, on the Tablelands near Cairns, a fortnight before. Just driving into the carpark was like easing into a cool bath on a hot day.

Erin killed the engine. 'I love it here.' She got out of the car, more relaxed than I'd seen her yet. 'I keep getting caught up at work and forgetting to come here and recharge.' She glanced up the hill towards the entrance, then left at the planetarium's white dome.

'Now where? This is a huge place. It could take ages to find him. Hunting for him telepathically would warn him and he'd run again.'

'Give me a sec,' I said. I walked over to a tree that stood as a little island in the carpark and touched its trunk, using it as an anchor point and beacon in the *sianfath*. Working cautiously, careful not to disturb the darkness behind the last block, I slid fingerlings of myself into the *sianfath*.

The invisible overlay was a rich cacophony of non-colour. Every bush, tree, blade of grass and person shimmered with their own aura of energy. I tied a thread of myself firmly and stepped free of my body. Spreading myself into a thousand delicate tendrils, I followed subtle trails of energy through the park. The reds, oranges and golds of human energy could be safely ignored. Instead, I sought the distinctive greenish-silver signature of someone with significant sidhe bloodlines.

There. It was tempting to sneak through his shields and comfort him; or even remove the memory of his father's actions. But I wasn't sure of his reaction, or if I could even do such a thing. I didn't have enough experience or skill as a technician to be sure of the result.

The thread to my body twanged as the dark-remnant of Calain sought to find its way out of imprisonment; to use this skill of mine for its own ends. I eased myself back, reeling in the extensions slowly this time to prevent the usual migraine and disorientation that went with falling back into the mortal clay of my body.

When I opened my eyes, Erin was staring at me in puzzlement tinged with horror.

'What *are* you?' She shifted back a step. 'You just weren't *there*. Your thought-house felt…*empty*. Where did you go?'

'He's this way.' I ignored the question. Pushing off the tree, I stumbled a couple of steps until I regained control of the heavy flesh holding my much-smaller mind imprisoned. The skin on the back of my skull tightened and I rubbed at it. My head ached as well. I drew from the *sianfath* and the pain faded.

Erin hesitated, then followed me. We hurried through the gate, past brilliant roses and soft lavender, and through garden beds containing herbs of a dozen countries: mint, rosemary, curry, and coriander; heady in the afternoon heat. Down a hill to our left lay a pair of lakes, dotted with vibrant green and pinks of lotus flowers; noisy with the calls of ducks, swamphens and excited children. I veered right, running through a covered cactus house, past stone and gravel display beds full of the exotic, twisted, spiky plants. I stopped before an enormous dome made of hundreds of curved glass panels set in white steel triangles. It rose high and reflected back the hot, blue afternoon sky.

'He's in there. The tropical dome.' I rubbed the back of my skull, unable to ignore a growing pressure. A warning, building like the threat of a thunderstorm. Around us, the many paths to this place held nothing but elderly couples, linked arm in arm; harassed mothers leading crying toddlers; and a young man engrossed in photographing the sharp leaves of a yucca plant. Nothing dangerous. Not yet.

Erin took a step closer to the closed glass door. I grabbed her arm, digging into the pressure point at her elbow. She flinched, yelped and glared at me.

'Quit it!'

'What can you do besides telepathy?' The push on the inside of my skull increased. When she hesitated, I shook her arm. 'This is no time to be modest, Erin. I'm a precog and I'm telling you we have company coming. Do you have any skills or weapons? What can you do?'

'Nothing,' she snarled at me. 'Nothing you'd call useful, anyway. I have psychometry.'

'What's that?' I checked around but there were no overtly suspicious people lurking behind any bushes.

'I can "read" objects to tell you about their history or find their owner.'

I curled a lip. 'Well that might have been handy when we were looking for Logan.'

'Did any of you happen to be carrying something belonging to him?' she snapped. 'I find most people don't.'

'You had his damned DNA. You don't get much more belonging.'

'I didn't think of it.' She twisted her arm free. 'Are you going to bitch at me until this alleged company appears, or are you going to go in and get your boyfriend out before he commits suicide?'

I bit back a hasty reply. She was right, but we needed to be ready in case they arrived before I could convince Logan to come out. Pulling my karambit blade out of its place in my bra, and a boot knife from the sheath strapped to my calf, I offered them to her.

'Which one?'

She gaped at them. 'I don't know how to use those.'

'Fine.' I stowed them away. 'Then you're better off without one because it would just get used against you. Can you fight?'

'No. I'm a scientist. I can't believe you're carrying knives!'

'Oh, for...What the hell was your father thinking?' I scratched my scalp underneath the wig.

'He was thinking we'd leave the Hunting to Maeve's people and we'd fight the Mors Ferrum in a more civilised way.'

'Oh? By boring them to death? Shut up.' I waved her into silence as she protested again. 'We need to get Logan out of there, but I can't leave you out here alone. We'll have to go in together. You keep watch by the door while I try and convince Logan to come out.'

I yanked the heavy glass door open and plunged into a wall of hot, damp air. Even drawing a breath took more effort in this place. The rich scent of moist earth, water, and mulch filled my lungs and poured energy into my body. Overhead, the ceiling arched in a beautiful geometric pattern of steel triangles and blue sky. A pair of concrete paths curved away, left and right, rising and overhung by deep green, lush foliage. Ahead, a round glass window, set into a concrete wall, revealed murky water behind.

I ran up the right-hand path, leaving Erin attempting to jam a broken branch through the door handles. Drops of water fell on my arms as I brushed past huge green leaves and brilliant red flowers. The top of the path opened to reveal the edge of a huge water tank that occupied the dome's middle. The dark surface was half-hidden by enormous lily pads, some at least six feet across.

Logan sat on the tank's concrete edge, staring into the water. A third-empty bottle of cheap scotch waited on the ground beside him. As I approached he lifted bleary, reddened eyes and groaned.

'Go away, Rowan. Let me be.'

I picked up the bottle, took a swig and coughed at the harsh, alcoholic burn. I tipped it into the pool. The brown liquid gurgled and splashed. There would either be some very happy or very dead fish. Logan ignored me, leaning his elbows on his knees and dropping his head onto his hands. I put the bottle down and folded my arms. I'd never been very patient with people wallowing in self-pity, even myself.

'Clear the alcohol out of your system and get up, Logan. We don't have time for this.'

'I said: go away,' he muttered.

'I heard you. I'm ignoring you. Get up. You can freak later.'

He glared at me, eyes puffy and bloodshot from more than alcohol. 'You don't get it, do you?' He choked and averted his face again, hiding from me. 'I'm...I can't...'

I crouched before him and grabbed his chin so he had to see me. 'Really? You think *I* don't get it? I spent the first eighteen years of my life an outcast amongst the people I thought were mine – humans. Then you came along and I thought I had a family I could belong to.' I fought against the tightness in my throat. 'Then I learned what I *really* am. Now I have no-one to trust and no-one who trusts me.'

He groaned. 'What if I end up like him? What if I hurt you, or Jennifer?'

I pushed aside the precog of him slapping me. I wouldn't let that happen. 'So you found out your father was a bastard and you *might* be in for mental health issues someday?' I snorted. 'Welcome to my world – almost.'

He rocked back. 'Rowan! I'm sorry. I didn't—'

'Enough.' I cut him off with a brusque gesture and checked the door. 'We don't have time, you don't need my sympathy and I don't want yours.' I kissed him hard, trying to soften truth's sharp sting. 'I love you Logan, but you have to pull yourself together. We need to get out of this kill-box. Bad things are about to happen.' I grabbed his elbow and hauled him to his feet. 'You can have a breakdown later, or beat the crap out of me in the dojo if that will make you feel better. For now, I need you compos mentos. There are people on the way.'

'People?' He frowned. 'Who—'

'Mors Ferrum, I assume.' I didn't bother to hide the sarcasm. 'Unless you've been making more enemies I don't know about?'

'No...' He closed his eyes for a second and I felt him draw from the *sianfath* and rearrange the alcohol in his blood into simple sugars. 'I meant who told them where we are?' His words were less slurred now. He screwed up his nose and ran his tongue over his lips. 'Have you got any water? My mouth tastes like I've been chewing dry old socks.'

'Do that often?' I yanked a half-empty bottle from my pocket and thrust it at him.

Erin appeared at the top of the path, her eyes wide and scared. 'They're coming. Eight men, all in black military gear and carrying guns. Heading straight for the dome. We can't get out of here without being seen. I can't find any other exits. What do we do?'

'What the hell are you doing here?' Logan stalked towards her, his brow blackened. 'You *knew!* All these years and you didn't tell me what my father'd done?'

Erin backed away. I grabbed his upper arm. He jerked free. I grabbed again and twisted his arm behind his back. He glared at me.

'Don't do this, Logan,' I muttered into his ear. 'We have more important things to worry about. This can wait. Eight guys won't. Especially if they're Eisen's men. They'll have those damned trank guns again. We need a plan.'

TWELVE

<Is it done?>

    [Almost. Although... I'm not certain... No, I'm sure it's fine.]

    <What, Ian?>

    [I believe our man may have had his hand forced. He may not be able to take care of this phase himself.]

    <And?>

    [The result may not be quite what we expected.]

    <Is Logan in any danger?>

    [...possibly. Either way, the situation should cause her to react appropriately. No cause for alarm yet.]

Logan didn't stop watching Erin, but he did relax. I released him. He rubbed his forehead.

'No emergency exit, huh?' He swept a narrow look around the thick-glass dome and the wall of lush jungle. 'Erin, you get behind the strelitzia plants. If you're lucky they won't see that damned red dress in among the red flowers. Whatever happens, stay there. You'll just be a liability. When it's over get out and tell...' He grimaced in distaste. 'Maeve.'

'But I—'

'Shut up!' His lips stretched into a snarl. 'Stay out of the way, Erin.'

Erin shrank from him, wide-eyed. She wriggled behind the plants, curling in to a small ball. I rearranged the leaves to hide her as best I could.

'Keep your head down,' I muttered. 'Cast a glamour of yourself as plants. Might work.'

At the bottom of the path, the door rattled once, then again more sharply. Erin must have managed to fasten or lock the door, somehow. It might buy us some time, but to do what?

The door glass flexed again, more violently this time.

'Can you do anything?' Logan sent me a half-wary, half-hopeful look from beneath his lashes.

'It depends.' Sarcasm didn't hide my fear. 'On whether you want the kind of help that could well suck you dry as well as those men?'

'At this point,' his voice was dull, 'I don't much care. Can you do it and keep control of Calain?'

'Are you asking me to kill those men – and possibly you as well – when you know I said I won't do that again?'

'Yeah.' His lip curled. 'Well, I vowed to kill every Dark sidhe I met, and now I am one. So where does that leave me? We're both good hand-to-hand, but we can't take on eight with tranks in this space and you know it. And, frankly, I'm in the mood to kill someone.'

'Logan, I'd rather be tranked and taken alive than let Calain loose again. You don't know what you're asking.'

He directed a fierce glare at me. 'And you have no idea what it means to be in their power.'

'Really?' I returned disdain. 'And I thought you'd seen my memories of Japan.'

He gripped my arm. 'That was *nothing*. A guy groped you. When I helped free Tom and those other sidhe from the lab in Sydney three years ago...what had been done to them. We had to...' He swallowed, paling. 'Give mercy to one of them.' Fear flickered in him. 'Whatever happens, Rowan...Eisen can't take you. Release

Calain if you have to, but *don't* go with them. Not even to save me. Understand?' He shook my arm.

The door burst open, glass shattering as it crashed into the wall.

'Let's make sure it doesn't come to that,' I muttered, twisting free. 'Here.' I offered my boot knife. He refused, revealing a wicked blade of his own.

Then he eased himself into a stand of plants, fading out of existence. I had to squint to see him. I found my own spot and tried to emulate his ninja skill. Could we hide from them? Unlikely, given they clearly knew we were here and there was only one exit. I slid my throwing knives free of their sheath around my waist.

Stealthy footsteps scuffed on the concrete paths. I stretched out my senses. Eight people, alright, including the sidhe from last night. Three coming each way and two at the door. All of them mentally shielded from any sort of standard telepathic communication. No chance to frighten them with a pithy speech inside their heads. Clearly Michael had thought of that and used his pet sidhe to protect his men. Shit.

The oldfashioned way, then.

The first man came into view. I tested the block holding Calain and my *shadow-thought* gift back. It seemed strong enough. But Calain could break free if I was under too much stress. Above anything, I had to prevent that. If he took over here, in the midst of so much life-force, he would be – I would be – powerful beyond belief. I tried to settle the race of my heart. Calm. I was calm. My palms were slick and hands trembling, belying my self-talk.

'Check behind the plants,' the leader muttered, gesturing at Erin's hiding place. 'You know how hard these animals are to spot when they're in their natural habitat.' He tugged on the low, dark tail of his hair. The sidhe who'd chased us at the MJE facility. His mind was the same: cold and emotionless. But his face was oddly pale and smooth-skinned, with deepset eyes and a slit of a mouth. Ah. He wore some sort of silicone mask. Why?

I kept my thoughts shielded and fought the urge to spit at him. Animals, were we? Fine. Animals with the ability to use tools then. I gripped a knife handle, measuring the distance between me and the man closest to Erin. He peered into the vegetation, pushing leaves aside, dart-gun ready. Too close to her. A few more steps and he'd trip over her, glamour or not.

I've got four knives to throw, Logan. Here goes the first.

I lifted my arm to throw. The leader's head snapped around, his shadowed eyes laser-focussed on me. He raised his gun. I threw the knife. The blade took him in the forearm as he squeezed the trigger. He yelped. The dart stuck into the soft trunk of a tree fern next to me.

I threw the second blade at the man near to Erin. It found its mark in his calf, severing the Achilles. He dropped to one knee with a muffled shriek. His dartgun fired in my general direction. The dart missed. Logan appeared and slit a throat without hesitation, blank and grim. He vanished back into the greenery before the body fell. Blood darkened the grey concrete to black. The metallic smell mingled with the warm scents of wet earth and water.

The third man – no, woman – dashed at me, gun raised. My third blade lodged in her shoulder. The gun clattered to the concrete. She ran on, yanking the blade free and yelling obscenities.

The block in my head trembled as Calain's darkness awoke, ready, watching. I quashed fear and gritted my teeth against the flash of pain. Now was *not* the time to let loose the dog of war.

An arm snaked around my throat from behind. A gun muzzle pressed against my neck. Shit. The darkness rattled its cage. I winced and tried to think calm thoughts.

'Move and I'll do more than dart you.'

Hot breath, stinking of cigarettes, fanned my ear.

'If that's a dart gun,' I said mildly, 'and you pull the trigger from that close, you'll rupture my jugular. Eisen won't be happy if I'm dead.'

'No-one gives a crap if another sidhe animal dies. We're not after you. We want the other one. Where'd he go?'

Why you, Logan? Why not me?

They probably don't know who you are. Remember, Eisen should still think you're dead. But why me? I don't know. Time to find out.

No! Don't come—

'Here.' Logan reappeared, with his arm around the sixth man's throat, knife pressing into the jugular. He backed away, keeping all four other survivors in sight. 'Let her go or he dies.'

The leader swapped his gun to his left hand. He pointed it at Logan and squeezed the trigger. Logan shifted and the needle landed in the thigh of the man he held.

'I can still kill him.' The tip of Logan's blade drew blood and the man in his arms waved a feeble protest, eyes rolling into his head as the lids fluttered closed.

The leader shrugged, loading another dart. 'Go ahead.' He waved his gun in my direction. 'Then I'll kill her. Or you can let him go and we'll let her go – if you come peacefully.' He produced a standard, silenced nine millimetre pistol and shot in the head the man whose leg I'd cut. Blood sprayed shocking scarlet on the plants. Then he waited, unperturbed. The woman retrieved her gun and pointed it at Logan as well.

No, Logan. Don't. We can do this.

We can't, Rowan. Not with two more at the door as well. There's no way unless you're prepared to let down that block. You can control him, you know.

No...I—

Didn't think so.

Logan dropped the unconscious man, who folded to the ground. The sound of his skull hitting the concrete echoed in the space. Logan raised his arms. He habitually wore a high-tech bulletproof vest, but the material was thin and flexible and not designed to stop the fine point of a needle. The leader darted him in the body, then used the regular gun on the insensible man at Logan's feet. Three dead. Logan flinched and swore as he yanked the hypodermic out and inspected the empty chamber.

He staggered towards me, his focus on the man holding me. The gun at my throat shifted, as though my captor debated whether or not to point it at Logan instead of me. His hold on my neck loosened a fraction. I jerked my head back. My skull broke his nose with a satisfying crunch. His finger twitched on the trigger. The dart skimmed my chin and broke on a window, splashing golden liquid onto the glass triangle. I jammed my last throwing knife into his stomach and yanked it out again. I spun and kneed him in the cheekbone as he bent over. He dropped.

'Kill her.' The leader wasn't even paying attention to me. He hoisted Logan's unconscious body over his shoulder. 'And dump all the bodies into the tank. And that idiot, too.' He indicated the man I'd stabbed, then strode down the path as though Logan's weight was nothing.

In desperation I threw my knife at the back of his legs. It missed, vanishing into the plants.

'No!' Erin appeared through the plants, pale as death. 'Logan!'

The black-clad woman, gun in her left hand and blood glistening on her shoulder where my knife had hit, pulled the trigger. The dart pierced Erin's back. She screamed, twisted, plucked it free and threw it back, point first, hard and fast. The woman tried to dodge but it took her in the neck. The dart was empty, of course, but Erin smirked in satisfaction.

She turned towards the path again. A puzzled frown crossed her face.

With a soft sigh, she collapsed sideways, onto the tank's edge. She teetered on the rim, then slipped into it, landing on a giant lilypad. For a second it looked like she would stay atop. But she was too far to the side and the leaf slid out from under her. She vanished beneath the surface of the dark water.

THIRTEEN

<Is it done?>

[Yes, but not quite the result we hoped for.]

<Did she...?>

[No. But Logan is still alive. And Erin.]

<Time to set stage two. Are you certain of our man's loyalty?>

[As certain as one can be in these circumstances. You should know better than I, anyway. His allegiance is dependent on your skill as a psychiatrist.]

<I wish I could be certain Logan will be safe. He wasn't supposed to be taken, just threatened so she would—>

[And that didn't work, did it? She controlled it. This is war, my dear Maeve. You've said it before. Sacrifices must be made for the greater good. He's a Hunter and a flawed one. This was always a possibility and you knew it from the day you adopted him.]

The wounded woman fled, following her boss and leaving her unconscious and dead companions behind.

I hesitated in the middle of the carnage, surrounded by bodies, and blood-spattered plants and concrete. I glanced at the door, swore long and loud at Erin, then vaulted into the tank.

Even in the murky water, Erin's red dress was visible, billowing softly. I snagged it and hauled her to the surface. Stinking, rotting plant matter swelled up, disturbed by my kicking, brown in the cold, dark water. Bits of weed clung to my hair as I struggled with Erin's dead weight. Climbing out, I dragged her over the edge and draped her, face down, across the seat. Water poured from her mouth. Once it stopped, I shoved her off and she crumpled into a sodden pathetic heap on the concrete. She coughed a few times then breathed normally and slept on.

I slumped on the ground beside her and leaned on the tank's concrete wall. Tears of anger and despair blurred my vision. Erin lived but Logan was gone. I could have got him back if I'd followed straight away. She'd picked *the* worst moment to come out of hiding. Damn her!

I contemplated her bedraggled, skinny body. Could I just leave her to explain in this bloodbath to the police? No. And I didn't have time to wait for her to come around.

Shoving to my feet I found her ridiculous little handbag, then my knives. I collected the three dartguns and all the full darts I could find and stuffed them into my pockets and belt. No point in giving more humans access to a drug that affected the sidhe as strongly as this one. There weren't many darts; six in total, but that was six less in Eisen's inventory.

One man also carried a nine millimetre silenced pistol. I took that as well, along with the three spare clips in his pockets. What the hell. Guns were difficult to buy in Australia, legally or illegally. I was a decent enough shot – good enough I could wound without killing. More reliably than with my Calain-controlled psychic power, anyway.

Logan's scotch bottle went into the tank. His knife I wiped of prints and placed in the lax grip of the man I'd wounded – the one the sidhe had then shot. With any luck, the police would blame him for one murder. With no pistol on the scene they'd know there was at least one more person present. But Eisen could afford to either have the survivor silenced in prison, or lawyered up so fast the police wouldn't know what hit them. Either way, four of his damned minions were out of the picture.

With one last check to make sure I'd retrieved all evidence of our presence, I picked Erin up. She weighed very little, even wet. Her short, black hair was plastered to her slack face and the dress clung to her curves in a way bound to shock anyone seeing us leave. How the hell was I going to get to the car carrying an unconscious woman? We were the opposite of glamorous in our sodden clothes and dripping hair. We'd be noticed for sure – and later tied to the death of the men whose blood stained the concrete at my feet.

Glamorous. Yes. I wasn't yet good at casting a glamour, and the illusion wouldn't fool cameras, but I could alter our appearance to look ordinary to any bystander.

At the bottom of the path, I found the locked manual controls for the sprinkler system. Breaking the cabinet open, I opened the controls to full and water poured from every possible site in the dome. Pinkish water trickled down the path and into a drain at the bottom. Good. That should take care of any DNA trace from us. I dabbled my shoes, washing off the blood.

Gathering Erin into my arms again I concentrated on building a detailed image of a middle-aged woman carrying a child of about four or five. Hopefully a normal enough image to get me to the carpark unnoticed.

As a bonus, I spotted a 'closed for maintenance' sign tucked away next to the door. With Erin's limp form over one shoulder, I staggered out and hung the sign over the door handles. There was no-one nearby so I hurried to the carpark, keeping the *glamour* in mind. We'd have to come back, with the spare key, for Maeve's hire car later. Hopefully it wouldn't get towed in the meantime.

My runners squelched unpleasantly as I walked, fuelling irrational anger. The more I saw of the sidhe who were supposed to be my allies, the less I liked them. With the exception of Logan, and possibly Jennifer, they were cold-hearted, self-centred know-it-alls who didn't give a damn about me or my mother. Logan's insistence they could help was becoming laughable. Because of Erin, he was captured. Because of Maeve, my mother was in Eisen's power as well. Who would be next?

I was better off working alone.

'Oh, my dear girl!' Ian snatched open his front door the instant my foot was on the step. 'Come in! Quickly. Lay her on the couch. Harry! Bring blankets and some tea for Miss Gilmore.'

'I'm fine.' A shiver belied my words as I dropped Erin on the gleaming dark leather and sank into a chair. I couldn't entirely blame the bone-deep chill on being wet. Harry wrapped a blanket around my shoulders and pressed a cup of tea into my hands. I thanked him, warming my fingers.

Ian sat on the edge of the couch, chafing Erin's wrist. 'What's wrong with her? What's happened? Where are Maeve and Logan?'

'She's been tranquillised. Maeve's on her way over.' I sipped my tea. 'I'll explain when she gets here.'

Maeve arrived shortly after and thrust a bundle of dry clothing at me without speaking. She fussed over Erin, taking her pulse, tucking the blanket around her, and towelling her hair dry. She touched the bruise purpling the left side of Erin's face from where I'd dropped her out of the water tank. The bruise faded to yellow.

'If it was only one dart it should be a matter of waiting a little and she'll recover.' She glanced around. 'We need to make plans. Wait, where's Tom?'

Ian's hands fluttered in voiceless frustration. 'When I contacted him, he asked me why. I said I assumed he wished to be informed about his sister's affliction.' He grimaced. 'He said I'd assumed wrong; that he was in a tutorial and would come home when he was done. He was quite brusque.' In an aside to me he added, 'He's doing his postgraduate studies in linguistics and etymology, even though I pointed out how useless that is to our long term goals.' He frowned, then his expression gentled. 'Pray, child, tell us what happened.'

I shivered again. 'Logan's been taken. We have to get him back – and Anna. We can't wait or Eisen might kill them. Or move them somewhere else and we'll never find them. Erin'll be fine.'

'Logan! But he wasn't—' Maeve shut her lips and ran her palms down the front of her flowing silk overshirt, leaving sweat-stains on the pale green cloth. When her grey eyes met mine they held all the worry and fear I could wish for. There was something else, too: uncertainty. That bothered me more than anything. In the short time I'd known her, I'd never seen her unsure of the next step. Serene, secretive, manipulative, focussed on what she thought was right, yes. Hesitant, no.

She swept a strand of hair from her face. 'Of course, you're right. We must find a way to get into the MJE compound and release Logan...and Anna. I just—'

'Maeve,' Ian interrupted her, thoughtful. 'How did they know where Logan was?'

Maeve hesitated for the merest fraction of a second, then gasped. She dragged her attention from Ian and stared at me.

'Hey! Don't look at me. Someone must have been watching us.' I folded my arms and glared back. 'They waited until we were separated then went after him, specifically.'

'After Logan, but why? Tell us the rest.'

I gave them a synopsis and, by the time I was done, Erin began to stir and moan. As Maeve and Ian checked her, I threw off the blanket and paced the hardwood floors.

'As to why they wanted Logan…I don't know.' I chewed on my lip, trying to think of all the possible angles. 'They knew I was sidhe, but they didn't want me. I don't think they even knew who I was, so Eisen might still think I'm dead. But why Logan? What's special about him?'

Maeve sank back into her chair.

'Oh…'

'What?' I leaned in. I needed the ability to get through her shields and see what she was thinking, without the pain of using *shadow-thought*. I doubted, somehow, she'd let me in just for the knocking on her shields, as per sidhe etiquette. She trusted me as little as I trusted her.

Her focus snapped back to Ian. 'The Dark gene. That has to be it. It's Eisen who's been taking them. Somehow he's found out about Logan and taken him, too.'

Ian agreed, the lines around his mouth deepening.

'You're not making any sense, Maeve,' I said, impatient with her dramatics.

She pressed her fingers to her lips.

'I think I can shed some light,' Ian put in, watching her, melancholy. 'As you know, for some years now we've been trying to track those responsible for kidnapping sidhe. That's why Maeve and Logan were in Cairns.' He cut me off as I opened my mouth to speak. 'And, of course, that's how you came into this. But what you don't know, is our suspicions about what's being done to the sidhe they take.'

'Logan mentioned something about labs.' I shuddered. 'I thought it was about tapping into our powers – telepathy, strength, lifespan, healing. That sort of thing. Do you think that's where they've taken him?'

'Yes,' Ian said. 'For the last ten years or so, we've been hearing reports of young sidhe working for the Mors Ferrum – kidnapping and doing despicable, horrible things to us, their own kind.'

I frowned at him. 'But we know that. We already ran into one – last night. He was there again today. Wearing some sort of silicone mask. I couldn't see his face. What does this have to do with Logan?'

Ian's high forehead creased. 'We believe the Mors are taking sidhe with the Dark gene on purpose. Those that aren't Dark they use as laboratory experiments, as you suspected. Those that *are* they somehow switch the gene on *and* brainwash to strip away any sense of morality. Then they set them against fellow sidhe. They're creating super-soldiers – out of our people.'

Blood drained from my head and I had lean on the chairback to stay upright. I tried to sip my tea, but my hand shook so I put aside the cold, over-sweet drink.

'You're saying Logan was targeted because of his results today?' A shiver sluiced over my skin. 'But how did they find out so fast?'

Ian shrugged. 'No way of knowing. They could have a spy in Erin's lab. That's the most likely explanation.' He dismissed the question, apparently uninterested in what I thought was crucial. Didn't he care that his daughter was being spied on?

Erin, finally awake and lucid, protested. She sat up and leaned on Maeve's shoulder. She closed her eyes and I sensed her drawing from the lush gardens around the house, using the *sianfath's* power to heal herself and flush the drug from her system.

'How do we get him out?' Erin's voice broke. The leather chair beneath her creaked as she leaned forward. She pointed at the three of us. 'I mean, it's not like we have enough people to take them head-on, even if we were a skill-match. You might be able to fight,

Rowan, but Tommy and I were never given the sort of training you and Logan had.' She tugged the blanket close about her.

Maeve straightened and cleared her throat, although she still seemed abstracted.

'Ian, did you get those plans?'

He started, then regarded his laptop in distaste. 'Yes, I believe so…that is…my associate said he emailed them to me. I can't seem to…'

'Oh, for the love of…' Erin struggled from her place on the couch. Stumbling over to the roll-top desk she flipped open the laptop and tapped at the keyboard. We all waited in silence while she wrestled with the software and swore at the cheap little printer tucked into the back of the desk space.

'Maeve,' I said. Something was missing. 'Where's Jennifer?'

Her lips pressed tight. 'She was being childish. I left her at home, having a tantrum in her room.'

'You're an idiot, Maeve.' I pulled out my phone. It stayed blank. Water dripped from it and I groaned. It'd been in my pocket. 'My phone's fried. Call her.'

She released a frustrated sigh and pressed a speed dial number on her phone. A few seconds later she held it away from her ear, redialled and listened again. Irritation flashed and she tucked it away.

'She's probably just sulking.' She pushed pillows behind her back and sipped her tea, ignoring me.

'Maybe,' I said, 'or she could be in trouble. If they followed Logan then they may have followed you as well. Don't dismiss my ideas because you don't like me, Maeve.'

Maeve's eyes widened. She stared off into middle distance for a moment then caught her lower lip between her teeth. She leapt to her feet, snatching at her purse. True fear now flickered in her.

'I can't *read* her either. The house is well within my range. She's just…gone.'

FOURTEEN

<Ian! What if—>

[*Hush, Maeve. You're ahead of yourself. They have no reason to go after Jennifer.*]

<*Except that she's sidhe as well, you fool!*>

'She could just be asleep,' Ian said soothingly. 'Don't fret yet.'

She headed for the door. 'I have to call a taxi—'

Erin crowed in triumph and snatched at several pieces of paper as they shot from the printer and wafted to the floor.

'The floor plan to the MJE buildings. *Now* we're cooking.'

I wavered and ground my teeth in frustration. If ever I needed to be in two places at once, this was it. Maeve didn't have the fighting skills to get Jennifer out if she was in trouble. But someone had to plan the incursion into MJE to get Anna and Logan back.

'Maeve.' I yanked my sodden blonde wig off and threw it aside. 'I'll go get Jennifer. I've told you about the external security we saw at MJE. I'm assuming you've worked with Dante in planning rescues like this?

She nodded.

'Right,' I said. 'If anyone's at the house with Jen I'm better equipped to deal with them.' I patted the throwing knives around my hips.' I'll be forty-five minutes, max. I'd like to have a workable plan by the time I get back.' I snatched Erin's keys and the dry clothing and headed for the downstairs bathroom without awaiting a reply.

A few moments later, I slipped into the driver's seat and a knock on my mental shields startled me.

Maeve?

<You need to know...> She hesitated and I sensed worried ambiguity. *<Logan said there was a second* sidhe *at the MJE complex last night. An older, stronger, almost-invisible mind. Be careful. If Eisen's men are at my house they may not be alone.>*

I swore, aloud and silently. She withdrew, offended and anxious.

I wound my way out of the leafy, idyllic riverside suburb and into mainstream traffic, cursing every car that dawdled in front of me. Where was Jennifer's telekinetic ability when I needed it? Probably not capable of throwing a car out of the way anyway. She'd Gifted me the knowledge of how to use telekinesis, but I hadn't been able to make it work. Half-heartedly, I gestured at a car that cut me off. Nothing happened. So much for being Jedi. Well, at least I wasn't Sith, like I'd expected.

The moment of dark humour lifted my spirits and I wished Logan was here to share it. Then again, he *was* Sith now, so he might not appreciate it.

When I arrived in Paddington, I stopped a few houses up the steep, narrow street from Maeve's place. No signs of intruders. A telepathic check revealed nothing; not Eisen's people or Jennifer. Either she was gone or she'd somehow developed mental invisibility. Even if she was asleep I should be able to detect the quirky, gingerbread cottage shape she used as a shield.

Maeve's Paddington house was a graceful old wooden structure in white, with deep verandahs and ornate scrollwork fringing the eaves. The purple-flowered jacaranda towered above, clashing with the red corrugated iron roof and the orange-yellow flowers from the neighbour's silky-oak tree. High brick fences surrounded the property on four sides and security cameras covered the gated front entrance.

Using the remote on Maeve's spare keys, I disarmed the external perimeter alarms and vaulted the neighbour's low front fence. Scrambling through their overgrown back yard, I found the rear of the Freyson property and the small emergency exit tucked into one corner. The security code for the front gate also worked on this and it opened without a squeak.

I snuck through the transplanted rainforest and peeked into the dojo. My eyes adjusted to the gloom.

'Jennifer!'

She started, leapt to her feet and clutched a book to her stomach like a shield.

'You scared the cr…scared me, Rowan.'

I grabbed her by the shoulders. 'We've been trying to reach you. Why haven't you answered your phone?'

She shrugged. 'Left it in the house. I didn't want to talk to my mother.'

'I know how you feel.' I grimaced. 'And you're welcome to swear in my presence. I don't care.'

She giggled. 'Mother says a lady doesn't swear.'

I threw her an ironic look. 'Your mother was born in 1736, when being a lady meant playing music, embroidering in tiny stitches, and being brainless. You don't have that luxury. You need survival skills. Swearing is useful in its place.'

'Y'know what?' Jennifer marked her place in the book with a scrap of paper. 'I'm starting to think you're right. Mother doesn't get what it means to be a woman these days, does she?'

'Well,' I temporised, 'she's not stupid.'

'No, but—oh!' She gasped. 'Logan! Did you find him? Is he ok?'

'Yes.' I pushed back my wet hair. 'Actually, no.'

'Huh?'

'I found him, but Eisen's men captured him.'

She paled and took a step back. 'Oh. What…what are y—we going to do?'

I admired her for changing the "you" to a "we". She was only a kid. Not equipped for this, but she was still willing to help, even after her ordeal in Cairns. I hugged her, swift and hard. She clung to me, shaking. I stroked her hair and rubbed her back until she relaxed.

'Sorry,' she mumbled, sitting on the bench and wiping her eyes. 'Why is your hair wet? And smelly.'

'Not important and there's nothing to be sorry about.' I dropped beside her. 'Truth is, that's how I feel as well – scared shitless.' She opened her mouth. I cut her off before we could get into the inevitable conversation about who was more scared. 'I came to get you. We're worried Eisen's men might be following Maeve and Logan. Which means you shouldn't be alone here.'

She started to rise. I grabbed her wrist. A vision of her future flashed. I grimaced and bit my tongue, literally, to hold it still. The vision I thrust to one side for later consideration. It made no sense, anyway, merely an impression of fear, determination and a long, white corridor lined with doors. I needed to get better at controlling when these visions appeared. They were distracting and not always useful.

'How come I couldn't find you?' I tapped my temple.

Her normal, irrepressible grin surfaced. 'It worked? Cool.' Hefting the book, she opened it and spun the age-spotted pages to me. 'I borrowed this from Tom's library. Since you Gifted me the *Henath* language yesterday, I thought I might read some of his old books. There's some great ideas – but some I can't work out how to do. See here? It's called *folach.*'

'Hidden,' I translated, reading the instructions. It sounded easy and useful. A technique rendering the usual protective "house" style of shield invisible, along with the mind inside. I tried it. My father's castle still looked the same. I checked with Jennifer. Her eyes glazed then she smiled.

'You're gone.'

'Huh. Nice find.' It must be the technique used by this "invisible" sidhe Maeve mentioned.

She beamed. 'The book says it only works as long as you remember to keep it going, or until you fall asleep.'

I traced out the name on the cover. '"*Mod an Meonn*". *Method of the Mind*, by Aeona Silverblade. I wonder why that name keeps coming up?'

'Does it?' Jennifer peered over my shoulder.

'Mmmm. Maeve said she was the last one known to have the *shadow-thought* skill I have. Ian had that book from her sister. Now this.'

'Maybe the Universe is trying to tell you something,' Jennifer said brightly.

'The universe doesn't give a damn about humans or sidhe, Jen. It's a big collection of stars, rock, ice, and vacuum; nothing else. Faith in yourself is far more useful than faith in anything, or anyone, else.'

I rubbed the back of my neck and rose, keeping hold of the book. Outside, the sultry, golden afternoon sun speared dust-filled beams through gaps in the leaves and picked out the brilliant orange flowers of a bush next to the dojo. A black and white bird landed nearby and warbled a beautiful song. But I couldn't ignore the feeling something was very wrong – or about to be.

'I think we should go, Jen. Throw everything you need into a bag. I'll grab some things for Maeve and Logan. Is there anything sensitive or valuable Maeve always takes with her?'

'The EM-proof room has her laptop and backups of her research, and our new identities.'

'You get those, then.' I checked my watch. 'We need to be gone in ten minutes. I have a feeling this place is under surveillance. Meet me back here.'

We parted ways inside the house. I shoved the book and my meagre belongings into my tattered gym bag then stuffed as many of Maeve's and Logan's things as I could into another bag. All of us were used to travelling light, so there wasn't much left behind when I was done. Jennifer appeared, puffing and shouldering two bulging bags, as I arrived at the dojo.

The pressure on the inside of my skull increased as we headed for the hidden back gate, but no-one broke in the front door. Hopefully we'd got away in time and the house could be re-used in the future. I didn't want to be the one to burn another of Maeve's safe-houses to hide our trace.

We ran through several back yards and emerged onto the street six doors away. I paused behind a tree and sent out cautious, questing tendrils of myself into the surrounding area, checking for spies. It felt clear. Only a few people were home and all of them were thinking mundane, ordinary thoughts. Wincing, I gathered myself into wholeness again and rubbed at my head. What was causing this feeling of impending doom, then?

Erin's cherry-red convertible grumbled to life. I dropped the clutch and squealed the tyres by accident. Cursing, I slowed to legal speed and checked the mirror. No tails, yet the pressure increased. I drummed on the steering wheel as the urge to run grew and the prickling beneath my skin became almost painful.

It got worse the further we went from the house.

No. It got worse the *closer* we came to Ian's house.

Crap.

The weight of expectancy vanished, leaving me lightheaded. We were still a good five minutes away.

Double crap.

I drove past the gate to Ian's house at normal speed. Around the bend until the house was out of sight behind a copse of trees. Then I pulled off and bumped the too-red car over the rough-mown verge. The tangled, weedy undergrowth provided cover. I killed the engine.

'Lock everything in the boot.' I threw my bags in. Two dart guns went into the waistband of my shorts. 'We're going in light. Something's happened.' I hesitated over the nine-mil pistol, then left it behind. Too much chance of a stray bullet hitting the wrong person. I tugged the karambit out of its sheath under my breast instead.

Jennifer shivered. 'What's going on?'

I shushed her and waved her to my side as I edged through the trees. A low timber fence bounded Ian's property. That was the problem with a big property: harder to secure. We climbed the fence and pressed against the trunk of a large eucalypt.

Can you cast a glamour?

Yes, Jen's thoughts whispered. *What of?* She shivered.

We'll be dogs. Hang on a sec. I stretched out telepathically. Seven minds. Three shielded human ones I didn't know. Plus Maeve, Ian and Erin, all in a drugged sleep. And Harry, Ian's man. He was sidhe, and well-shielded behind a Norman era motte-and-bailey fortress. He wasn't drugged, but hovered on the edge of unconsciousness, bathed in pain, shame and anger. That didn't bode well. There was no way of telling if an eighth mind – an invisible sidhe one – was there or not. And a *glamour* wouldn't work on another sidhe.

Here. I passed Jennifer my boot knife and her throwing-dart belt. *Remember the work we did this morning with your telekinesis? Now's the time to use it.* I brought her up to date with the possible existence of a brainwashed, psychically-invisible sidhe. She paled and clutched the knife.

I'll go in first. I gripped her shoulders. *Stay outside and keep your mind hidden. There are at least three of Eisen's men in there. All of our people but Harry are unconscious. So Eisen's people are waiting for us. Use those weapons and make them count. Try not to kill if you can avoid it.* I squeezed her shoulder. *The nightmares are a bitch. Stay clear of darts. Use telekinesis to point the gun at them instead.*

Her head bobbled like one of those dashboard figurines, her eyes wide and terrified.

'It'll be ok, Jen. It's just a precaution.' I hesitated, afraid to scare her more. 'Here's another one. If anything goes wrong with me...If I can't control Calain...Trank-dart me as many times as you can. Then run. Got it?'

She swallowed hard, but managed another nod.

'Good. Follow me.' I built an image of a golden retriever and broadcast it, along with feelings of goodwill.

We jogged across an expanse of mown lawn, around to the back of the house. Less ornate than the front, it still boasted an impressive kitchen garden, golden sandstone walls and a wrap-around verandah. The rear door stood open.

Keep the glamour going as long as you can. Hide behind that chair on the verandah. Take out anyone who comes through the door. Got it?

Jennifer bit her lip, her whole body shaking, but she slipped behind the furniture.

FIFTEEN

[Will she break her vow not to kill?]
   <If he gives her enough incentive.>

I reinforced the *glamour,* raised a dart gun, and trotted into the kitchen, trying to behave with the unconcern of a stupid family pet. Lying on the black-and-white tiles, Harry opened one faded-blue, dark-rimmed eye. The other was blackened and bleeding. His bruised lips twitched into a small smile. A gentle, very formal knock touched my shield and I opened a window for him.

/My lady, have care. There are three left. All in the library, I believe. Please.../ Blood coloured his lips. */Don't let them destroy the book collection. It must be saved at all costs./* His gnarled fingers wrapped loosely around my wrist. */There are books in there you, especially, must see./*

Me? "My lady"? You know me? No, it doesn't matter. I checked the door to the rest of the house. Still clear. *Can you heal yourself?*

His lips twisted. */I'm old, my lady. Drawing on the sianfath becomes more difficult each year. I'm too weak to reach far enough to draw what I need. I'm dying./*

Not if I can help it. I have questions for you. Here. I hid behind the table and dropped the *glamour.* Working carefully, I extended into the *sianfath,* excluding my people, but including the men in the other room. I drew the energy Harry would need to repair his injuries. Not enough to drain all three humans to unconsciousness, unfortunately. I could only draw what Harry needed. Any more and

I'd have nowhere to release and would cremate myself from the inside out.

I'd created a reinforced room in my thought-house and now stored the energy there. I gritted my teeth against the flare of pain. The beast that was my father rattled his cage and screamed his desire for power. He urged me to drain every living thing and lay waste to the humans and their destructive march against the natural world.

I peeled back Harry's torn, bloodied white shirt, exposing his shrunken, blood-smeared chest. Bruises darkened his side. They'd kicked an old man? Rage built and with it the urge to reduce the men in the next room to lifeless husks. Ruthlessly, I shut out my father's voice. My own bloodthirsty tendencies were bad enough without his encouragement.

Touching Harry's arm, I slowly fed the silver-green life-force into him, letting it spread throughout his body. I didn't know how to heal his wounds in a precise way. So I envisioned the energy speeding his metabolism, encouraging his cells to heal themselves. His eyes flew open, his shock undisguised. The damage faded, bruises yellowing and gashes closing. I trickled more energy into him with painful, painstaking care and control. Finally, all that remained was drying blood on his skin and a blinding headache behind my temples. I massaged my neck, fighting to stay conscious. I clutched at the table for support as the floor tilted. My legs shook and knees ached on the hard, cold floor.

'Let me, my lady,' Harry whispered. He touched my forehead and sloughed off the migraine, much as Maeve had done for me in the past. He sat up, patting himself in bewildered pleasure. 'I feel better than I have in years, my lady. Thankyou. How did you do that?'

'Maeve says I have the *shadow-thought* gift,' I murmured, swallowing against the inevitable post-headache nausea.

'*Skath-sheel!*' He used the *Henath* words, paling as he said them. 'But Aeona was the last and she died six hundred years ago.'

'You know of her?'

'Of course!' He sounded affronted. 'My family have served the Silverblades for four thousand years.'

I opened my mouth to ask more but the sound of coarse laughter from the nearby library stopped me. 'We need to talk, Harry, but not now. Go out the back. Jennifer's waiting. Stay with her until I come.'

'But, my lady…' He struggled to his feet, somehow still dignified even though his clothing was bloodied and tattered, his white hair matted with gore. 'You must let me assist.'

No, Harry. Go. That's an order. I'll be fine.

He pursed his lips, then bowed. Light-footed, he eased out the back door.

Edging along the hall, I paused outside the library door and listened. The three men weren't saying anything profound. Something about waiting for someone; and about being well-paid for this job. Nothing useful. How did Eisen and his men know where Ian lived? And why had they only sent three men?

How had three humans overcome *four* sidhe? Harry, Ian and Maeve hadn't lived this long by being oblivious. I brushed the thought aside for later consideration. Right now I had three men to dispose of in the least-permanent way I could. I produced the two dartguns.

I swapped the karambit to my left hand and lowered myself to the cool, wooden floor. Dart gun ready, I peered around the doorframe. I could, of course, go screaming in at high speed and outpace pretty much anyone. But it would only take one obstacle to trip me. And one human with a quick trigger finger would end everything. If I took out two from here things would be a lot easier.

Two men, dressed in black and wearing bulletproof vests, stood in the centre of the room. I couldn't see Maeve and Ian. Erin lay on the couch, asleep. One of the men stood over her. He flipped back the blanket Erin still wore. Even in her waterstained dress, with her hair wild and her mouth slack, she was pretty. I cringed as they discussed her in crude terms. My finger curled around the trigger.

The third man was posted at the window, staring out over the garden towards the visible part of the road. He would have seen us drive past in the red convertible. Hopefully he hadn't heard the engine's distinctive roar stop close by.

One man tugged at Erin's dress strap. I took careful aim at the back of his thigh and squeezed the trigger. He jumped, yelled, and flailed at his leg. Brandishing the dart, he glared at his companions, who stared back in shocked denial. I swapped guns and made the second shot. The second dart took his companion in the upper arm.

The third man shot at me. I ducked out of sight. The dart smashed against the wooden floorboards, inches from my face. There were two thumps, which I took to be two bodies falling, then silence. Damn. Now what? He might be on his own, but he had three hostages and no other exits, apart from barred windows.

The empty dartgun went back into my belt. I climbed to my feet and took a cautious step away from the door, considering my options.

I bumped into something large and soft.

I spun and slashed left-handed at a grey-suit-clad arm. The short, curved blade of my karambit sliced through cloth and skin. Red stained the fine material. A large hand clamped onto my wrist. The bones ground together.

Flexing an elbow, I levered against his thumb. But he was even stronger than Logan and held fast. His grip tightened. My fingers numbed. I lashed a straight-kick at his knee. He shifted aside and twisted my arm into a lock. The knife dropped from my nerveless grip. He caught it and tucked it into a pocket.

Pain lanced through my arm and I cried out, angry at myself for doing so. I glared at my captor, searching for a weakness to exploit.

He was huge – well over six foot and almost as broad. This must be the other sidhe Maeve had mentioned. Like the one who had taken Logan, he wore a too-pale, silicone mask that hid his features. But behind the mask, there was no mind. His body stood before me, but he didn't exist. That rendered him more horrifying than the worst of humanity I'd ever met.

His free hand latched onto my throat. He hoisted me into the air. Pushing me up the wall he watched without emotion as I scrabbled at his arm. Blood roared in my ears. Terror welled. The bright hall dimmed and the world faded. My heels drummed against the wood and panic flooded in.

Deep in my mind the caged beast broke its bonds and surged out. I almost welcomed it, for it seemed less frightening than the monster strangling me. But the essence of Calain paused and retreated. It vanished back to its cell without intervening.

I was so shocked I could barely think. I forgot everything I'd ever learned and simply dangled at the end of his arm. My father had abandoned me? He'd always been there every other time I'd been in danger. Why not now?

As the world darkened, defiance surged. No. I was better than this. I didn't need to wait to be rescued by my father's memory. I didn't need him.

I grabbed the arm, tightened my stomach and flung a leg up. Wrapping it around his neck, I jerked his head back. He released me. I let my shoulders fall, bringing my other leg up as my upper body swung down. My momentum tipped him off balance. He staggered and bent but didn't fall. I released my leg-grip and tumbled free, rolling to my feet a few metres along the hall.

Gasping and coughing, I massaged my throat. The world slowed its spin and the ringing in my ears subsided.

We regarded each other warily.

'Rowan?' Jennifer appeared in the back doorway, anxious.

A real gun appeared in the sidhe's hand. Aimed at Jen. She shrieked and froze. A throwing-dart clattered to the floor.

A red haze of anger and fear clouded my thoughts.

His finger curled around the trigger.

I hauled open the last block in my mind and drew on the *shadow-thought*. Tendrils of my self speared into the *sianfath;* into the enemy, drawing life from all of them.

The three men in the study died within seconds. Their life-energy was now a glowing ball inside my body, fizzing, tasting of lightning. But something protected the sidhe from my powers; his shield, maybe. He was immune. He remained untouched, alive.

I closed the gap between us and drove my open palm into the sidhe's broad chest. That strike would cave in a human sternum. He didn't even flinch. Glaring into his cool eyes I poured the stored energy into him. It should incinerate the man. But something interfered, dampening and diverting the power, reducing its strength. Some earthed in the wall behind him. Paint peeled and timber smoked. Some energy forked away and vanished into the study, where glass smashed and books thudded to the floor. What was left exploded against his body.

His white shirt burst into flames. He stumbled backward, hitting the wall with a thud that shook the pictures. The gun went off. Jennifer screamed and Harry's deep voice echoed her. The sidhe batted at the smouldering ruin of his shirt. His skin was blistered and red. He ran at me. I sidestepped and stuck a foot out. He leapt over and continued, heading for the door. Wood splintered and metal pinged as he tore it open. He vanished through the opening. Vaulting the front gate, he disappeared down the driveway, shirt flapping.

My punishment began. The consequence of using *shadow-thought* without care for the last psychic block protecting it from release. A sledgehammer smashed at the walls of my core-mind. The migraine exploded in my brain and I sank to my knees, retching helplessly. I went into darkness unsure if Jennifer had survived, knowing I'd just murdered three people to save her.

SIXTEEN

[By God, Maeve! Did you see those men? Nothing but husks. It's incredible.]

<*Yes...Yes, I saw.*>

[Not getting squeamish are you, my dear? They're only Mors Ferrum.]

<*But what of Jennifer and Harry? They almost died.*>

[Don't lose sight of the goal, now, my dear. Just help her realise her potential.]

I awoke to find Maeve and Erin bending over me. I sat up and they withdrew, expressions of cautious fear in their faces. The walls swayed so I stayed on the couch. We were in the library. I'd been out long enough for it to be put to rights. The room was reassuringly normal and free of dead bodies. A framed watercolour, sans glass, leaned against one wall as the only evidence of the destruction I'd wrought.

'Jennifer? Is she ok?' I half-rose but my legs gave way so I sat, frustrated by my weakness.

'She's fine. She deflected the bullet and is very proud of herself. She's making you tea.' Maeve's calm reply did much to soothe my fear.

'How long was I out?' I accepted a glass of water from someone and drank without tasting it.

The leather beside me creaked as Maeve sat. She folded her fingers in her lap with an air of suppressed excitement at odds with how I felt.

'Only about twenty minutes.'

I scowled at her. 'But how... You were all sedated. It takes longer than that to shake it off.'

Maeve waved my question aside. 'Harry and Jennifer healed us. We thought it best to let you recover naturally.'

More likely they'd wanted a chance to discuss me without being overheard.

Erin sat on a chair opposite, her arms folded and legs crossed. 'What'd you do? You killed those three men but there's not a mark on them.' Her chin lifted. 'And why the hell is there a bloody great burn on the wall and the door ripped off its hinges?'

'Erin!' Maeve's tone was hard. 'I believe we can do without your charming presence. Go tell your father to start packing. This house is compromised. You'll need to move.'

Erin glowered at her, mouth set mulishly. She unfolded her arms. 'Fine. But you can't tell me she's normal or safe. I've always told Father you're crazy and now I know it's true. You want to use her in your stupid war but you can't control her, can you?' She rose and snorted a bitter laugh. 'Well, don't blame me if your weapon of mass destruction explodes in your face.'

She stalked out and stomped up the stairs. A few seconds later the sound of running water attested to her whereabouts in the shower.

Harry entered and passed me a hot cup of tea, but I shook so much I couldn't hold it. He set it beside me and patted my wrist. There was a warning in his expression I couldn't interpret and I was disinclined to let anyone into my shields at the moment.

A long silence followed. I avoided Maeve's speculative gaze.

'You saved Jennifer's life,' she said, 'and mine – again. I'm in your debt, you know.'

I couldn't speak. My throat was too tight. I curled into myself and dropped my head onto my forearms, on my knees. My chest constricted as the enormity of what I'd done broke over me. Did saving five lives outweigh taking three? Were Maeve and Ian any better, as people, than Michael Eisen's mercs? Who was I to choose who lived?

And yet, in a single moment of stress, I'd done exactly that. Without a second thought. My choices had seemed clear and justified – and without the influence of Calain's darkness. I did what I had to.

My mother had often said – "your worst moments can define what sort of person you are." So, in spite of Logan's assurances and my efforts, that's who I was: a killer. All this agonising over taking lives was pointless. The fear of Calain's influence was wasted.

He wasn't the monster, I was.

I shuddered and clenched my teeth as my whole body shook with reaction. No. I would not dissolve in front of Maeve. I swallowed the bile of my self-hate and the salt of tears. Revulsion I shoved deep into my gut and buried it beneath bleak acceptance. Well, if I was prepared to kill, I may as well stop fighting myself and get used to it. I was what Erin had named me: a weapon of mass destruction.

I straightened, then pushed to my feet, cold and detached. I thrust stiff fingers through my tangled, still-damp hair. My hands hurt and I stank of wet weeds and burnt cloth. I inspected my palms and found them blistered and red. Healing was no effort but the stench lingered in the back of my nose, reminding me of the power I could wield.

'I need a shower,' I said. My voice was surprisingly steady, even unemotional.

Maeve regarded me narrowly. Her mind touched my shields. I held them firm and brushed her aside. She hesitated, then pointed.

'Down the hall. When you're done we'll help Ian finish packing and we'll all go to a new safe-house.'

'Then we'll plan Logan's rescue.'

'Then we'll plan Logan's rescue,' she agreed. The gleam of excitement in her had, if anything, grown.

An exhausting hour later most of us, including Tom, crowded around the chrome and glass dining table of a hastily-hired AirBnB house in Chapel Hill. Maeve had decided Logan's capture meant any of her Brisbane safe-houses presented a risk. So she and Ian rented a five bedroom, glass-and-steel monstrosity tucked away in the hills. Not one of the graceful, older houses preferred by Maeve and Ian. Erin, Tom and Jennifer, however, inspected the property with evident delight in its modernity. Jennifer was already splashing in the huge indoor pool.

In the old house, Ian's multitude of books and antiques were now being packed by removalists for storage somewhere in another suburb. There'd been a major argument between Tom and Ian over that. Tom wanted to retrieve some of the *Henath* books and Ian wouldn't let him. I didn't care about their squabbles or the house. I wanted to get on with the business of saving Logan and Anna. Getting to a safe house had already taken too much time.

I scrutinised the faces around the table. Tom was sullen and distracted, pressing one fingertip to the middle of his forehead as though to relieve a headache. Erin had regained her aloof disdain but was studious in avoiding my eye. Maeve was calm, as ever, but still with that suspicious air of repressed excitement. Ian seemed determined to dislike every plan anyone put forward for getting into MJE. He listened politely to every idea, then proceeded to pick it apart in meticulous, patronising detail.

The only one I wanted to hear from was Harry. But he was relegated to the kitchen and, by the sounds and delicious smells, was preparing dinner. I rose from the table, leaving the others arguing over the building plans, and strolled into the gleaming kitchen.

'Can I help?' I selected a knife and pointed at the small pile of carrots sitting on the white granite bench. A huge pot bubbled on the induction cooktop, its contents giving off a meaty, salty aroma that made my mouth water.

Harry smiled. 'Thankyou.'

We worked in silence awhile and I found the mindlessness of it soothing. In the room next door, voices rose and chairs scraped. Hasty footsteps echoed across the hardwood floor. A door slammed.

'Are they always like this?'

Harry chuckled. 'Oh yes. Master Tom and Miss Erin have been at each other's throats since they were born. And Master Ian does enjoy setting them at it. They need to get out from under his thumb and find who they are, but...' He pursed his lips. 'I shouldn't speak out of turn.'

I considered him curiously. 'You said you've worked for this family for a long time?'

'Yes, indeed.' He shot me a quick, mischievous look. 'Apart from a few years in the early eighteen hundreds when I worked for your father.'

'Dare I ask why?'

Harry raised a shoulder. 'Master Ian had decided to reside in a Buddhist monastery for a while. He sometimes goes on these spiritual searches.' His mouth twisted in wry humour. 'Trying to find a meaning to life. Many sidhe who have lived a long time away from their native forests do the same. They never understand life has no point, except to nurture the *sianfath* of the great Mother Earth that sustains us all. Anyway.' He shrugged. 'He wasn't allowed a servant, so I sought out your father. I'd always admired his work.'

'And?'

'Calain was a good man. We fought together against Napoleon. If I had to choose anyone to have my back, it would be Calain Gilmore. We remained friends for a very long time.' He laid a sympathetic hand on mine. 'I was sorry to hear he'd passed. I tried to find your mother and offer help, but she'd already moved on – protecting you, I assume.'

I nodded, my throat thick with emotion. I couldn't bear to think of her, still in Eisen's power. What was she suffering because of my mistakes? Was she even alive? Surely I would know if she'd died? Even the thought of losing her hurt. Clearing my throat, I went back to cutting carrots and sought a safer topic of conversation.

'What was Aeona like?'

He paused, staring out the window at the thick bushland outside. A small brown bird alighted on a branch nearby and twittered its song before flitting off into the greying landscape. Harry shook himself.

'She was most truly a lady. Gentle and kind. It broke her heart to be used in the wars as she was. Mine too, my lady.'

'Why did she let them?' I stopped for a second. 'And please call me Rowan. Being an Earl's daughter is a bit pointless these days.'

'Miss Aeona was born in an age where women didn't mean much, except as bargaining chips and mothers.' His precise chopping became more forceful and a piece of zucchini flew off his board onto the bench. 'As soon as her *shadow-thought* gift became known, she was whisked off by the local lord and his Dark sidhe advisor, Tordal Ivaldison, to be a weapon in their wars. She was only seventeen at the time. Poor lass. We didn't see her again for a very long time. When she came home a hundred years or so later she was broken.'

'Do you know what happened to her after that?'

'No-one does. She simply left. Best not to ask questions.'

'I'd like to know, though, Harry.' I stopped cutting and pinned him with a stare. 'What happened to Aeona?'

Harry said nothing but stew splashed onto the stove as he stirred too vigorously.

I persisted. 'Did she leave in the middle of a battle in Wales? That's what Maeve said. What about her child – the one they held hostage?'

'She was with Tordal Ivalidson and his son, Kieran, in Wales,' he said wearily. 'In 1404 Tordal hired her to England to help quell the Welsh rebellion. There was no child. That's why she came home to Scotland. She said the child had died. Without the babe to be held against her, they couldn't stop her leaving, though they tried.' He sighed. 'But she only stayed home a few months – long enough to help Miss Mairi finish her book of visions. We awoke one morning and she was gone. Miss Mairi was devastated. She couldn't even reach her telepathically. Miss Mairi never saw a single vision of her sister after that, either. That's how we knew she must be dead.' He knuckled an eye and went back to cutting. 'Seven years later, Miss Mairi disappeared as well, leaving me to raise her son, Master Ian's father.'

I stayed silent, touched by the story. I had a dim understanding of how Aeona must have felt. Trapped as a pawn in the wars of others, helpless to change things or escape.

'One thing I will say about her.' He shifted his weight to one leg and faced me, his expression knowing and sympathetic. 'For all the horror she went through and all the lives she took, she never became hardened to death – human or sidhe. She was remarkable. She had a boundless capacity for love and forgiveness I've never seen since.'

There was nothing I could say without sounding bitter and resentful, so I kept silent and blinked away tears I couldn't even blame on onions.

Handing the carrots over, I cocked an ear towards the dining room. There were only three voices now. It sounded like Tom had left. I ought to check on him. I still had his Aeona Silverblade book in my pack, but I was reluctant to give it back without reading more. There must be something in there I could use against our enemies.

'How would *you* go about getting Logan and my mother out, Harry?' I studied Harry's craggy profile. He must have seen a lot in a very long life. It seemed crazy not to ask.

He smiled, wryly. 'I'm honoured you've asked.' He stirred the pot and added a dash of some dried herb. Tasting it he smacked his lips, then offered me a spoonful. It tasted as good as it smelled; salty, meaty. He laid the spoon aside and put the lid on. He gripped my shoulders.

'There are times when a team is required.' He lowered his voice. 'And times when, perhaps, it's not. I'm not certain which of those this is. I think you should weigh the benefits and drawbacks for both. Whichever you decide on, commit to it wholeheartedly, for a team is only as strong as its weakest member: be it a team of one, or of seven.'

He kissed my forehead, his dry lips scratching against my skin. His expression held old pain and much sadness. He tucked an auburn curl behind my ear.

'Calain would be proud of you. He mentioned you once, you know?'

'Really?' My heart leapt.

'He'd been badly injured in the battle of Waterloo. I was nursing him for we were far from any large stands of forest and he had little connection to the *sianfath* to work with for healing.' Harry smiled in reminiscence. 'I told him he wasn't allowed to die. He laughed and told me not to worry. Said he had yet to meet his daughter and he had no intention of dying until he'd had that pleasure.' He tilted his head. 'I'm not sure how he knew, but he did. I think the idea of you kept him alive that day.'

Tears clouded my vision and I leaned on his convenient shoulder. 'Thankyou. I always thought he didn't want me. My mother said it took her three years to convince him to have me. Then he left when I was four.'

Harry wrapped a wiry arm around my waist. 'Never that, my dear. He was afraid that being his daughter would make your life unbearable.'

He released me, stirred the pot, and cleared his throat. 'Please run along and tell Master Tomas and Miss Jennifer dinner will be ready in ten minutes. My thanks for your kind assistance.'

Dismissed, I left the kitchen through the other entrance and leaned over the balcony to yell at Jennifer, still splashing in the pool. Then I ran up the floating glass staircase to the third floor. Tom sat on the back deck, moodily overlooking the manicured garden of clipped hedges and short lawn. Beyond it, bushland whispered its chaotic, wild defiance; far more appealing and powerful than the imprisoned garden. I tasted its eucalypt scent and drank its energy, letting silvery warmth seep through my tired body.

'Sorry I wasn't there.' He didn't bother to look around and his tone was harsh. 'At the house, before.'

I got the impression he meant his apology but expected me to condemn him anyway. I sank into a white wicker chair next to him.

It creaked alarmingly beneath me. The sun's last red rays snuck through the surrounding hills, half-blinding me. I shifted the chair.

'No way you could have known, Tom. I don't blame you.'

He snorted. 'You're the only one, then. Father and Erin have spent the last couple of hours treating me like I'm Typhoid Mary.' Leaning back, he folded his arms over his chest. 'What was I supposed to do? Erin was wet. What, was I meant to rush home and blowdry her hair?'

I bit back a hasty reminder that Erin being wet was hardly the issue, Logan's abduction was. The Fairchild sibling rivalry was so strong it clearly ranked higher than anything else in their minds. Instead, I chuckled dutifully and waited.

When I didn't react, Tom relaxed. He glanced sidelong at me. 'Anyway. I am sorry I wasn't here to help you.'

'I don't know you would have been able to do anything. They would have just darted you as well. How'd the tutorial go?'

Tom shuddered. 'That's the thing. I had to say something.'

'What do you mean?'

'Y'know how we talked about my memory and the gaps?' His expression was stricken. 'I can't remember. One minute I was on my way to Uni for the tutorial.' He spread his arms. 'The phone rang then…then I'm in my car, somewhere over the south side, and my phone's still ringing on the seat next to me. But it was two hours later. I have no idea where I was or what I was doing. But if I'd said that, the lecture on my stupidity would still be going on. Nothing I do is right, so I'd rather not give him an excuse to throw this in my face.'

I waited a minute, debating how to give him advice he wouldn't want to hear.

'D'you think, maybe, it might be worth talking to Maeve?' I said, trying to sound casual. 'Whatever happened to you in that Mors Ferrum lab obviously affected you. PTSD and all that?'

'This from you? I can tell there's no love lost between you two.' He waved aside my half-hearted protest. 'Either way, you're probably right. But I think it can wait until all this is over.'

He stood and held out a hand to me. I took it, blocking any precogs before they could happen, and let him tug me to my feet. He crooked an elbow and tucked my arm through it.

'For now we'd best go plan a rescue, and eat dinner. Harry hates it when people are late to the table. He gets horribly polite and makes us all miserable. I'd rather not upset him. He's about the only person here who cares about me.' His mouth twisted into a little grin. 'Present company excepted, I hope?'

I laughed. Truth was, for all his childish sulkiness and insecurity, I liked Tom far better than his sister or his father. Trusted him more, too.

SEVENTEEN

[If we play this right, Maeve, we can retrieve your precious nephew and wipe out Michael Eisen's operations in one incursion.]

<I agree, but we can't risk her losing control and losing sight of who the true enemy is. She could kill all of us in a moment.>

[Quite. But perhaps there's another solution. One that poses no risk to us at all. What's her range with the shadow-thought?]

<I'm not certain. At least a few kilometres, though she may not know that yet. But she can't use it without risking releasing Calain. At the very least it causes her a great deal of pain, and her mind shuts down – as you've seen.>

[Hmmm…I'll think on it.]

I disengaged my arm from Tom's before we entered the room but Erin aimed a haughty, suspicious stare at us anyway. Jennifer, grinning and damp-haired, patted the seat next to her. I dropped into it.

We ate and little was said beyond trivialities. I inspected each person at the table and considered Harry's words about teams. Who, out of these people, did I trust to have my back if we went into MJE? The answer came down to two people who were ineligible because of their age – one too old and one too young. The others were practically useless in a combat situation. Plus, Erin was likely to abandon me out of spite. Tom might suffer whatever was causing his memory lapses at a crucial moment. Ian was a foppish old fool with a stick up his backside. Maeve clearly still had some hidden agenda.

Decision made, I went through the motions of listening to and agreeing with their plans and strategies after dinner. I had no intention of letting any of them know what I actually wanted.

I memorised the building plans to the MJE complex.

Hours later, after the arguing petered out and a plan of action for the following night had been grudgingly agreed on, the party split and went to their separate bedrooms. I was, supposedly, sharing a room with Erin. Instead, I chose the oversized bed-couch in the home theatre room and no-one said anything.

I wasn't sleeping, anyway, but read Aeona's book, and wished I had even a few of the amazing abilities she described. Death-warning, fire-working, trans-location, levitation; and something she called 'slipping' which sounded almost like a version of time-travel. All the skills were way cooler than an iffy precognitive ability.

She even devoted a whole page to various techniques for merging with the *sianfath* and returning to the body, stressing each time how important a lifeline-tether was. I shuddered. How cavalier I'd been with my skills. She touched on the ability to release or cut the tether and still return to the body, but it sounded painful, difficult and unlikely to succeed. To be used only in desperate circumstances. I flipped the page, hoping for something more promising.

Unfortunately, there was nothing about the *shadow thought's* other aspect: the ability to drain life.

After midnight, a cautious telepathic sweep of the house showed everyone asleep. I eased out from under the blankets and pulled on my sneakers. Checking I had all my knives, I swore softly when the sheath sewn into my bra turned up empty. I'd forgotten. The invisible sidhe-bastard had pocketed my karambit. Nothing I could do about it now. I lifted Maeve's keys from a large clay bowl on the kitchen bench and closed the front door softly behind me.

Twenty minutes later, I doused the headlights and rolled the car off the road, into the deep shadows of the forest next to the MJE complex. After sitting for a moment, I unclenched my fingers from the wheel, got out and thumbed the button to open the boot. I'd placed Logan's bag of useful items there earlier in the day. Clearly, I'd already known what my path was, even if I hadn't admitted it to myself until later.

The boot popped open, loud in the warm, silent evening.

I jumped back and swallowed a scream.

'Jeezus, Jen!' I glared at the girl, curled up in the boot of her mother's car. She squinted at me, a mixture of defiance, fear and excitement bubbling in her expression.

'I *knew* you'd ditch us!' With a groan, she unfolded herself and stood beside me, stretching and bending. 'You were way too quick to agree with everything Mother and Erin said after dinner. I snuck out and fell asleep in there. When you started the car it freaked me, though.'

'*You're* freaked?' I lowered my voice and inspected our surroundings. About two hundred metres away, through the bushland, the MJE building lights glowed. Off to the west, a flicker of lightning illuminated clouds piling on the horizon. The faintest smell of rain wafted on a breeze that carried the distant rumble of thunder.

I unzipped Logan's bag and stuffed things into my pockets and belt. The nine-mil gun I left behind again. Something in me was reluctant to use it. It seemed too final and, for all my realisation about my willingness to kill, I still struggled with the idea of shooting someone. Both dartguns and the remaining four darts might be useful, though. Using the *shadow-thought* to drain the MJE staff would incapacitate me at the wrong time.

Jennifer reached past me. I grabbed her wrist.

'No way, kiddo. You are *not* coming in with me. You stay here. I'll be back with Logan and Anna and we'll need to get away fast. You can keep the engine running for me. That's it.'

Her mouth set in a mulish pout and she wrested her arm free. 'I'm coming and you can't stop me.'

I brandished a dart gun. She narrowed her eyes. A knife drifted from the boot and hovered next to my jugular. I grinned reluctantly and tucked the gun into my waistband.

'You catch on fast. Fine. Here.' I passed her the belt of throwing-darts. 'Stay behind me and keep a *glamour* in place. Be invisible.' I thought about it. 'Actually, can we do that?'

Her voice shook as she buckled the belt around her hips. 'Sure. Sort of. But you'd have to know what you're standing in front of all the time, so you can make yourself look like that.'

'Ah.' I considered it. 'Too complicated. We'll have to go as security guards. I'll give you the image of the ones we saw the other night. I wasn't close enough to see the detail on their badges, though. If we meet a real guard, change your image to suit.' I indicated a spot above her head. 'And remember to be about a foot taller than you are.'

She gave a slightly hysterical giggle.

'Here. So the cameras don't face-capture you.' I tossed a black ski-mask to her and pulled one on as well. She'd had the sense to wear long, dark clothing.

I inspected her. 'If we survive this, your mother will kill me. You know that don't you?'

She shrugged. 'If we bring Logan home, I think she'll forgive a lot.'

'How'd you get so people-smart?' I pressed the boot shut.

'Hanging around with a two-hundred and eighty-year-old psychologist helps.'

I snorted a laugh. We were both being ridiculous because of an excess of nerves. After adjusting my ski mask, I squared my shoulders.

'Ready?'

'Guess so,' she said.

'You can still wait here.'

'Not a chance. Rowan? Did you know I'd be here?' She tapped her temple.

I lifted a shoulder. 'I had a precog involving you and a long, white corridor. Not too hard to guess where. I tried to avoid it by leaving you behind.'

'Oh.' Jen shuddered. 'Did you see anything…else?'

'No.' There was no need to tell her about the vision of Logan's cruelty, or of my capture. All I could do was hope I could avoid falling into that one. There was no way of knowing what would trigger it. Sneaking into MJE was a pretty obvious one, though. Was I being too predictable? Had they broken Logan? Would he tell them I was alive? Would they be expecting me? Probably. I had to try, stupid as it sounded.

We eased into the open forest and my worries about Jennifer's ability to go ninja dissolved. She may not have had any training from Maeve on the unladylike skill of sneaking, but her sidhe heritage made it natural. She glided from shadow to shadow like a wraith and it took her only a few moments to get the hang of walking without crunching the brittle leaves and bark underfoot.

Keeping our communication silent and short, we lowered ourselves into an overgrown stormwater easement and padded east along the fenceline. In the far eastern corner was the worst-lit section of fence. That was my goal.

We reached it without incident, stopping once as a two-man patrol strolled past inside the fence. Then Jennifer kept watch while I used wire cutters. The blueprints hadn't shown any alarms wired into the fence, but that wasn't a guarantee. Nothing happened. We scrambled inside and twisted two thin strands of wire around the fence-loops to hold it together enough to pass a superficial inspection.

The tap-tap of boot heels gave ample warning for us to duck behind a waste bin. A one-man dog patrol sauntered past. The German shepherd sniffed the air in our direction more than once. The man paused and spoke to him encouragingly. Jennifer glared. The dog lost interest and tugged his handler off in a different direction.

~The guard's mind is shielded, but the dog's isn't, Jennifer explained. *Dog-brains don't make a lot of sense, but I made it think it heard something over the other end of the building.~*

Now I am *glad you came.* I squeezed her shoulder. Her teeth flashed white against the dark mask.

Lightning flickered to the west. I gave the sky an uneasy glance. A storm could mean flash-flooding in the storm drain and cut off our escape route. We'd need to be quick.

For the next minute or two, we traversed the stark, concrete spaces between the buildings in a pattern that, to an onlooker, would have seemed bizarre. I was, in fact, treading a path that led us through as many camera blind spots as possible. Four times Jennifer had to use her telekinesis to either unscrew lightbulbs, or rotate cameras to let us sneak past unseen. By the time we reached Building Three, she was panting and trembling. Not only was she under emotional stress, but this was the most she'd ever had to use her abilities with such precision.

You should wait here. I peered around the corner, gauging the distance to the door. *If all hell breaks loose, run for the cut in the fence and get away. Ditch every weapon and find a house nearby. Get in and play the lost child to the hilt.*

~*Stop it, Rowan.*~ She sounded like her mother. ~*You saw me in a white corridor, so that's where I'm going. I'm not deserting you or Logan.*~

I gripped her arm briefly and we made the final dash together.

Getting in proved relatively easy. Jennifer's telekinesis took care of the lock and the alarm trigger. Inside, we stole along a white corridor lit only by three dim knee-high night-lights. Only one camera covered the entire space. Jennifer switched it off. The vast warehouse was mostly empty to the roof where huge lamps hung unlit. The only sound was the low-pitched hum of airconditioning and the whisper of our clothing as we moved. Dust and the faint scent of antiseptic tainted the cool air. The corridor existed because a dozen or more rooms had been built inside the space. They were wood-framed, plasterboard boxes with silvery airconditioning ducts snaking across the low roofs. All the doors were closed, leaving us with too many choices and little time.

We split up and checked each one for occupants. We couldn't risk a telepathic check in case the brainwashed Dark sidhe slept there. They would sense our intrusion. Most were empty offices and labs. By the last six rooms, my heart was in my throat. What if Logan was right and they'd moved Anna because of my little act of stupidity the other night? What if he and Anna had already been shipped off to a different country altogether?

The pounding of blood in my ears almost overwhelmed other sounds.

~*Here!*~ Jennifer's exultant, silent shout made me jump and I almost swore aloud. I closed the door to the room I'd checked and hurried across to hers. She waved me over, eyes wide with a mixture of horror and excitement.

One dim downlight lit the stark room with a sickly blue-white light. The room contained nothing but a bed, an open shower, and toilet. On the narrow cot-bed lay a woman, asleep. She wore a loose white tshirt and grey long pants. She was curled on her side, her legs tangled in a thin grey blanket, as though she'd had nightmares. Her wavy red hair, splayed across a white pillow, was a splash of colour in the bleak space. One bruised wrist was handcuffed to the metal bedframe.

I froze for a moment. Then I bade Jennifer to watch the door and ran forward, yanking off the ski mask as I went. From a specially-designed pocket in my bra I produced a pair of lockpicks, then crouched beside the bed. Putting a palm over the woman's mouth, I whispered her name.

'Anna? Mum? Wake up, it's Rowan.'

Her eyelids fluttered then flew open. She sucked a breath through her nose and her mouth moved beneath my palm. I clamped down harder, preventing a scream as her body stiffened. She squinted and nodded, relaxing. I removed my hand and shushed her. Relieved tears flooded her blue eyes as she watched me work on the handcuff lock.

My fingers trembled as I struggled with the double-locked cuffs. They clicked open, sounding too loud in the suffocating silence. Anna eased to her feet. She threw her arms around me and we clung to each other in silent joy, not needing words. A sense of security filled me as I breathed in the scent of her skin and held the soft warmth of her body. She finally drew back and wiped fresh tears from her cheeks, kissing mine away as she'd done when I was small.

EIGHTEEN

[They have Anna Gilmore.]

   <They?>

   [Jennifer is with her.]

   <Jennifer! How-?>

   [I planted the suggestion in Jennifer's mind that she go along. Rowan needed someone with telekinesis and she wouldn't have allowed you to go.]

   <How dare you endanger my daughter without my permission!>

   [As you so frequently point out, Maeve, this is war. She is quite capable. More than you seem to realise. They're doing fine.]

   <...>

'We have one more person to find,' I whispered into Anna's ear. 'Have you seen a guy, about my age, with similar eye and skin colour? Short, dark hair? His name's Logan.'

Anna gasped. 'They brought him in this morning. I saw him go past my door. Somewhere to the right.' She bit her lip and shuddered. 'I don't know what they did but he screamed for a long time.'

I swore and Jennifer blanched. She looked at me beseechingly. As much as I wanted to get Anna out of here as fast as possible, I had no intention of leaving Logan behind. We slipped from the room.

The next door down was locked but simple enough to pick. After a quick check, we all eased in and closed it behind us. The setup was identical to Anna's room, but with the substitution of a hospital bed for the cot, and a medical trolley in the corner. Logan lay, strapped to the bed, a drip feeding into his left arm. He was shirtless and wearing the same sort of gray pants as Anna. His head lolled to one side, facing away from us. But if the bruises on his torso were any indication, he'd been beaten and hadn't been able to heal himself.

Anna undid the straps while I removed the drip. He didn't stir. Jennifer, who'd been inspecting the medical trolley, passed over a bandage. I withdrew the needle from his wrist. Even that didn't wake him and I began to worry. How the heck was I going to get an unconscious, grown man out of this compound without being seen?

In the distance, a door slammed and two pairs of boots clumped on concrete. The three of us stared at each other. Then Anna ducked behind the hospital bed and gestured furiously to me and Jennifer. I taped the drip tube onto Logan's wrist and restrapped his arms loosely. Jennifer hesitated, then pointed at the door and the lock clicked.

I joined Anna behind the bed, pulled out a dartgun, and checked the chamber. Jennifer wriggled in. I made camera-clicking gestures to her. She gave a thumbs up. We'd agreed to keep telepathic communication to a minimum, in case the sidhe working for Eisen could possibly hear or sense us, but it made some things difficult. Hopefully she'd switched the hall camera back on.

The footsteps neared. The door handle rattled.

'Still locked. It's fine.' A man's voice, light and with an edge of irritation.

'We should check, though,' a second voice, deeper and calmer, responded. 'You know how the boss gets about these animals escaping.'

'It's just a bloody camera glitch. Happens all the time,' the first replied. 'Anyway, you heard John, the feed's back now.'

The door lock clicked and it opened. An overhead light flicked on, flooding the room with brilliant, eye-aching white light. Jennifer and I flinched. All three of us squashed ourselves lower. On the bed, Logan groaned and stirred.

'See?'

The light vanished, leaving the room in gloom.

'Yeah, but maybe we should check the woman, too.'

The first man sighed. 'I checked her twenty minutes ago. Besides, she's human. It's not like she could get out without anyone seeing, with or without cameras. C'mon. I need a coffee if I'm going to make another three hours of this shit. Especially if William creepy-guy and Eisen are coming back in the morning to work on this kid again. I almost feel sorry for him.'

There was a short silence.

'You shouldn't call him "creepy-guy",' the deeper voice replied, tinged with worry. 'He knows when people are disrespectful behind his back. You notice that?'

There was a snort. 'That's one of the things that *makes* him creepy-guy. It isn't *right* to be able to get into someone's head and know what they're thinking. Violation of privacy. Plus, he's like a damned ninja with how quiet-like he sneaks up on you. Scares the crap out of me. Him and his offsider kid. Tell *me* they aren't just like these damned animals? What I don't get is why they hate them so much when they're the same?'

'Shut up, Matt. Stop thinking stuff like that. You're asking for trouble. Let's tell John it's clear and get back to patrolling.'

The door shut and the footsteps disappeared along the hall, carrying a laconic argument between the men with them.

We waited a minute or so longer. The outer door slammed shut and we breathed a joint sigh of relief. Jennifer trembled so much I was surprised she could even stand. Anna's fingernails dug deep marks into my arm.

As I straightened, I checked Logan. His eyes, swollen and bruised, were open and fixed on me. His bloodied mouth twisted into a painful smile and he reached feebly towards me. I unstrapped him, clasped his hand and tried to hold back a cry of despair at his pain.

I kissed his temple. 'Can you heal yourself? We need to get out of here.'

'No. There was something in the drip. A drug that suppresses our abilities.' His voice was husky and cracked.

'Damn. Must be the same thing Eisen put in my drink in Cairns. I'll have to—'

His fingers tightened around mine. 'No. You can't use your gift here. You know what it does to you. This isn't the place to be unconscious and vulnerable.' His mouth twisted again. 'Believe me. Get me home and we can worry about my health issues later.'

'Can you walk?' I moved to the other side of the bed and finished unstrapping him. Drawing his arm over my shoulder I helped him stand. Jennifer hovered nearby and Anna listened at the door.

'Watch me,' he said grimly.

'Jen, camera?' I jerked a chin at her and she nodded.

We eased out the door and locked it behind.

'Rowan, wait.' My mother tugged on my sleeve and pointed to the door opposite her room. 'There's someone in there. I saw him...her...I don't know, being wheeled in on a gurney. I couldn't see the face.'

I hesitated. I wanted to get Logan and Anna out. But I couldn't, in good conscience, leave one of my own people in Michael Eisen's control. I transferred Logan's weight to her shoulders and dug out my lockpick again.

'Take him to the door. I'll be there in a minute.'

Slipping into the half-lit room, I tiptoed to the bed. This room was much nicer than the others, boasting a television, fridge, bedside lamp, a colourful duvet, and several books – all recent-release action novels. On the bed, a young man lay rolled onto his side, facing away. He too had a drip in his arm. Instead of the dark hair I'd come to expect on a sidhe, his was fair. Perhaps a quarter-caste? So why did Michael want him?

A medical chart hung off the metal tube-frame bed. I lifted it, angling the page into the bedside lamp's dim light.

I almost dropped the chart. Paul Eisen. Michael's *son?* I read the paperwork closely. There was a lot of medical jargon I didn't understand, but three words stood out: "possible Huntington's disease?". I had no idea what that was, but apparently Paul had undergone a battery of tests in the last couple of weeks.

When he'd taken me on our one and only date, two weeks before, in Cairns, he'd made light of a bandage on his inner arm. He'd complained his father was forever making him take blood tests for some unknown reason. Could this be why? Had Michael Eisen known, somehow, his son had this Huntington's thing?

The sleeper sighed in his sleep and slumped onto his back. Definitely Paul; thinner and with dark circles beneath his eyes. I froze, waiting for him to wake. His brow twitched into a frown and he muttered something incomprehensible.

For a moment, I contemplated taking him hostage, but I had Anna and Logan. There was no point in triggering an all-out war with Michael we weren't yet ready for. I hung the chart back on the bed and exited the room, locking it behind me. I ran along the long corridor and joined the others at the door.

'Who was in there?' Anna whispered.

'Michael's son, Paul,' I said shortly. 'He's sick. Having treatment. He doesn't need our help. Let's go.'

Jennifer's eyes widened. Logan didn't comment. His head hung low, his eyes closed and mouth set in a grim line. I ducked under his other arm. He winced with each step. His jaw worked and his breath came in short pants, interspersed with swearing.

Outside the building, we retraced our steps to the fence, only once having to avoid the dog-security patrol. Jennifer used the same trick, fooling the dog's mind into believing it heard something a long way away. She became a little more reckless with redirecting the cameras, but I didn't much care. Thunder rumbled overhead and a light rain spattered the warm ground. Speed was the issue now and, even with Anna holding Logan on the other side, progress was difficult. Neither of them wore shoes and the rough gravel had to hurt their feet.

We re-opened the gap in the fence and tied it shut behind us. It might gain us some time if the escape was discovered. Getting Logan into the easement and back to the car proved the most difficult. The ground was so steep and uneven I couldn't carry him. Watching him struggle down the first slope and back up was heartbreaking. Jennifer offered to help with telekinesis, but she was exhausted and couldn't do more than steady him when he stumbled.

With every step I expected the wail of sirens, the flare of lights and the chorus of dogs on our heels. Instead, there came only the crunch of dead leaves, the rumble of thunder, and the hoarse rasp of our breathing. Not even my precognitive ability predicted anything bad. There was not the slightest sense of unease or pressure.

Was it possible we'd get away unnoticed? It seemed so unlikely that I checked behind half a dozen times. Even once we got to the car and I drove away, into suburban normality, I couldn't shake the feeling it had all been far too easy.

NINETEEN

<They did it, Ian. They're on their way back.>

[See? I told you. Now we can refocus her on destroying the Mors Ferrum.]

<You may find that harder than you think. She's not exactly excited to be working with us. Now she has what she wants, she may leave.>

[Well, we shall have to convince her otherwise. I'm sure Logan will help us.]

The clock ticked over to two o'clock as we arrived at the Chapel Hill house. I'd gone a circuitous route to make sure we weren't followed. As we coasted into the driveway, the front door flew open. Maeve, fully dressed and heavy-eyed, hurried out.

She opened her mouth when she saw me, then shut it when Logan emerged, leaning heavily on Anna's shoulder. Jennifer flung open her door and threw herself into her mother's arms, crying and babbling incoherently. I left them to it and helped Anna get Logan inside.

We laid him on the couch in the theatre room and covered him with my blankets. He muttered 'thanks' as his eyes drifted closed. Maeve bustled in with an order to let her check him. Resentful, I retreated and watched her work. Her hands hovered an inch above his battered body as she assessed his internal injuries.

'Rowan?' My mother's soft question drew me and I stepped into her arms. She burst into tears on my shoulder.

We stayed that way a long time, with me stroking her hair like I was the mother and she the child. Her sobs eased and she leaned back, sniffing and wiping her nose with the sleeve of her shirt. I laughed, for she'd often reprimanded me for doing the same thing as a child. A quick hunt produced tissues. I left her blowing her nose and grabbed some spare blankets and two cups of hot, sweet tea from the ever-prepared Harry – who still managed to be dignified even in blue-striped pyjamas. Then I took her out onto the back deck and we sat at a table, with blankets around our shoulders. We spoke in whispers so as not to disturb Maeve, inside.

'Mick told me you were dead.' Anna's voice caught on the word. 'I woke up in that bed. He came in and said…he said you'd fallen off the top of his house and died. He *smiled* when he said that. Then they injected me with something and asked me questions. I don't remember much but I know I talked a lot. He kept asking about that *ocair* thing you've been chasing information about for years. Mick wasn't happy when I couldn't tell him anything. I don't understand what's happening. I haven't seen anyone but him and a female nurse for days.' She studied Maeve. 'Who are these people? What's going on? Where are we?'

As succinctly as I could, I brought her up to date, filling her in on what happened in Cairns, on my father's history, and the existence of the sidhe and their factions. She heard me out in stunned silence as I explained the Freysons', Fairchilds', and my own psychic gifts. It came out jumbled and half-incoherent in my relief to unburden myself to her, but she seemed to understand the gist.

When I'd dribbled to a halt she inspected my face with thoughtful interest, faintly coloured by fear.

'So that's why you and Calain understood each other so well, even when you were a baby? Telepathy?'

I nodded. 'And when he left he put blocks into my mind, so I wouldn't be able to use my gifts by accident. He was trying to protect me but it kind of backfired in some ways.'

'Yes,' she murmured. 'I can see that. What an idiot! Why on Earth didn't he trust me enough to tell me? I loved him to pieces. I would have done anything to protect both of you.'

'I think he was worried he'd hurt us if he stayed and the Dark gene overcame him.' I leaned on her shoulder. My tension dissolved with the touch of her lips on my forehead and the sound of her sigh against my hair. I buried my face in her shoulder and we sat in comfortable silence in the cool predawn. I hadn't told her everything – not about my ability to kill. I wanted to. Desperately. But I couldn't bear the inevitable condemnation. She'd always been adamant I restrain myself to ensure my superior strength didn't hurt anyone. She'd be appalled by what I was; who I was.

'And this *ocair* thing? What is it?'

'A key of some sort.' I yawned. 'It's supposed to be the salvation, no *deliverance*, of those that dispossess the sidhe. Don't ask me what that means. Logan thinks the *ocair* was Calain but, if he's dead, it can't be.'

There was a long silence before she replied, 'No. How could it?'

The patio door's metallic slide signalled the end of our tete-a-tete. Maeve emerged and spoke softly, but with overtones of stiff disapproval.

'Rowan, Logan's asking for you.'

'Is he ok?'

She lifted her chin. 'I did what I could, but my ability to draw from the *sianfath* and feed it to others is limited.' She gave me a haughty look. 'He has two fractured ribs, a fractured cheekbone, bruised kidneys and a tear in the liver. I stopped the worst of the internal bleeding. That's all I could do. The suppression drug is still in his system so he can't draw fast enough to heal himself. He needs you. Call me when you're ready to start.' She went back inside without awaiting my acknowledgment.

'What's her problem?' My mother's defensive tone made me smile.

I snorted a laugh. 'I don't know where to start on that question. She doesn't like it that I can heal him, where she can't. She's angry I took her daughter, Jennifer, with me tonight – even though it wasn't my choice. Plus, she's too used to having her own way. She hates it when I do my own thing – especially when it works.'

Anna chuckled. 'Now *that* I can empathise with. I might go meet her officially and leave you with this Logan boy.' Her smile was knowing as she followed Maeve into the kitchen.

I hurried inside and sat on the couch's edge, staring at Logan. Was he sleeping? No, I sensed his mind, hovering between pain and oblivion. He had his shields raised. Probably didn't want me sharing the agony he must be suffering, both mental and physical.

I laid a hand on his chest. Slowly, delicately, taking care in working around the block, I extended myself and drew from the nearby woodland's pulsing energy. A little from every contributor to the biomass did no harm to them and gave me enough energy pass on so Logan could heal himself.

My head thumped in warning and the energy prickled under my skin. I gritted my teeth and pushed on, storing what I needed then trickle-feeding the power into his body. As with Harry, I encouraged the *sianfath* to do its thing, while having no idea how it worked. But it did. Little by little, his bruises healed, the cracked ribs knitted and the internal damage mended. The frown creasing his forehead eased as the cuts to his face vanished. His eyelids lifted. His grey eyes were clear.

He stroked my cheek as I released the last dregs of energy and sagged. Groaning, I screwed up my face against the pain slicing into my brain.

'If you need to let go and sleep it off, go ahead,' his deep voice reassured me. His thumb brushed my lips. The other hand rubbed my back in long, comforting strokes. 'I'll be here in the morning, I promise. Lie down.'

The black hole of unconsciousness tempted me as an end to the agony. The world faded into greyness.

'Rowan!' Maeve's voice had a sharp edge.

Light from the kitchen stabbed through my eyeballs. Irritation flashed across Logan's face as he squinted at the doorway and Maeve's silhouette framed in it.

She strode in, poked a fingertip to my head and siphoned off the pain. 'What were you thinking? You should not be doing that without supervision. Have you forgotten you're missing that regulator organ? Drain yourself too far and you'll die. You could have killed Logan or impaired your own abilities.'

'And perhaps,' Logan said. He struggled to his feet. 'You'd like to tell us which of those is more important?' His tone was quiet, deadly-polite; his expression flat and cold. But the tension in his shoulders told a different story.

Maeve backed away, her eyes wide.

'Logan, you're exhausted. Get some sleep and we can talk about this in the morning.'

'About what?' he said coldly. 'About my father murdering my mother and you hiding it from me? Or about you lying to me for the last twelve years about my own genetic heritage. You must have known I'd inherited the Dark gene.' He brandished his inner elbow at her. 'You took my DNA sample when you first adopted me. You said it was a routine blood test. But you were checking. You *knew!* I trusted you and you made my whole life a *lie*.'

Maeve paled. 'No, Logan. I did what I thought was right. I was trying to equip you. To help you be ready to take on the Mors Ferrum.'

He laughed, not with joy, but with derision and scorn. 'Oh, you prepared me, alright, but the result may not be quite what you were expecting.'

'What—'

He waved her words aside and scrubbed at his hair. With a narrow look at me and another at her, he flipped a hand at her. 'Nevermind. Go to bed. You're right. This can all be dealt with in the morning, when everyone's awake.'

With obvious reluctance, Maeve backed out, her eyes darting between him and me. My mother appeared. I kissed her on the cheek and bade her goodnight. She followed Maeve up the stairs, glancing back twice. I closed the door and pressed a button to shut the blinds on the huge picture window.

Logan paced the room like a caged wolf, his expression black. I waited. He sighed and the anger faded. He raised rueful grey eyes to mine.

'I think I'm understanding what makes you so wary of Maeve. Sorry.' He opened his arms.

I laughed and fitted myself against him. 'I don't think she's entirely to blame. I have my fair share of paranoia.'

He grinned and slid his fingers to the nape of my neck. My heart thudded against my ribs and my cheeks flushed hot under his scrutiny.

'Thank you,' he murmured, 'for coming after me. That took guts. You're a good person, Rowan.'

'You're welcome.' I pressed against his lean form, riding the rush of desire and excitement that flared at his touch. 'But you're wrong about me.'

'Oh?'

I couldn't bear to tell him the details of what I'd done at Ian's house. I looked away.

'I had to kill some of the Mors people to protect Jen. Three of them.' The memory of it sickened me but, with each retelling, acceptance deadened the guilt. 'So you're wrong. And I was wrong. I am a killer.'

To my surprise, Logan chuckled. 'You know I never shared your moral high ground on this one, Rowan. I supported you because you didn't want to kill, even when your enemies had no hesitation. If you've accepted your abilities, that isn't bad a thing. On the contrary.' He kissed me softly, his eyes gleaming. 'It makes you even more interesting.' He kissed me again and I trembled. 'To me, anyway.'

I no longer cared about the right or wrong of what we were going to do next. It didn't matter. When he'd been taken all I could do was regret what we hadn't shared and hope for the chance to get him back so we could. More than just sex. I wanted to share a future with him. And now I had both him and Anna back, there was nothing keeping us from doing that.

I stood on tiptoes and wrapped my arms around his neck. He kissed me, hungrily, with purpose and expertise. Overhead, the storm that had been threatening all evening, broke and poured a deluge on the house.

TWENTY

<Ian, I have a bad feeling about this.>

[Oh? I thought you'd be happy. Logan's back. The only downside is that our little charmer didn't obliterate the whole base while she was there.]

<That's what I mean. It was far too easy. You know, as well as I do, the sort of security the Mors Ferrum usually have around their facilities.>

[You think they were followed?]

<No. I've been checking and I know Rowan was careful. She is about these things. It's just...>

[Pfah, my dear. You're becoming worse than Harry. It was straightforward and you're paranoid. Let's redirect our thoughts towards how to remove Mr Eisen from the world.]

I woke to a still-darkened room, with a hint of light flickering around the blockout blinds and beneath the door. Smiling and stretching languorously, I swept an arm across the double-bed-couch – and found nothing but rumpled blankets. The room was empty, too. Logan was gone.

Sickness twisted in my stomach. Had I misjudged him?

Wait. Erin's words came back to me. I checked inward. There. A brilliant green thread now shimmered from deep within my mind, through the *sianfath*, to where Logan was, in the garage. He re-entered the house, climbing a flight of stairs that would bring him into the kitchen. He hadn't left.

I flung the blankets aside and yanked on my clothing in a hurry. A quick trip to the bathroom behind the theatre room and I was ready to face him – and everyone else. Trepidation seized me as I twisted the door handle. Everyone but Anna would be aware of the new connection between Logan and I, and the significance of it. How would Maeve react? And Erin? Anna was no fool, either. She'd see it in my face.

With a sheepish laugh to myself, I threw back my shoulders and opened the door. So what? I was eighteen. As far as I was concerned, all was right with the world and nothing anyone did this morning would change that.

The dining room was redolent of bacon and eggs when I entered. The whole family, barring Erin, were already there and picking from a veritable smorgasbord of food. Harry greeted me with a nod as he placed a platter on the glass surface. Logan, seated at one end of the massive table, pulled out the chair next to him. When I sat he leaned across and kissed me, ignoring Maeve's sharp intake of breath and Ian's uncomfortable throat-clearing. Jennifer giggled, snorted milk through her nose and dissolved into a coughing fit. Maeve fussed and remonstrated. Anna's mouth twitched into a tiny smile. Tom said nothing, staring at his untouched food in morose distraction.

We broke apart, me flushing and Logan apparently unperturbed. Erin appeared in the doorway, yawning and wearing a scarlet silk robe over white silk short pyjamas. Her jaw dropped open.

'Logan? You're here! How…?'

'Hail, hail, the gang's all here,' he muttered. He put his fork aside, leaned back with an air of satisfaction, and grinned raffishly. 'Come on in, please. The more the merrier. You all need to hear what I have to say, anyway.'

Erin dropped into a chair like her legs had given way. She glanced at me and her eyes narrowed.

'I see. Well, that's as stupid decision, Logan. She'll bring you nothing but trouble.'

I ignored her and forked a mouthful of herbed, scrambled egg into my mouth, basking in the glow of Logan's affection. His knee pressed against my thigh beneath the table and his bare foot swept across mine in a distracting fashion.

Erin caught sight of Anna and blinked. Anna introduced herself and gave a brief synopsis of what Jennifer and I had achieved by way of explanation. Erin gaped.

'So...' Erin said. 'You're telling me Rowan and *Jennifer* got into a high-security compound on their own, weren't discovered and managed to get you both out without being detected?' Her scorn swept everyone at the table. 'Seriously? Doesn't anyone find that the least bit unbelievable? This is the Mors Ferrum we're talking about. Logan.' She glared at him. 'When you and Dante went in to get Tom, you had a team of five and only three of you came out. And Dante's people were all experienced and bonded by his ability to pull a team into the *lorntinn* – the unity. But they still got trashed.'

Maeve bit her lip. Jennifer folded her arms with an audible *humf.* I kept my mouth shut, but the seed of my own doubt from last night grew under the chill rain of Erin's derision.

'My daughter is *extremely* skilled,' Anna said mildly.

Logan laughed and threw back the last swallow of his coffee. He leaned back in his chair, exuding some unshared, unspoken humour.

'Tom,' he drawled. Tom looked up, his expression haunted and wary. His eyes were dark-shadowed and his skin sallow. He swallowed hard, his adam's apple bobbing.

Logan pushed himself back from the table in a leisurely, catlike manner. He collected a piece of toast and took a bite. He paced away to the window overlooking the street, then returned to the table.

Then he downed the last bite and brushed crumbs off his dark blue t-shirt.

With a sly, amused look at me, he said, 'Tom, Mars is rising.'

I blinked at him and switched my attention to Tom. His expression shifted into cold blankness and he shot to his feet, standing to attention like a soldier on parade. Everyone at the table gaped at the pair, confusion uppermost in their expressions. Harry, standing in the kitchen door, frowned. He knocked brusquely on my shields.

/Get out, Ruadhán. Now./

What? Why? I don't—

A soft explosion by my ear sent me jerking backward in shocked reaction. Several voices screamed at once. My chair tipped. I tucked my head in as the chair smacked to the floor. Rolling to my feet, I lifted my hands, prepared for the threat. A second blast was followed by the distinctive sound of swearing and a scuffle. What was happening?

Maeve lay slumped across the table, moving, but feebly. A dart protruded from her arm. Anna snatched at Jen and dragged her to the door. A second dart quivered in Jen's chair back. Either she'd ducked or deflected it. Erin struggled in Tom's arms, scratching and shrieking obscenities at her brother. His face, behind her shoulder, was unemotional. Ian shouted instructions everyone ignored.

On the floor at my feet, Logan and Harry writhed, locked in grunting, messy ground combat. I took a hesitant step forward, not sure who to help. What the hell was going on? Harry and Logan rolled towards me. Sunlight flashed off the dartgun in Logan's hand and my heart dropped. Logan struck Harry's white head with the butt. Harry slumped into unconsciousness. Logan shoved him off.

Run! I threw the thought at Jen, hoping she had our thought-window open. *Get to the bushland out back. I'll find you. Keep Anna safe. Let me deal with this.*

Jen yanked at Anna, hauling my mother out the door in spite of her obvious reluctance. I glared at Anna and mouthed 'go'. She, hesitated, pressed her lips together and nodded. They vanished out the door.

A fist took me in the diaphragm and breathing became more important. Grunting, I folded around the pain. A knee rose towards my face. I threw myself aside and rolled behind the table.

Footsteps neared. Sweet air flooded into my lungs and I straightened. Logan's open palm rammed at my nose. I batted it aside and slid an arm over his and around his neck. If I got a sleeper-hold on him... He jabbed an elbow into my ribs. Something cracked and agony speared through my body. I coughed, tasting blood. He struck again in the same place. Pain hazed my vision into sepia.

Backing away I searched for help. Erin dangled in the crook of Tom's elbow, insensible. Ian stood with his back against the wall, mouth agape.

Logan strolled over to me, his smile brittle. He fisted my shirt and shoved me against the wall. I could counter but I didn't want to hurt him. He had no such qualms. My head hit the wall and glittering lights sparkled behind my eyes. His knee drove into the nerve bundle in my thigh and I gasped. A soft, metallic click sounded next to my ear. His forearm pressed against the pressure point behind my jaw, blinding me with pain.

It would be so easy to drain him to the point of weakness. I could. It would take only a second and the threat would be over. Darkness stirred deep in me. I fought to hold it in check. Whatever was going on, I didn't want Calain killing everyone in the room to protect me.

'No.' Logan's breath brushed my cheek. 'Don't hold back, sweetheart. Don't let Calain out to play, but you'll have to do something special in order to beat me. It's the only way, you know.'

'What...' My voice broke and I whimpered as he pushed harder against my jaw. '...are you *doing*, Logan?'

'I thought it was obvious,' he murmured, his lips touching mine softly, in awful parody of our time together last night. 'I'm doing my job – bringing you, and all the others, in.'

I lifted a hand. He pressed the gun muzzle harder into my forehead. A nine-mil this time. The one from the boot of my car. 'No. Use the shadow-thought. Go ahead. You won't beat me any other way. We both know it.'

Calain-inside rattled his cage. I swallowed my fear, holding hard to my anger.

'Don't do this, Logan,' I managed. Every movement shot stabbing pains into my back and stomach. I couldn't concentrate enough to heal myself lest Calain take advantage of my divided attention and escape. 'Whatever the Mors Ferrum did to you, you aren't this person.'

He laughed softly, genuinely. 'Yes.' His answer was simple and honest. 'I am. I'm my father's son. As you're Calain's daughter. Michael Eisen showed me the truth of who I am. And he's right: we're destined for greater things. You've already admitted who you really are. Own it. Stop being so afraid. You have the potential to be the strongest sidhe that ever lived. With you, we can run the whole damned world right.'

I fought for breath. 'I always thought that was an overrated pastime. All the paperwork.' I tried to buy time, hoping Harry or Maeve would wake; or Ian would find the guts to do something heroic. But Tom now had a dart gun trained on his father, unmoved by the older man's begging.

Logan kissed me again. I couldn't turn away. 'We'll have people for that. But right now…' He cocked his head at me. 'I need to work out how to get you back to the facility. Calain'll come out if we try and dart you, won't he? I wonder.' He stepped back, the gun still trained on me.

I slumped against the wall, coughing. Blood sprayed onto the gleaming white floor. Tears of anger and frustration gathered. I wiped them away and pushed myself straight, glaring at him defiantly.

'I won't go with you.'

Logan's grin twisted. 'Not even if I do this?' He swung the gun around, pointed it at Ian and squeezed the trigger. The report echoed in the huge space. I jumped. Ian gaped at the red stain blossoming across his white shirt and clasped his hands across the wound in his stomach. He slid to the floor and sat, staring stupidly at Logan. Blood smeared the white wall behind him.

Calain strained at the block holding him back. I struggled against my own protective instincts and against Calain's murderous ones. Releasing him wasn't what Logan wanted, either. But he knew if I drew too fast on the *sianfath* – as I'd have to in order to heal Ian – the resulting migraine would reduce me to helpless oblivion far more effectively than the darts.

I swallowed and ignored Ian's pleading, his burbling cries for help.

Logan raised his brows. 'Impressive. But I suppose you don't really care about him, do you? What about this, then?' He pressed the gun muzzle into his own stomach.

'Logan!' I took a half-step forward.

He backed up. 'Thought that might do it. You're a fool, Rowan. You think you're tough-ass, but you're so damned needy it's pathetic.' He cocked his ear towards the door but kept his focus on me. Tyres crunched on the gravel driveway. Doors slammed. 'Ah. Reinforcements. Decision time. What's it going to be? Come peacefully or...' He gestured with the gun.

I closed the gap between us and wrenched the gun sideways. He pulled the trigger. Glass shattered, cascading in a waterfall of white-noise.

I hooked an ankle behind his knee and swept his foot. We fell together in a tangle of arms, struggling for control of the gun. His legs wrapped around my hips and he stretched out, forcing me away. Grimly, I hung on, driving an elbow into his jaw. His eyes glazed and his grip on me and the gun weakened. I tore it free and sent it clattering across the floor. The gun skidded under the glass railing and splashed into the pool below. Wriggling free of Logan's legs, I rolled and sat astride his hips.

On the house's lower level, timber splintered – probably the front door. Deep voices shouted orders.

Logan blinked and refocussed. He slid a hand through my guard, going for the strangle. I swore and slammed an elbow into his temple. His eyes rolled back and he sagged beneath me.

Clambering to my feet I recoiled as a dart-gun muzzle appeared, inches away. Tom's cold, unyielding gaze focussed on me. His mind was now the dual, unthinking drone-mind I'd felt first at the MJE complex three nights before. Now his memory losses made sense. They'd brainwashed him with some sort of post-hypnotic suggestion when he'd been captured. He was a sleeper in our midst the whole time.

There was no point in trying to reason with him.

He was standing too close. I struck at the inside of his wrist and twisted the gun free. I darted him without compunction.

Footsteps clattered up the stairs.

With one last, despairing glance around the room, I ran. It was that or let Calain loose. I was in too much pain to control him any longer.

In an all or nothing moment, I chose the nothing. To release Calain would endanger everyone, not only the Mors Ferrum. And I couldn't bring myself to kill either Logan or Tom by accident. There wasn't enough time to go carefully into the *sianfath*. If I went quickly and killed the men on the stairs, I'd succumb to the after-effects and be unconscious when Logan came around.

So I abandoned my allies and ran. Or rather, limped, out the back door, out the back gate and into the bushland behind the house.

TWENTY-ONE

[Oh god, Maeve! Help me! What have we done?]

I staggered through the open forest, searching for clues and a hiding place. I needed to find Anna and Jennifer. Even more, I needed somewhere safe to hide so I could concentrate on healing myself. From the feel of it, Logan had done serious internal damage. Each breath was agony. Twice I stopped and vomited, blood colouring the bile brilliant red. Not a good sign.

Simply being in the forest wasn't enough this time. All my concentration had to stay on keeping Calain locked away. If I relaxed enough to let the *sianfath* do its thing, he would come roaring out to protect me and all my actions of the last ten minutes would be wasted.

Then there was Logan. How long did I have before he came hunting for me? Not long, I suspected. My only hope was to get far enough away and buy time to heal before he found me.

So I staggered on through the forest. Twigs scratched my bare calves and stones stabbed into the soles of my feet. I wiped my mouth and leaned on the smooth, silvery trunk of a soaring eucalypt. When I took my hand away, it left a scarlet print. Swearing at my own stupidity I veered in a different direction and tried to tread with more care. Logan was a skilled tracker, though, so I was probably wasting time.

Doggedly, I plodded on.

Was it my imagination, or did someone call my name? Logan? Panic seized me and I froze, fighting my own internal demon. The world tilted as I lost control of my body in the effort to contain Calain. I fell, not even able to catch myself or roll. I hit the hard ground. Beneath me, bark and leaves crackled. The scent of broken, dried eucalyptus and damp earth filled my nostrils. The forest crown swayed overhead. Blue and grey-green; soaring silver and red trunks; restless leaves, stirring in the breezes.

I fought a silent, grim battle with darkness under the canopy's beauty.

Faces filled the sky. Anxious, appalled. Red hair and black hair. Female. Jennifer and my mother. Together they dragged me into a small, sheltered space, hidden from the world on three sides by bushes and a fallen log. Anna sat with her back against the log. She cradled me in her lap like I was a child, my head resting on her shoulder. She murmured useless reassurances into my ear. Jennifer hovered close by, casting anxious glances over her shoulder, starting at every bird alarm call or rustle in the underbrush.

When I'd mastered Calain enough and closed the dungeon door against him again, I stirred. Struggling off Anna's lap I leaned my back against the log and rested.

'What happened?' Anna brushed something off my forehead and picked a strand of hair from between my lips.

Taking shallow breaths, I closed my eyes to better concentrate. 'The Mors Ferrum got to Logan and Tom. I guess the reason we got out so easily last night was because they wanted all of us, not just me.'

'But why didn't they take you all at Ian's house yesterday?' Jennifer objected.

Even shaking my head hurt, so I didn't. 'Don't know. Doesn't make any sense to me, either. All I know is that Logan must have led them right to us today. He had backup. I had to get out or they'd have taken me, too. Or worse.'

'Worse?' Anna trembled as she gripped my wrist.

'Did they…' Jennifer's question ended on a gulp.

'Everyone was alive when I left. But I'm not sure about Ian.' I gritted my teeth. 'Logan shot him – in the stomach.'

'No!' Jennifer squeaked. Anna hushed her.

'Logan was trying to get me to overcommit,' I explained. An invisible weight sat on my chest, making it hard to breathe. 'He knows he can't threaten me too much or the corruption of Calain will act to protect me.'

'What are you talking about? Overcommit how?' Anna scowled.

I coughed, then swallowed blood. The taste made me ill. 'I have an ability. I can kill people by draining their life-force. But when I do it conflicts with the last block Calain left in my head. And with his presence – his memories. If I do manage to drain people, I always end up unconscious. Logan knows it's the only way to get me back to the MJE compound.'

'Drain…' Anna's mouth fell open. Then she gathered me into her arms. 'Oh, my poor baby. You must be terrified. I'm so sorry I haven't been there when you needed me. This is all my fault. If I hadn't fallen for Mick in Cairns. If I hadn't been so flattered when he went to such effort to find me and offer me the job. I was a fool not to see it.'

I managed a weak laugh. 'Hardly your fault, Mum. Mine for trusting the Freysons in the first place.' Jennifer bit her lip. I squeezed her hand. 'Not you, kiddo. Sorry.'

'I'm sorry my mother has been so horrible. And Logan! I can't believe he—'

'Not his fault, Jen. Mors Ferrum has a way of switching on the Dark gene, remember? And they've brainwashed him as well. Don't hate him.'

'What are we going to do?' Her voice quavered and she fearfully checked the direction of the house.

'You two are going to get out of the country.' I frowned at Anna when she adamantly refused. 'I can't go after them if I'm worried about you. Jennifer, Anna will look after you, I promise.'

'No!' Jennifer wailed. 'I *won't*! You're not my mother and I wouldn't go even if *she* told me to. I *won't* let you face this on your own. I can help. I already have, remember? You need me.'

Anna squeezed Jen's shoulder but her eyes were on me. 'Rowan, you can't do this alone. From what I hear, Jennifer can help. And I'm not leaving you again. I might not have psychic powers or super-strength but there has to be something I can do.' She grimaced. 'Even if it's get you to a doctor.'

'No.' I grabbed at her shirt when she started to rise. 'I'll be able to heal myself in a minute. I need to rest a little to make sure I can control Calain. Look…' She opened her mouth and I waved her to silence. 'I can't have you both near me. I…you make me vulnerable.' I held their gazes, one at a time. 'I make stupid, lethal choices when I'm forced to protect you. I've killed people to save both of you and I don't want to do that again. I might be a killer, but I don't have to hang that on you two. Go.'

Anna stroked my hair. 'You have a choice, Rowan.'

'I know,' I said bitterly, 'and I've proven it three times now. If my worst moments determine who I am – as you've always said – then I'm a murderer. There's no pretending otherwise.'

'I said,' Anna put in, gently, 'your worst moments determine who you are – if you *let* them. Don't forget that last bit. It's the important part. Everyone makes mistakes. You can either learn from it, or let it decide your life for you.'

I couldn't stand her sympathy any longer and closed my eyes. The heaviness in my chest was almost unbearable and I could only breathe in short, shallow pants. I had to heal myself and risk releasing Calain before it was too late.

'Rowan!' Jennifer's urgent whisper forced my eyelids open. She was staring at me. 'Logan's coming after you.'

'I know,' I muttered. 'If I can heal myself we should be able to get away before he gets here, though.'

'But he'll *keep* coming after you. The thread...' She pointed at me. 'We can all see it.'

Swearing, I groaned. 'I forgot.' I concentrated for a few seconds on dragging breaths, barely hearing Jennifer's hurried explanation to Anna of our new connection.

'We need to get you as far away as we can,' Anna stated in a tone that brooked no argument.

I argued anyway. 'No. I know what to do. Jen I'll need your help, though. Anna, you keep watch.'

'What can you do?' Jen asked.

'To cut the connection to Logan I'll have to die.'

We then wasted several precious moments in pointless argument over the inevitable. I cut Anna off with an imperious gesture.

'It's the only way.' I coughed and blood sprayed. Anna's eyes swam with tears. She rose to her knees and peered over the log.

Closing my eyes again I settled my heart. This had to work or we were all done for.

With painful slowness, I extended myself into the *sianfath*. Only this time I didn't tie a thread of myself to my body. This time I intended to let go and let my body die. Only my death would break the tie leading Logan straight to me. Hopefully, Jennifer would be able to bring me back. I anchored a tiny filament to her bright life and she squeaked. She would be my lifeline. Aeona Silverblade had mentioned the technique. A last-ditch act of desperation. This situation qualified.

Easing myself into the life of the forest, I touched on a thousand brilliant pulses and drew a little from each. Filling myself, healing myself, intertwining with them, I become one with what Aeona called the Great Mother. The world's heartbeat, slow and deep beneath everything, engulfed me.

When I was stretched as thin as I could, I delicately released my body.

I should have died.

But the block in my mind burst asunder and Calain roared out of his prison. Protective and fear-filled, his ethereal arms encompassed me. He wrenched me to earth and we tumbled back into his memories, still merged with the *sianfath.*

Calain threw his arms wide and laughed at the grey sky.

He was home.

Calain nudged the chestnut mare into a trot and followed the rutted track leading to Lothien. He surveyed the countryside and found it little changed. As he rounded the end of the ridge on which Lothien Castle sat, the village came into view. Several houses were now two storey half-timbered constructions with thatched roofs. The majority were still squat little huts huddled around the village green, minding their own tilled patches of earth encircled by low, drystone walls.

Women still clustered around the market space, gossiping. Now they wore cinch-waisted dresses and stiff, full skirts instead of tunic-dresses and felt caps, but the faces of these villagers were interchangeable with those of his youth. The coal-blackened smith who emerged, hammer in hand, appeared much like the old one.

Calain inclined his head, aware his fine garments, war-horse, and sword marked him as gentry. All doffed their caps or curtseyed as he passed. He suppressed a grin. Would that any of them knew his beginnings in this place.

Involuntarily, he sought the site of Mairi Silverblade's funeral pyre. Just dust and packed earth, well-trodden by over a century of indifference. Her death hadn't changed the village in the slightest; only him.

The road drove straight through the middle of the houses and ended at the church door. Calain regarded the building with distaste and scratched the back of his head. The church was new since he'd left. Catholic by the looks of it. Grey stone. Not a cathedral; a simple, rectangular building with a steep, crenulated roof and a few narrow windows. A tower adorned the western end. Not surprising to find the village still Catholic. King Henry's religious reforms had been rejected by the Irish. These folk would cause the young Queen Elizabeth much grief, he suspected. Small wonder she'd raised her fine-plucked brows at him when he'd requested Lothien for his reward.

Calain stroked his short, russet beard and grinned. It had taken all his hard-learned charm to seduce her out of irritation and persuade her to put pen to paper on the title deeds. And considerable tact to convince her she no longer needed his sword arm. But she'd taken to heart his comment about being seen as strong and independent; not requiring a man by her side to rule. Calain had left her putting on a show of listening to her advisors as they presented marriage candidates. They would have little luck for she liked ill to be mastered.

He straightened a spine wearied by many long days of travel and soaked in the power of green, growing things; the land's pulse. His land now. He was Earl of Lothien in perpetuity. He would need to invent a way to hide his unaging countenance. A way to pass his title and properties on to himself in the coming centuries. But time for that later. For now, he needed to meet his people.

Swinging down from the saddle he gestured to a reasonably-clean urchin and requested the child water the horse. Hurried footsteps echoed from the church's dark interior. Calain waited on the stoop, drawing off his gloves and stamping his feet to get feeling back.

'My lord! Thou art most welcome to our humble village. How mayst I assist thee?' The priest who squinted in the grey morning light bore no resemblance to the thin, intense man who'd burned Mairi. Tonsured and hale, this man's brown eyes were rich with secret humour and intelligence. His garb was plain and his hands un-bedecked by rings or jewels. Not one of the money-grubbing corrupt church officials so obvious in the old regime. Perhaps Henry's reforms had, at least, brought a little wisdom to the Church here.

Calain removed his soft hat and swept a bow. 'I thank you good Father. I come but to present myself to you. I am lately gifted the title of Earl of Lothien. Calain Gilmore, at your service.'

'Earl!' The priest's eyes widened and flicked to the stern grey castle watching over the village. 'We hadst heard of my lord John's death in England and did wonder what would become of his demesne. Art thou his heir?'

Calain shook his head. 'He had none. I am but a humble servant of our liege. Having done her a service, she hath bequeathed the lands to me and mine.' He bowed. 'So, the question dost become: how mayst I assist *you* and the good people of Lothien?'

The priest crossed himself. 'Bless you. If I canst be so bold, my lord, my parishioners wilt be overjoyed to hear the direction of thy bent is towards helping, rather than bleeding them dry, as wast the wont of our previous lord.' He crossed himself again and muttered. 'I shouldst not speak ill of the dead.' He pointed at the door. 'An it pleaseth thee, come in and partake of refreshments. Mayhap we might discuss the needs of thy folk over nuncheon. I am Father Paul O'Flaherty, my lord.'

'May I beg your indulgence, Father? I'm not yet a-hungered.' Calain smiled to take the sting out of his refusal. 'But I should like to walk in yon woods awhile.' He pointed at the forest and the thatched roof tucked in its skirts. When Father O'Flaherty frowned, Calain added, 'I'll return to partake anon. 'Tis only that I hadst the good fortune to pass by this way some years agone and met the family living in yon house. I hoped I might call on them before I must begin my official duties, for they knew me as but a humble traveller and yet made me welcome.'

O'Flaherty hesitated, then bowed. 'Certes, my lord. But the Williamsons passed away a year ago – scarlet fever. Only their daughter, Fionn, remains. She hath refused all offers of help or marriage, and doth insist on managing the property.' He sighed. 'Indeed, my lord, thine official duties could well begin an thou dost meet her, for she is the most resty of my flock. The one most like to argue with me on doctrine.'

Calain chuckled. 'Well, it behoves me to meet Mistress Williamson now, that I may stand in the good graces of even the most intractable of my people. I'll away and return anon.' With a bow he strode along the path. She sounded very much like he imagined his foster-sister, Grace, would have been as a tough old lady.

As he neared the little thatched cottage the forest's old draw strengthened. He'd spent too long in London. He'd lost touch with this – the source of life and strength. In time, he would spend a week or two in his old territories, high in the hills behind Lothien.

The stout timber door flew open before his knuckles touched it. A young woman appeared, an untamed mass of pale red hair loosely braided over her shoulder and a militant gleam in her hazel eyes. She studied him in silence. Her small mouth pursed. She folded freckled arms across her chest and thrust a bare foot out from beneath the raised hem of tucked-up, woollen skirts.

'So,' she said in a broad accent that spoke to Calain's early memories of this place, 'thou'st finally come, then. Fie! And time enow.' She jerked her chin towards the forest. 'Thou'st kept her waiting too long. She's been pestering me for weeks.'

TWENTY-TWO

Calain raised his brows. 'I believe you hast me at a disadvantage, mistress. It appears you wast expecting me? Or dost mean Mistress Williamson ha' been expecting me?' He tried to peer around her, into the house's murky depths. 'Is she in?'

The girl snorted. ''Tis I who live here, master lackwit. And 'tis *Miss* Williamson, to thee. Fionn Williamson. And 'tisn't *I* who awaiteth thee. 'Tis—'

Holding up a hand, Calain stemmed the flow of incomprehensible statements. '*Miss* Williamson, canst be you hast mistaken me for another? None knew of my coming.' He wavered between irritation and amusement at her insolence.

'Certes, I didst. You art Calain Gilmore, new Earl of Lothien. Tho you wert known as Calain Williamson once upon a time. Look.' She pointed at the door frame where the letters C and 1413 were scored into the oak. 'The mark to show you wert tall enow to draw a man's bow.'

Calain recalled the day his foster father had, grudgingly, pronounced him of a height to begin his bowyer's apprenticeship. But how did this girl, a hundred and fifty years or more later, know that?

Bereft of words, he waited in bemused silence. She chuckled and shut the door. Her derision softened into amusement and she gestured with a work-roughened hand.

'Come. Tarry not. She'll not stay long here. Ne'er doth.'

'Who?' He got the word out but his voice broke.

A dimple flashed.

'You wilt see.' She strode into the forest, glancing back twice as if to judge his acceptance.

Calain followed, studying her slender, swaying back in confusion. She had stopped speaking in the formal way of a peasant to her betters: with *thou* and *thee*. Now she addressed him as an equal but, for some reason, he didn't mind. After the Queen's court, her frankness was both refreshing and unsettling.

Deep into the forest she led him, sure-footed and unhesitating even in the trackless, wild places. The watered-green light through spring foliage shifted and flickered, tricking the eye. Silence and stillness marked her passage. Only his attunement to the *sianfath* allowed Calain the comfort of knowing where he was. An ordinary human would be long lost. Had she lured him here to lose him? She'd find her time wasted. He was more familiar with this place, even a century later, than any human could be.

Curious, he followed, astonished by Fionn's woodcraft. He'd met several sidhe since growing to manhood, but she was a match for the best of them. She trod lightly amongst the green-shadowed trees and made not a sound barring the faint rustle of her skirts, barely breathing hard. Cold air, smelling of wet earth and decomposing leaves, brought vivid roses to her pale cheeks and sharp little nose. Calain smiled at her robustness and said nothing.

By the time they'd climbed deep into the dark-forested valley behind the village, Calain was close to the end of his patience. He was travel-wearied and had yet to inspect his domain before sundown. He was about to demand an explanation when she stopped and pointed.

'She's within. She's expecting you, so be not afeard.' Her smile turned cheeky. 'She doth not bite.'

Calain examined the small stone cottage dubiously. He had used it for a few weeks after leaving the village. A hunters' rest, even then it had been neglected, its roof half-rotted. Someone had now made repairs, but only enough to render it barely habitable.

He chuckled. When had he become so nice in his tastes?

Before he could duck to enter the darkness within, a woman emerged. She straightened, brushing at her plain, dark-woollen dress. Patting back her waist-length rich brown hair, she lifted her head. Her dark-grey eyes, shadowed by anxiety, met Calain's.

Grabbing at the trunk of a sapling, Calain held himself up by sheer force of will.

'Aeona? Mamai?' The same word he'd uttered to Mairi Silverblade so many years ago, said in the same tones of hopeful disbelief.

The woman before him resembled Mairi closely – same warm cast of skin and angular bone structure. She even seemed a similar age, though tell the age of a full sidhe by looking was near impossible. Tears spilled onto her cheeks and she stretched out her arms.

'Yea, certes, 'tis I.'

Assailed by conflicting emotions: anger, disbelief, joy, and hurt, Calain stared at her for a long, unspeaking moment. His legs gave way and he collapsed onto a fallen tree trunk.

'Why?' His voice was low and harsh. Of course, he knew the answer, in general terms. He'd long since locked away the worst of her memories lest they send him insane. But he wanted to hear it from her.

Aeona raised her face to the trees, old pain tracing lines around her mouth. She lifted her arms.

The forest groaned. Leaves drooped, branches cracked, the bright green of spring new-growth darkened and aged. Birdsong ceased. The *sianfath's* warm pulse thinned and cracked, shrivelling into brittle death.

Calain shot to his feet, his body wracked with a thousand aches. Fionn appeared unaffected, save for a slight creasing of her smooth brow. But all around them, the forest died, its essence pouring into Aeona's slim form.

'That is why.' His mother's voice was taut. The silvery-green aura every sidhe possessed gleamed so brightly about her that Calain had to shield his eyes. Surely she couldst not contain such power for long?

'Stop!' Calain hesitated to touch her. Would the power earth through him?

She splayed her fingers. Hair lifting in an intangible breeze, she released the power back to its place. Branches straightened. Leaves returned to green life. Birds twittered again. The *sianfath's* rhythm resumed its steady, slow heartbeat.

Aeona sagged and Fionn wrapped an arm around the older woman's waist. The lines on Aeona's face deepened and her skin greyed.

'My lady!' Fionn said. 'Thou shouldst not waste energy on such a wild demonstration. He'll not appreciate it, anyway.' She shot Calain a wrathful look from beneath sandy lashes.

'Now, Fionn,' Aeona replied faintly. 'Hold thy tongue.' She slumped.

'The *skath-sheel* doth take a toll on a body, m'lord.' Fionn pursed her lips. 'You men and your wars. They almost killed her. 'Twas only your birth that gave her the strength to escape. Even a hundred and sixty years of time in these forests hath not restored her strength. Do not ask her to do anything for you.'

'Why would I?' Calain regarded both women in bewilderment. 'I lack for nothing now. The time of needing a mother is long past.' He didn't mean the words to sound as bitter as they did.

Aeona scrubbed at her cheeks. 'Forgive me. We acted as we thought best at the time. I'd no notion the blocks my husband put in thy mind would cause thee such pain when they broke. I wished for thee to have as normal a childhood as was possible. A safe one.' She raised wide, frank eyes. 'I was no longer strong enough to protect thee from Tordal.' Her fingers crumpled and twisted her skirt. 'The Darkness took my husband from me thirty years after we left thee. He departed to fight in the wars and wast reported killed, in France.'

'So why ha' you sought me out now, after all this time?' Calain couldn't hide the hurt from her. He rubbed at the back of his neck, trying to ease the stress.

'Because thy daughter knows not how to release thee. She doth *dulin* - slip in time in thy memories. Though time and place is meaningless in the deepest part of the *sianfath.*'

'Daughter! But I…' He paused, recalling the first day of his awakening, here in this very place. He'd been certain he would, one day, have a daughter and she would help him unlock the solution he needed.

Aeona nodded. 'E'en now she is with thee. Canst thou not sense her presence? I mayst only speak to her through thee and the *sianfath.*'

'Slip?' Calain scoffed. 'How canst one slip through time. 'Tis not possible.'

Her lip curled. 'Says thee, who by human mores hast lived already three lifetimes and wilt live another forty at least?' She sighed. 'Slipping is something one canst only do to the limit of thine own memories. But she hath thine also, so she canst slip further than most.'

Calain stroked his beard, frowning. 'Why then canst I not do this *dulin*; this "slip" of which you speak? 'Twould be useful to warn my younger self.'

''Tis connected with those who have the Sight. The Sight is, I believe, but the future self slipping back to warn the past unconscious self.' Aeona grimaced. 'We waste precious moments for our two times do march apace. She must be taught before she wakes. Thy well-meaning desire to protect her mind will be her death, an we do not show her how to release thee.'

She rose, refusing Fionn's help.

Aeona held out a slender hand to Calain. 'Wilt thou assist me?'

He was half-minded to refuse. It was an uncanny thing to be called on by a mother long absent, to assist a daughter unborn and unknown. What if this was all some sort of trick? Calain smiled wryly. He'd been at court politics too long. These qualms were mere childishness, born of fear and naught else.

He took her thin fingers in his, sensing through them her feverish energy. Aeona was a sputtering torch; the fuel sustaining her almost consumed. Calain bowed low.

'I'll assist thee, my own heart's root.'

Colour flushed into Aeona's cheeks at the familiar pronoun and the term of endearment. Behind her, Fionn's lips curved into satisfaction. She gripped Aeona's hand and extended the other to Calain, a challenging gleam in her hazel eyes.

'We need Fionn,' Aeona explained when he hesitated. 'She carries a mote of sidhe heritage in her blood. Enough to sense the *sianfath* and hear my thoughts from afar. But her humanity wilt help us find my grandchild in the *sianfath*.'

'How?'

'Thy daughter is half-human, of course.' Aeona's brows twitched together. 'But her strength is astonishing for a half-caste. I wouldst be unsurprised to learn her mother is more sidhe than not. Come.' She closed her eyes. 'Think on her, Calain. Her name is Ruadhán.'

He started. How ironic he would give that name to his daughter. The name of his people. The name humans had given to a tree thought to protect them against witchcraft and fae influences. He allowed himself a brief flare of amusement. Would he have named her thus had this moment not happened? Would he even have had a child? He would never know, for her birth must now be inevitable. But when?

Fionn crushed his fingers and he brought his attention guiltily back, concentrating on Aeona's thoughts and the *sianfath's* silvery-green luminescence. She drew Calain and Fionn deeper into it until he was lost to the real world. Panic surged. Aeona's warm mind embraced his.

(Thou art safe here, in my care. But stray not from my side lest thy mind wander an eternity without anchor. Fionn? Canst thou find her? My strength is little.)

=Aye, my lady. She ist entangled there within Calain's thoughts, buried deep. Help me pluck her free that we mayst converse with her shade.=

At their instruction, Calain held himself still in mind, focussing on nothing but an illusory candleflame Aeona set before him. It served to hold his attention long enough that the women were able to pick the strands of Ruadhán free of his own. It was an uncomfortable sensation; as though a long string were being drawn from deep within his mind.

At last, the ghostly image of a young woman appeared in the centre of their little circle. She stood a full head taller than Aeona and Fionn, but barely topped his shoulder. Her auburn hair was cut unwomanly-short and curled about a face both piquant and fierce. Dark-rimmed grey eyes, so like his own, stared back.

She spun in a circle, gaping at them. Then she plucked at the long, full-skirted gown she wore.

Where am I, who are you and what in God's name am I wearing?

TWENTY-THREE

Calain blinked at the blasphemy. Fionn flinched. He'd long ago given up belief in the gods of humankind, but found the language uncomfortable naetheless. What era was this girl from that such terms fell so easily from her youthful tongue?

(Thou dost wear what is seemly in this age, child. 'Tis of no importance. That was Aeona, with a touch of astringency in her thoughts. *As to who we art—)*

Wait! The girl's mouth dropped open. She pointed at Calain, joy lightening her visage. She placed an insubstantial hand on his chest. It passed through and she snatched it back, her expression falling into misery.

Father. Her thought was a hopeless whisper. *I'd forgotten you were so big.*

-Not yet your father.- He responded with a formal bow. *-But one day, yes.-*

Huh? She screwed up her nose. *Well that made no bloody sense at all. Will someone tell me what's going on?* Her focus fell on Fionn. *Hey! I know you. You're…Fionn Gilmore. Calain's first wife when he became Earl of Lothien.*

Fionn flushed pink, avoiding his eye.

Ruadhán spun in a circle again, inspecting each person. *We're in the* sianfath *aren't we? How did Fionn get here? Are you sidhe as well? Hang on…Have I slipped again? Wait? How can I slip through Calain's memories and be outside him at the same time?*

(Cease your chatter, child!) Aeona's sharp thought cut through the girl's and Ruadhán flinched.

Calain thought it a little harsh. He was quite impressed with the girl's intelligence. She had understood her situation far faster than he expected. Aeona should speak more gently to her. He opened his mouth, intending to say so, but refrained, for Aeona swayed on her feet. Her skin was pale and bedewed with sweat; her fingers trembled in his. He gripped them tighter.

(In the sianfath *there is no time and place as thou dost know it. 'Tis possible to be both within Calain's memories and without, at once.)*

That makes no sense, either. Ruadhán frowned. *But not much has—*

('Tis of no account, Aeona snapped. *There is no time for debate. Thou art bonded to thy father unnaturally and must release him if thou art to survive to save thy loved ones. Thy life and theirs art at risk an thou dost not. My task is to teach thee how, but we must proceed apace for my strength doth wane more speedily than I thought.)*

And who the hell are you? Ruadhán placed her hands akimbo, her pointed chin thrust forward.

(Aeona Silverblade.) Aeona lifted her head, regal and haughty. The resemblance between the two woman became pronounced. *(Thy grandmother and one who knows thy gifts well. Well enow to know the dangers thou dost face. Well enow that thou must shut thy mouth and listen close.)*

Aeona! Her jaw dropped. *Grandmother? I'd wondered. Ok. What do I do?*

(Thou must remove the final block in thy mind. Release Calain from his bondage in the dungeon of thy thought-fortress. His essence is consuming thee. Together thou art too dangerous. Release him.)

Release him! Ruadhán shrank away, casting a fearful glance at Calain.

Of what was she afeard? Had he, as a father, injured her? His heart sank. Had the Darkness overcome him and wrecked this precious part of his life-to-be? He wanted to ask; wanted to know; wanted to avoid the mistakes, but a warning thought from Aeona silenced him. She was right. He could spend his life second-guessing each action. No, he must plough on his chosen path, knowing that one day, at least, this fair child would come into being and he would do his best.

But if I release that block, Ruadhán said, *the result could be...catastrophic.* She flicked a glance again in his direction.

Aeona pursed her lips. *(Naetheless, child, thou must. Trust thyself and thy father. Thou hast the strength to control both.)*

Ruadhán grimaced. *Alright. So when do I do this?*

(Thou wilt know the time, I assure thee,) Aeona replied dryly.

A shudder passed through Ruadhán and Aeona at the same moment. Calain felt it too: the bond between them weakening.

(Thy time here is done, child.) Aeona smiled sadly. *(Would I couldst know thee better.)*

Ruadhán cocked her head. *I know you pretty well. I've read your book.*

(My book? But I've written none.)

Well, you'd better get started then. Ruadhán shrugged. *Because it will be very helpful.* She gasped, laying one hand on her stomach. *What's happening? I feel...thin.*

Aeona stared off into nothing. *(Thy body is healed, but the Mors Ferrum ha' drugged thy blood. Thou must return now lest thou art separated from thy clay. Rejoin Calain and thence to thy mortal form. Hurry, child.)*

Ruadhán approached, staring at him. Calain studied her, committing her visage to memory for the future.

-*Tell me who ist thy mother, child?*-

Anna. She glanced at Fionn. *Anna O'Reilly. You'll meet her in London...but not for a few centuries. You'll save her from being run over by a car...carriage. She has red hair, too.* She scowled at him. *She'll love you very much so be nice to her. Don't lea...* She stopped and sighed. *No, I suppose you will, because you have. I hate time paradoxes.*

With one last look over her shoulder at Aeona, Ruadhán stepped into his mind and body. The sensation lasted barely a moment then Calain felt an odd sense of completeness. She was part of his future again.

Around them, the *sianfath's* silvery light shimmered and dissolved into reality. Aeona's eyelids fluttered closed and she collapsed to the ground, pale and senseless.

'My lady!' Fionn dragged free of Calain's grip and fell to her knees, scooping Aeona's slight form into her arms. She touched the pulse at Aeona's neck. 'She lives yet, but she's so cold.' She raised and accusing glare to Calain. 'Canst you do nothing?'

Calain glanced at the darkening woodlands. 'What, pray tell? I canst carry her home.'

Fionn growled, low in her throat. 'Dost know nothing of your heritage, sirrah? She Gifted you her life story. Ha' you not studied it? She drained herself to save your unborn daughter. The least you canst do is give some of your own life-force to sustain her 'til we get her home.'

'Why canst she not draw what she doth need from the forest?'

'This is more than mere sleep!' Fionn snapped. 'Do as I bid. When she wakens she'll draw what she needs, but for now you must suffice. Hurry, man!'

Calain knelt and touched his mother's flat stomach. He had little experience with this and feared a misstep. Carefully, he poured some of his own energy into Aeona's frail body, until she took on a more healthy silver-green aura.

'Stop!' Fionn gripped his wrist. 'Do not drain yourself. She'll do now. Draw what you need to recover and we'll go before darkness hides the path. 'Tis not long 'til suppertime and you canst see in the dark, but I cannot.'

As Calain straightened with a groan, she spoke again, gruffly. ''Twas well done. You ha' saved her life, my lord.'

Calain laughed weakly. 'My lord? I'll begin to think I've offended, an thou dost address me so formal. Mend not thy tongue now, sweeting.'

She flushed and checked Aeona's pulse again before laying her on the ground. Rising, she brushed at her skirts and threw back her shoulders.

'You need not mind Ruadhán's words, my lord,' she said. 'There's no reason you shouldst marry the likes of me, just because her history says it was so...will be so.' She laughed. 'I cannot make my mind understand that she wast your daughter, from the future.'

He chuckled. 'Nor I. What dost thou mean "the likes of you"?' He deliberately used the more intimate, 'thou', personal address form. In the very short time he'd known her, he'd come to admire Fionn's courage and fire. It would be a relief to be with a woman who understood his true nature; to not have to hide. Her finger twisted her skirt into knots so he plucked them free and held them still. 'Surely Aeona hath told thee I'm no more nobility than thee, for all I ha' a high-sounding title now.'

Fionn pursed her lips but her expression softened to wry humour and her voice held a caress. 'Nay, thy human title is naught, 'tis true.' She gestured to Aeona. 'But thou art the son of a truly noble woman. The fae folk are the beautiful people. Thou art far more worthy of respect than humans, who claim land by force of arms and wrest life from it for naught but profit.'

Calain grimaced. 'Not all of us have so beautiful a soul, if we ha' a soul at all.'

She stroked his cheek. 'Thou dost, my sweet. N'er doubt it, for I shall not. Recall, I saw into thy mind?'

He drew her into an embrace. 'Thy job will be to remind me, an I forget.'

She chuckled, her body trembling against his. 'I will. And thine will be to remind me I'm worthy of thee.'

He kissed the top of her head. 'I will.'

She stepped back with a gentle smile. 'Now gather thy mother and let's go home. I left a pot of stew warming by the hearth.'

'*That*,' he responded, lifting his mother's limp form, 'is the best offer I ha' had for many a long day.'

Fionn sent a twinkling look over her shoulder. 'But mayhap not the best one thou'lt get tonight, my lord.'

'My lady!' he replied in mock-affronted tones. Grinning, he followed her down the hill.

Thirty years later, he lay her to rest, deep in the forest they both loved, beside Aeona's cairn, and the graves of the two tiny babes who'd not lived past a year. Kneeling between the piles of lichenous rocks, he touched Aeona's and Fionn's graves. Tears fell unheeded to the wet ground as he mourned the two women he loved more deeply than he'd ever believed possible, and the two children who'd stolen his heart at their births and crushed it at their deaths.

Never again. No more wives. No more children. Not until his heart healed and his hand was forced by a future foreordained. Not until Anna O'Reilly.

He raised his head. Until then, his path was set. The wild places needed him.

TWENTY-FOUR

I awoke slowly enough to remember I hadn't fallen asleep naturally. To realise I wasn't in a comfortable bed. To not utter the stupidest words in history: 'where am I?'. My mouth tasted like dry old newspapers and a weight on my stomach made it hard to breathe. Staying still and keeping my eyes closed, I extended other senses in an attempt to work out where I was.

The red tinge through my eyelids suggested somewhere lit. The low thrum of airconditioning and a steady, mechanical beep, along with the scent of antiseptic and dust, spoke of a familiar location: MJE's warehouse. I tried a telepathic sweep but was unsurprised when it didn't work. My mind felt thick and heavy, my connection with the *sianfath* non-existent.

So, the dream-encounter with Aeona, if it was a dream, was right. I was in the power of Michael Eisen and the Mors Ferrum. Which, since I'd fallen unconscious in the eucalypt forest with Anna and Jennifer, meant they were, too. Every single person I cared about was probably here and I was drugged into powerlessness. I resisted the urge to grind my teeth.

Shit.

Shit. Shit. Shit. Shit.

I swore mentally awhile longer, in several languages. The beeping nearby quickened: a heart monitor. I'd given the game away to anyone listening or watching. An increase in heartrate equalled awake. Well, there was no point in pretending any longer.

I opened my eyes.

No surprises there, either. Overhead a white-plastered ceiling with downlights. Straps held me in place on a hospital bed. Someone had undressed me. I wore a plain white tshirt and grey tracksuit pants. My feet were bare and cold. I shivered, fighting against the creeping fear and helplessness chilling my stomach and clawing at my throat.

There was no escape from this. A drip in my wrist was in no danger of dislodging. There were no convenient scalpels lying around, no idiot henchmen to seduce, not even a way to remove the drip and stop the drug suppressing my abilities.

What the hell was I supposed to do? Terror and fury burned, displacing fear with temporary strength of purpose. Wrenching at the straps I tested their limits, making the bed rattle and the wall shake. The beeps went berserk. A yell of frustration forced its way from my throat as the straps held fast.

The door burst open and slapped against the wall. Two large men, wearing black military gear and carrying drawn nine mils rushed in. Two more followed. Impassive and visibly unimpressed they arrayed themselves around the bed, guns fixed on me.

I froze, trying to think.

Into this scene, Michael Eisen strode, with his pet sidhe in tow – one of them, at least. By his height and shoulder breadth he must be the same man who'd come to Ian's house. Once again, though, his face was hidden beneath a mask. Why? What was he hiding? He took up a stance beside the door, arms folded, legs shoulders-width apart.

'So!' Eisen strode over to me, rubbing his palms together. 'I was surprised when Logan told me you were still alive. I'm sure my man, Connor, dropped you off a three-storey building in Cairns.' He sat on the edge of my bed and patted my shin in a fatherly way that made me want to kick his teeth in. Cocking his head, he inspected me.

'I'd very much like to know what happened to Connor. He and two of my men went to search Anna's flat for the *ocair* and vanished.' He waited with raised brows, acting for all the world like we were having a polite conversation over coffee.

The last thing I wanted was for him to exploit the total control he had over me, so being polite was smarter than being an asshat back to him – deeply though I wanted to spit in his arrogant face. I considered lying – politely – but he had Logan, who would confirm or deny anything I said, so there was no point.

'To be honest,' I said, glad I sounded relaxed, 'they're dead. I have no idea what happened to the bodies, though.'

'Ah.' Eisen revealed nothing but civil acceptance. 'Pity. Connor was quite useful. Nevermind. I have a better replacement. Your young man, Logan.'

I couldn't help the quick clench of my jaw, or the curl of my fingers into fists. Eisen's expression shifted to mock-sympathy.

'Don't worry. He's fine. In fact, he's quite comfortable with his new outlook on life.'

'I'm sure,' I shot back. 'It's amazing what a little brainwashing will do.'

Eisen laughed. 'There was none required, my dear. A matter of hours after we'd finished the gene therapy he asked to help us bring you in.'

I reeled in my urge to yell defiance at him. 'So why didn't you take me when I came to rescue him and Anna?'

He shrugged. 'We needed to be certain where his loyalties lay. It killed two birds to let you rescue him then lead us back to where the rest of you were.'

'But if you wanted all of us,' I said, trying to piece it all together, 'why not send a lot more people to Ian Fairchild's house the same day you took Logan from the gardens?'

By the door, the anonymous sidhe twitched. One hand rubbed at the back of his head, then both dropped to his sides and opened, loose. His weight shifted to the balls of his feet.

Eisen shoved off the bed and sighed with the impatience of someone unused to having their motives questioned.

'By the time my men got there, you'd all moved on. Hence the need to let you rescue Logan. Enough of this. We must speak of the real reason I've brought you here.'

Bemused, I watched the sidhe a moment longer then switched back to Eisen. Could it be Eisen didn't *know* about the attack led on Ian's house by his own man? But surely Logan would have told him? No, Logan hadn't been there and we'd never got around to explaining to him why we'd shifted from Ian's place. He probably assumed it was because he'd been kidnapped and would give the location away.

But Tom. Why hadn't he told them? Was it possible he was able to fight the brainwashing and keep some control?

What the hell was going on?

One of Eisen's men brought in a chair. Eisen reversed and straddled it, then scratched at his crewcut grey-blond hair.

'Please.' I groaned. 'Spare me the "we can do this the hard way or the easy way" speech. Just ask. If I know the answer I'll tell you. I'm not the heroic type. I have no desire to be stoic under torture. Get on with it.'

What sounded like a real chuckle sputtered from his lips and he straightened. 'Fair enough. What's the *ocair?* '

'Logan and Tom have probably already told you,' I replied. 'It was in a prediction made by Mairi Silverblade in thirteen something.

It goes: "And in the year of our lord 1403 a key shall be born in the realm of the three crowns. In the embrace of the *sianfath* and the *lorntinn* that key may be the deliverance of those that dispossess the *Ruadhán Daoine sidhe*".'

'Yes, yes.' He dismissed my words. 'I've heard that bit. But what *is* it?'

'Well, Logan's theory is that it *was* Calain. But he died, so now it's non-existent. There is no such thing. No magical key to be the deliverance of humanity. Sorry.' I tried to sound casual, dismissive and uninterested. But Logan would have told him my fear.

Eisen's smile twisted. 'Nice try. It might have been Calain, but we both know it's now you. The question is, *how* are you humanity's deliverance?'

'You find out and we'll both know. I have no idea.'

'Hmmm.' He cocked his head. 'I actually believe you. Logan and Tom have both said the same thing. Well!' He slapped his palms on the chair back, stood and spun it aside. 'We'll have to find out together. I'm rather glad you didn't die, now.'

'I'm kind of regretting it, myself,' I muttered.

He jerked his chin at the sidhe, who opened the door. A white-coated woman entered, carrying a syringe full of straw-coloured liquid and wearing medical gloves.

Adrenalin surged through my blood again and I shrank away. 'What's that?'

She ignored me, inserting the needle into the cannula in my wrist.

'The antidote to the drug suppressing your sidhe gifts,' Eisen replied.

'Really?' That made no kind of sense at all. As soon as I had my abilities back nothing would prevent me from escaping and taking every one of my companions with me.

Completely at sea, I waited – for the antidote to take effect and for some sort of useful explanation to be forthcoming.

The woman left and an elderly man came in, wheeling a laptop on a stand. He positioned it close to my bed, plugged it in and passed a remote to Eisen, then left without saying a word. Eisen must pay people well if they were willing to ignore a young woman strapped to a bed.

Hitching his hip onto the bed again, Eisen pointed the remote at the computer and pressed a few buttons.

'Right now, you're wondering how long it will take before you can kill me and all my staff and escape.' He didn't wait for my reply. I wasn't going to answer anyway, so that suited me fine. 'But you're not going to kill anyone and you're not going to escape.'

'Really?' I repeated, this time loading the word with sarcasm.

'Yes, really. In fact, you're going to help me. Then, when you succeed, I believe we may know what it means for you to be the *ocair*.'

'Why the hell would I help you with anything?' The pain and anguish he'd caused me spilled out. My voice broke, much to my disgust.

'Because of them.' Eisen pointed at the screen.

The large image was broken into five smaller ones, each showing two people. Every scene was the same: Anna, Jennifer, Harry, Maeve, and Erin all lay, strapped to beds. They all appeared to be asleep, which was a small mercy. Beside each sat a guard wearing an Eisen company uniform and resting their hand on some sort of small, black box. Next to each victim's head stood a complicated piece of metal and electronic engineering. Holding a gun.

I swallowed but said nothing, merely waiting for Eisen to explain. So far I couldn't see any reason why I shouldn't drain everyone in the building who belonged to him, then blow the damned place up.

'You're going to help me because each one of my men holds a dead-man's switch.' Eisen spread his arms. 'It's quite simple. If they die, the switches trigger the devices holding the guns. The guns kill your friends.'

'What's to stop me killing you and everyone else, except them?' I tried to keep the quaver out of my voice, but his amusement said he'd heard it.

'Because the same thing happens if they stop hearing my voice in their earpieces.' He tapped his ear.

Could I cleanse the drug from Maeve and Jennifer and wake them at a distance? They could use their telekinesis to stop the switches. No, even if I cleared the drugs – which I wasn't sure I could from this far away – Jennifer wouldn't be able to stop more than one, maybe two switches. Her range was limited. Maeve was more experienced, but I had no idea what her ability level was. Contacting them presented too big a risk, with Logan and the big sidhe around to hear. If the plan failed it would fail in horrifying fashion.

I wracked my brain for some other option and came up with a big fat zero. As far as I could tell, Eisen had covered every contingency.

'What do you want from me, Eisen?'

'Wise girl.' He rose, leaving the screen on. 'You're going to cure my son.'

'What?'

He ignored me. 'The suppression should be wearing off about now. William?'

The large sidhe unstrapped my ankles, watching me carefully as he did so. I held still as he undid the other straps. I might be impulsive and have ten years of training, but even I wasn't stupid enough to start a fight with a sidhe twice my weight and backed by four guys with guns. They treated me like I was, though, which wasn't surprising.

I struggled off the bed and the guns muzzles followed me. The drip tugged at my hand. I ripped off the tape and yanked out the cannula, hissing through my teeth. Testing my connection to the *sianfath,* I found it restored. A great wave of relief and confidence strengthened my trembling limbs. Substantial bushland surrounded the complex. I drew, instead, a little energy from several of Eisen's men to purge the drug from my system and heal the cannula-exit wound. It might be enough to slow their reactions at a crucial moment. One of the guards stifled a yawn. The large sidhe, William, scrutinised him narrowly.

'Excellent,' Eisen muttered, staring at my wrist as the blood stopped and the wound sealed itself.

Two men entered the room and hope leaped. Logan and Tom. But Logan's expression held cool disinterest, and Tom's was blank. Hope vanished as fast as it had come. I tested Tom's shield and found it an impenetrable dome. Cold as they had been the first night I met him, here, outside the MJE compound, chasing me. If he fought the brainwashing, he gave no sign of it.

A small smile lifted the corner of Logan's mouth and I took an involuntary half-step towards him. He closed the gap and struck me across the cheek with an open palm. Tears, from more than just the pain, stung my eyes. He grabbed my shoulders and impelled me into Tom's grasp. Behind Tom the older sidhe, William, waited impassive.

My precog had come true. I hated that.

But maybe I should stop avoiding the precogs; use them to my advantage? I pretended to stumble and clutched at Tom's bare forearm, concentrating on the near future.

Darkness and isolation. A small, decrepit room in a dark building. Then over-bright lights and a sickening sensation of guilty awakening. Horrified familiarity; recognition of a bare room with downlights and a hospital bed. Fear. Blood. Distress.

Letting go I staggered under the vision's power, trying to interpret it. It seemed to be from Tom's point of view. The soul-deep fear and anguish in it shook me to the core. Something terrible was about to happen to Tom, but there wasn't enough information to work out what, where or when.

The darkness and fear at the beginning didn't feel right. More like metaphoric ideas of where his conscious mind was currently trapped – perhaps in the ruined part of his thought-house. If I could somehow find him in there and drag him to consciousness, would he revert to normal and be able to overcome the brainwashing enough to help me? Or would doing that somehow lead to the blood?

A hand shoved me in the back and I swung around, my anger only half-pretence. Logan gripped my upper arm. He was ice and mockery. Keeping eye contact, I grabbed his wrist and twisted free, concentrating to maximise the brief contact.

A blur of movement; the pain of blows struck and received. Fierce sense of triumph. A shocking report in a small space. A body on the concrete floor: Rowan's. Grief. Dismay. Doubt.

My legs collapsed this time and I couldn't stop the gasping denial that escaped my lips. Someone hauled me upright and Logan peered at me.

'Stop that,' he ordered. 'It won't help.'

'What's she doing?' Eisen demanded from behind me.

Logan shrugged indifferently. 'Trying to use her precog to work out what's going to happen. From her expression I'd say she didn't see a happy ending.' He directed his next, sneering, words to me. 'You won't escape. None of you will.'

I straightened, calm understanding now settling my nerves for the first time since I'd awoken here.

'I know,' I said coolly. 'And *you* will be the one to kill me.'

His eyes widened. Twisting free from his suddenly-lax grip, I let the other guard and Tom lead me from the room. Logan fell behind. He and Michael engaged in a heated discussion about the truth of my words and I allowed myself a small, satisfied smile. Anything that messed with their allegiance and their heads was fine by me. I wasn't certain Logan would be the one, but I now knew it would happen – and why. But when was another matter.

TWENTY-FIVE

We entered Paul Eisen's room to find him sitting up in bed, reading a car magazine. He glanced up with a bored scowl, then his mouth fell open. Tossing the magazine aside, he threw the blanket off his legs and swung his feet to the floor. A scrubs-clad male nurse, who'd been standing to one side, warned him against standing and practically forced him back into the bed.

Muttering disgruntled complaints, Paul complied but he never took his gaze off me. He dismissed the nurse and guards, but Tom stayed, silent and blank, a statue by the door.

Paul beckoned me closer, grinning. In full light it was shocking how much weight he had lost. Only two weeks had passed but he was now underweight, pale and heavy-eyed. His boyish good looks were lost to a sallow complexion, dark rings and lank blond hair. The *sianfath* glow about his body was a dark-rust colour and swirled unpleasantly, like coagulating blood. But his good cheer seemed undimmed and his smile lit the room. Even bearing in mind my doubts about his neutrality in this situation, it was impossible to return anger. It would be like kicking a puppy.

He patted the bed.

'Hey! You're back from Ireland already? How'd it go? Did Dad tell you I was here? Man, it's a pain in the arse, this being sick crap. I think—'

'Paul,' I interrupted the flow as I sat on the bed, 'I have to ask you something before your father comes in. Did you know about me?'

Genuine bewilderment clouded his blue eyes. 'Huh? What about you? All I knew was that you and Anna had to go back to Ireland. Is there something I *should* know?'

'What do you know about that night in Cairns?' I sought his mind. It had been shielded by someone, but not so I was completely blocked out. Thoughts and emotions leaked through: surprise, delight at seeing me, honest confusion. As far as I could tell, he had no idea what I was. Perhaps he wasn't part of this, after all?

He leaned back against the bedhead. The tube from his drip flicked the metal bedframe with a tinny ring that echoed in the bare room.

'I took Anna home then I went over to a mate's place for an hour or two. When I got back the house was quiet so I went to bed.' He shrugged. 'Next morning I got a call from Dad to say he'd gone to Brisbane. Two days later he called again to say my blood tests had come in and he was sending the plane to get me.' He waved at the room. 'I've been here ever since – charming place that it is. I've had doctors crawling over me for two weeks. So frigging over it. You have no idea how nice it is to see a familiar face who isn't telling me I'm going to die.'

'Die!' I gasped. 'What is this Huntington's thing, anyway?'

Paul rubbed his forehead. 'Who the hell knows? They're calling it that because that's the closest they can get to a diagnosis. My uncle died of the same thing at about my age. Evidently Dad had me tested the day I was born and found out I had the potential to get it. Wasn't sure it would ever come on full-blown, though. He's been paranoid my whole life and he's pretty much spent the last eighteen years trying to find a cure, just in case.' His mouth twisted and he plucked at his grey tracksuit pants. 'Turned out he didn't find it fast enough. Sucks to be me, huh?' He screwed up his nose. 'Can we talk about something else?'

I averted my face for a moment, trying to regather my composure. A lot now became horribly clear: Michael Eisen's obsession with the health industry in general, his study of the sidhe powers, even his seduction of my mother and abduction of me. He'd cited his parents' death as his reason in Cairns, and that undoubtedly played a part in why he'd chosen me to be his victim. But his hatred of my father wasn't the only motivation for finding me and experimenting on other sidhe. He was trying to find a cure for his son. How much must he have regretted having me thrown off a building when Paul's blood tests came back two days later.

Oh, my God. An offhand comment, made by Ian when I first met him, sprang to mind. He'd said seven people had vanished in Brisbane during the last two weeks. All the missing people must be sidhe or part-sidhe. That's how desperate Michael was. He'd probably had them under surveillance and took them when Paul's results came in. What had happened to them? Were they here in this complex or had Eisen deemed them useless and had them murdered?

Some of my horror must have shown because Paul sat back up and folded his arms.

'What?'

'Nothing.' A great surge of pity and dismay welled in me. Hopefully he'd never find out what sort of man his father was – or follow in his footsteps.

Michael had done appalling things in the throes of desperation and fear. Perhaps I could stop it by helping. Perhaps there was a way to resolve this peacefully, so I and my family and friends could walk free.

The question was: how far had Michael gone down the path of the unredeemable?

I sensed Michael's approach and stood before he entered. The big sidhe, William, trod in his wake. Michael sent Tom out and closed the door, leaving the four of us together. Part of me wanted to slap Michael. Part wanted to kill him. The sanest part held the others back and I said and did nothing, only watched him warily.

Michael's gaze darted to Paul then away again. He cleared his throat and stalked to the end of the bed, where he made a show of reading the medical chart.

'Feeling better, son?' He didn't look up.

Paul, who'd been watching his father with a mixture of pity and hurt, mumbled an unconvincing 'sure'. A bleak little smile flickered across Michael's thin mouth. He replaced the clipboard with precision and swung around to face me.

'Now.' Michael rubbed his palms together and showed me a bright, artificial grin. 'Ready?'

I folded my arms then recalled an old book I'd read on negotiating and opened my arms again. Palms out and facing up, I softened my body language and tried to seem gentle and non-threatening. Peaceful resolution. I had to keep that in mind.

'Can I ask two things?'

Michael's eyes narrowed. 'Make it quick.'

I lowered my voice, figuring he wouldn't want Paul hearing. 'First: as a show of good will, can you let two of them go, so I know you're for real.' It was worth a try.

He gave a cool, sardonic look. 'No. Second question?'

I glanced over my shoulder at Paul, so emaciated and yet still bright-eyed and worthy of life. I liked him. He didn't deserve to die; didn't even deserve the last two weeks of suffering.

'Why didn't you just *ask* me, in Cairns?' Would Michael give even a little in this game, or was he so focussed and so hell-bent on his purpose that everything else was irrelevant or an obstacle?

Whoever had shielded his mind had done an excellent job. The shield presented as a featureless sphere without a crack. Nothing I could get into and nothing of his thoughts leaked out. Since I couldn't afford to weaken myself by sliding into the *sianfath,* I had to rely on his expressions.

He frowned. 'Ask you what?'

'If I would cure Paul? You could have asked.' I pointed at the bed. 'I like Paul. Of course I would have helped. It would have been…inhuman not to.' I used the word deliberately but managed to keep the irony out of my voice.

Confusion flickered through him for a moment, then vanished beneath scornful disbelief. He pursed his mouth and lifted his chin.

'Oh yes.' The sarcasm was clear. 'Calain Gilmore's daughter would have voluntarily helped someone of the Mors Ferrum – me, especially. Sure.'

I bit back the urge to point out that, until the Freysons had come into my sphere, I'd been ignorant of the Mors Ferrum, or my father's part in any of this nightmare. There was no point. He wouldn't believe me. Or, if he did, he'd probably get defensive and angry for misjudging me when he could have saved his son earlier. He'd decided who I was. There was no hope of changing that image in a hurry.

I headed for the bed and sat again.

'What's going on, Meghan?' Paul studied me and his father.

I hesitated, working out where to start and how much to say.

'Well, for starters, my name's Rowan, not Meghan.' I held up a hand to forestall his astonished questions. 'Long story. Don't ask. Second, and better news is: I'm here to cure you. You good with that?'

'Wha…?' Paul scowled. 'Is this some sort of joke? There is no cure. Unless…' Hope leapt for a moment, then died away. 'No, you're still at high school so you can't be some genius wunderkind doctor.'

That made me smile and I shook my head. 'Again – long story. You're going to have to have a little faith and…believe in fairies.'

Paul snorted. 'Cut the crap, Meg…Rowan. I'd like an explanation, and maybe a beer, but stop spinning bullshit.' He looked over my shoulder at his father. 'What's this about, Dad? If you brought her in to cheer me up it's not working. This is a bit weird.'

Michael hesitated then walked around to stand beside his son. He stroked Paul's hair once, then pulled away.

'No, it's true. She's agreed to heal you.' A tight little smile stretched his mouth. 'And she's right: have a little faith. But there's something we must do first. Rowan, I need to borrow you for one moment.' He pointed at the door. 'There's someone in the room next door I'd like you to meet before we get started.'

I patted Paul's leg reassuringly, then followed Michael into the little boxy room one door away.

William dogged my footsteps, silent and intimidating.

'Rowan!' Anna tugged at the straps binding her to the bed and glared at her guard. 'Are you alright? Have they hurt you? Mick, you bastard!' She yanked again at the straps, her pale cheeks flushed and eyes bright. 'Let her go!'

'Anna!' I took a step forward but Michael barred my way.

He gestured to William. The sidhe paused, staring in Anna's direction, apparently transfixed. He cocked his head and, even the silicone mask's anonymity couldn't disguise he was doubtful about something.

'Anna.' His deep voice resonated in the chamber.

She sucked a quick little breath and stilled. Had they met when she was here before? Was there something between them? No, she seemed astonished more than anything. And she'd said she'd been kept isolated before, seeing no-one but a female attendant and Michael.

'William!' Michael's voice pulled the sidhe's attention back and William shook himself, rubbing at the back of his neck.

He opened the door and two more people were ushered in. Both wore the standard white shirt and grey pants of an MJE victim. They huddled together by the door, fear jumbling their thoughts and battering on my shields. One was a young man, maybe in his late twenties, with dull brown hair and dark eyes. The other an older woman, in her forties or fifties, with a smattering of grey in her short, black hair and an air of resignation about her thin-pressed mouth. She wore a wedding ring.

I felt a faint frisson as my heritage recognised another sidhe. A quick check on their minds showed no awareness of who they were and no training or psychic skills that could be of use. Quarter- or eighth-caste at best, then. So, who were they and why were they here?

I raised my brows at Michael. He gestured me away from Anna.

'They'll provide the energy you need for curing Paul,' he said in an undertone. 'I understand you need life-energy to perform the healing.'

'No! You can't—' Horror and disbelief choked me. My hands curled into claws and I had to force myself to stand still and not leap on him.

Beside the door, William's big body tensed and he took a half-step forward. Michael waved him away.

'Yes,' he replied, coolly.

TWENTY-SIX

'I won't kill these people, not even to save Paul,' I said. Sick fear weakened my knees and I trembled, fighting nausea. 'She's married for God's sake. She probably has children. You can't do this! I can take a little from everyone here and some from the forest outside.'

Michael looked down his nose at me. 'I don't trust you. You could kill Paul, or everyone in this compound and leave only me and the guards on your people. This way I'll have control over the situation, not you. You'll take what you need from these people or yours die. Your choice.' He pointed at the guard sitting next to Anna. Then he took out his phone, tapped the screen and showed it, revealing a close-up of Jennifer's sleeping face…and the gun-muzzle pressed to her temple. He swiped the screen and Harry's image replaced it.

I bared my teeth at him, helpless, horrified, sickened and angry all at once. 'You are a complete psycho, you know that? You don't *need* to do this!' I made one last appeal, infuriated when tears blurred my vision. 'I'll cure him anyway. I really will. Let them all go. You can even keep me. Please, Michael. Listen to reason. Please? Don't make me do this?' Tears blurred my vision and I dashed them away.

I hadn't meant to beg him, but I couldn't help it. And if abasing myself and begging would make this madness stop I'd do it. I couldn't do this. Wouldn't. Surely he wouldn't make me?

Something like empathy flickered in the icy depths of him. He seemed to see me as a person for the first time.

I actually prayed to whatever god would listen.

Then Eisen lifted a shoulder and jerked his chin at William. The sidhe manhandled the two prisoners into waiting chairs and handcuffed them, ignoring their fearful protests and pleas. My heart stuttered as the locks clicked shut. I felt their glowing life-forces, felt their fear and confusion, felt their desperation to live and their growing belief that they would not.

I looked to Anna and she gazed back, dismayed.

Taking hold of my arm, Eisen murmured. 'Now, you will drain them to cure Paul. If anyone else here is affected, or if you fail to cure him, one of your friends will die. Do you understand?'

'Please, Michael,' I whispered. 'Paul wouldn't want you to do this. I know he wouldn't.'

'Don't you *dare* tell me what Paul wants or needs,' he growled. 'He wants to live. And if you want your friends and mother to live, you'll do exactly as I say. Got it?'

Numbly, I nodded, my tongue thick and stilled by helplessness. William took my other arm and I walked between them to the door.

'Rowan.' Anna's chin lifted, her mouth set. 'Remember what I've always said.' Her gaze flickered to William and back to me. 'Your worst moments can define what sort of person you are, but only if you let them. Do what you have to, sweetheart. It will be ok.'

Beside me, William stiffened.

'Hey!' Paul's voice lifted in concern when he saw me. 'What's the deal? What've you said to upset her, Dad?'

I sank onto the bed and managed to stem the flow of tears by sucking a deep breath and pasting on a determined smile. The ache in my chest intensified and the burn of self-hatred threatened to consume my thoughts. I closed my eyes for a moment and cleared my throat. What choice did I have? Two people's lives for six. Not even any way to take my own life to prevent being used. There was no choice.

'Nothing, Paul. I'm fine.' I squeezed his arm. 'Just worried I might not be able to fix you.'

He scowled at his father. 'I don't get it. Will someone explain what the hell is going on? How can you fix me?'

I hesitated.

Eisen shook his head in the barest hint of negation. My heart heavy and throat thick, I watched my thumb sweep over the back of Paul's blue-veined hand.

'You'll have to trust your father,' I murmured, 'and me. I can't explain any more. Close your eyes and relax.'

His gaze darted between me and his father a few times before he lay back on the pillows with his eyes shut.

'Won't hurt will it?'

I gave a weak chuckle that ended on a half-sob. 'Me more than you, I think.'

After one, last, despairing look at Eisen's granite expression, I closed my eyes as well.

I wanted to draw the power slowly so I could manage Calain-in-my-head and the pain from working around the block. But if I did that, the two prisoners would die slow and painful deaths. They would scream and suffer horribly, in front of my mother. I couldn't bear to have her know I was responsible. Or to hear the screams.

Yet, if I drew it fast I'd pay the price and I didn't want to be unconscious again. But I couldn't see any other option.

Clamping down on the block to strengthen it I stretched into the *sianfath* and sought out the two fear-muddied, bright lives beyond the thin wall. Oh, it would be so, so easy to suck the life out of Michael Eisen, a few feet away from me. No. I shut the thought out. That was my father talking, not me. There were too many lives at stake. I would *not* sacrifice the Freysons, Fairchilds, Anna and Paul for revenge against one man. Still, Calain's voice whispered soft encouragement: drain them all, walk out free and unencumbered to rule the world. I shut him out and reached for the prisoners.

Tears coursed afresh down my cheeks as I tore the light from them and stored it within, holding the sum of two souls in my mind. I'd destroyed their lives. Resolutely I forced my attention back to Paul and shut out the awareness their bodies now lay as lifeless husks on the floor. The dungeon door in my head rattled as the imprisoned, ruthless spirit of my father sensed the power. I held firm and lay a hand on Paul's stomach, baring my teeth against the blossoming agony pounding in my skull.

His skin fluttered beneath my touch. Cautiously, I released the brilliant, silvery-green energy into him, tasting lightning, guiding it to damaged organs, driving it deep into cells, encouraging it to seek out and fix DNA. I had no idea how to imagine the DNA that caused the genetic disorder he carried, and I wasn't telekinetic, so I could only hope my vague instructions were enough. It had worked with Harry and Logan. But they were sidhe. The *sianfath* seemed to understand. It responded, even seeking out places and damage I hadn't seen. Could it be sentient somehow, or was that my imagination?

Paul writhed. His back arched and he groaned. It went on forever, but we were deep in the *sianfath* and time had little meaning there, so it could have been seconds. We were close to restoring his health, though. I sensed it; tasted it in the blood-metallic, ozone tang in my mouth; heard it in the whispers of his deepest mind; felt it in the surge of blood and energy through his exhausted body.

He shrieked. Behind me, Michael bellowed, yelling at me to stop or he'd kill Anna. I was too entrenched in the process to respond, unable to control my mouth. My entire concentration was caught up inside Paul. If I left now it would all be undone and unfinished and Paul would die. Then those two prisoners would have died for nothing. In a twisted way, curing him was the only way I could make their deaths worthwhile.

Pouring the last of the life-energy into him, I managed to stay awake long enough to see him draw in several gasping breaths. His eyes flew wide. Michael called his name. Then the wave of pain broke through my mind, tearing open the block. I released consciousness in order to hold back the darkness.

Who was the worse monster, though: Calain or me?

I woke to a dim room and the sensation of restraints on my wrists and ankles again. This was getting old. I should have taken Maeve's offer, two weeks ago, to removed that damned block. My own fear of her and of Calain's potential – of *my* potential – had put me in this vulnerable position. I was an idiot.

And now I was a complicit, murderous idiot.

I pounded my head against the hard pillow a few times in an effort to beat out the image of the nameless woman and man I'd killed. It didn't work. Hot tears burned down my temples and I swore at myself. The ache in my chest grew. So much for being resigned to who I was. So much for being a ruthless, hardened killer. Would this ever get easier? Did I want it to?

The doorknob rattled and the door cracked open. Someone came in and the door snicked shut again. The drip stand and heart monitor obscured in my line of sight. All I could do was wait, tense and breathless, as stealthy footsteps approached.

The dim overhead light fell on lank blonde hair.

'Paul!' I spoke too loud and we both flinched.

'Shhhh. Keep it down. I snuck out, but someone will check on me soon for sure. Here.' He fumbled with the leather around my wrists. 'It worked.'

'What did?' I lifted my arm free and freed the other wrist as he tugged at the ankle straps.

'Whatever you did to me.' He sounded surprised. 'It hurt like hell, but after they took you out the doc came and did another test.' He flipped the straps open and threw his arms wide. 'I'm better.'

'Oh.' I sat up and rubbed at my wrists. 'I'm glad.' It would take a while to regain his old muscle tone and healthy good looks, but his eyes had regained their sparkle.

He helped me stand, steadying me when my knees shook. I couldn't draw from the *sianfath*. They'd drugged me again. Spotting the medical trolley, I pulled open a couple of drawers until I found one with a small phial of straw-coloured liquid. After a moment's hesitation I found a syringe and injected it into the cannula. Then I yanked the needle out and pressed my thumb against the bead of blood.

'What the *hell* is going on?' Paul watched me in horrified, fascinated silence the whole time. His whisper sounded loud in the silence.

'It's a long story,' I replied. 'What time is it?'

He checked his watch. 'A little after nine pm. Why?'

I searched the room again in the vain hope my clothes and throwing knives would materialise. No luck. 'Where's your father?'

Paul shrugged. 'Dunno. He and that big guy, William, went off into town for some reason an hour or so ago.'

'Right.' I grabbed a syringe and filled it with something labelled Sidazolam. A type of benzodiazepine. I had no idea what that was. Perhaps the drug that suppressed our abilities. At this point in time I didn't care. It was my only weapon until the antidote kicked in. 'That means now is the time to get out of here.'

'Rowan.' Paul gripped my elbow. 'What's going on? Who are you?'

I shook him free. 'Not now. Thank you for releasing me but I don't have time to explain. I have to get my mother and my friends out before Michael comes back. If you're not going to help, then get out of my way.'

Instead, he folded his arms and planted himself in front of the door. 'Not until you tell me what my father did to you. Why is he holding you like this? And I heard Anna's voice in the room next to mine. What'd he do to upset you so much?'

I swallowed hard against the memory of the two people who'd given their lives for his. 'It doesn't matter. I need to get out of here. Move.' Without waiting, I grabbed his shoulders and manhandled him aside, ignoring his astonishment. My strength was returning, at least.

Before I could open it, the door burst open. Logan rushed in, knocking aside my hand so the syringe flew free and broke against the wall. A feral grin distorted his handsome features as he bore down on me. He jabbed at my stomach but it was a feint. My reactions were still slow. I almost missed the real strike: a straight kick at my knee. A shin-block stopped it.

He lashed out with a knife-edge-hand at my cheek. I struck it aside and followed with a forearm under his jaw. He twisted, enough to stop the strike from being a knockout, but it still stunned him. He staggered back, working his jaw.

Michael and Tom entered.

'Don't kill her, Logan. She's the *ocair*. I need her alive.'

TWENTY-SEVEN

Tom! Tom, help me! Please?

There's no use, Rowan. He can't hear you.

Logan? Stop this, please? This isn't you. Michael's twisted your mind. You know what the Dark gene does. You're brainwashed. You know it's not who you are. If you care for me at all, please let me go.

Oh, not brainwashed. Just awake, now. And I do care. I just think there's more to being sidhe than acting as caretakers for nature and having sidhe babies. Maeve was right: you're far more useful as a weapon.

I won't. Whatever Michael wants me to do, I won't.

You will. We have your mother and even if you run, you can't hide from me. I knew you were awake. I knew you were trying to escape. Wherever you go, I'll find you. We're connected, remember?

'Dad!' Paul grabbed at his father's arm. 'Call him off. What are you doing? What do you want with Rowan, anyway?'

'She's mine son,' Michael replied. 'She's the key to everything I need to set this world to rights and I'm going to be the one controlling her. I'm going to be the one the world turns to. Keep out of it. You have no idea how important this girl is. Don't meddle with what you don't understand.'

'But—'

'Don't you see?' Michael pointed at me. 'She can cure every disease. Can you imagine what we can do? People who shouldn't die, won't. We can control the population growth to something sustainable. We can grant long life to those who need it. We can run the damned world as it should be run.'

Paul's mouth dropped open. His released his father's arm and took a step back.

'And who decides who needs long life?' he said. 'Who decides who's allowed to have kids and who's not? You? Christ, Dad. What is *wrong* with you?'

Michael curled a lip. 'I didn't expect you to understand. You're too young. You will, eventually. Then you'll thank me.' He gestured to Tom, who stepped behind Paul and twisted his arms into a lock. Paul gargled, standing on tiptoes, his face a rictus of agony.

Logan and I circled each other, wary. He snatched at my shirt. I fended him off and drove a fist at his diaphragm. He slapped it aside and latched onto my wrist, twisting my arm into a lock meant to dislocate my shoulder. I jumped over, landed on my feet and used my momentum to unbalance him.

One foot against his ankle, I dropped to my back and planted the other in his stomach. He flew over my head and crashed against the medical cart. Instruments, bandages and phials of medicines spilled from the drawers in an appalling cacophony. I leapt to my feet. Logan lay, sprawled and stunned on the floor. Had I hurt him? My heart skipped.

I risked a look at Paul and Tom. Paul gaped at me. Tom was cold and distant. Could I reach him? I had to take the chance. It was only a matter of time before someone showed up with those damned darts again.

Holding the dungeon shut I extended myself carefully into the *sianfath*. Tom's energy was a dull, grey-green, his mental house hidden behind that smooth dome. I broke through and found his house dark and smaller than I remembered. I pushed through his walls as though they weren't there. The gothic, gloomy mansion was empty. I ran from room to room, calling Tom's name.

I headed for the derelict wing, running faster as a sense of impending doom pressed at me. I didn't need my precognitive ability to tell me something was about to happen, but it did anyway.

Kicking in a half-rotted door, I fumbled in the darkness, calling out. At last, a faint answer and his image appeared in the gloom.

You must come back, Tom. You've been brainwashed. I need your help.

{I can't, Rowan. I...I've done awful things. I'm sure I have.} His expression twisted into fear. *{No, don't tell me. It doesn't matter. I can't find my way back, anyway.}*

Take my hand. I'll guide you. I held his trembling fingers in my own. *I'm in trouble and I need your help. You want to make up for what you've done? Now's the time. Will you help me?*

{...What do I have to do?}

I'll show you. Be brave, Tom. I have faith in you.

An arm snaked around my throat as I came back to myself. No! If Logan got a rear naked choke on me... Digging my nails into his skin, I tensed my stomach and threw my legs high into the air. Using every ounce of weight and momentum, I dropped, bent and flung him forward. This time he landed lightly and bounced to his feet, snarling in anger.

'You can't beat me, Rowan.' He was panting now. 'You know I'm faster and stronger than you.'

'So why are you the one bleeding all over the place?'

Blood dribbled down his neck, onto his collar. He touched it and inspected the crimson smear. I used the moment of distraction and swarmed in, reaching for his neck. He was too quick. His fist flicked at my eyes and I flinched. He grabbed my arm and wrenched it into a lock. I spun out and reversed it into a lock on him. He slapped the heel of his free hand into the pressurepoint on my jaw. My head snapped back and I cried out. I let go, backing out of reach.

He closed again, arms up to protect his throat. I snaked a hand over the top, smacking the forehead pressurepoints. He reeled back, guard dropping for a moment. I could follow through with a neck-strike, but I didn't want to seriously injure him. There had to be a way to get through to him.

Could I bring him back as I had Tom? No, his mind was different. Tom had no Dark gene. He had been transformed into a drone-soldier, his free will locked away. Logan wasn't brainwashed and his thought-shield was intact – in fact it was stronger than ever. I could get through it using the *sianfath,* but I'd be left vulnerable and there was no point. His thinking was clear, but faulty and twisted. I needed to find a way to switch off that gene again.

Logan drove a quick palm strike to my chest. The power of it knocked me down. I rolled to my feet, coughing. My ribs hurt – broken again by the sharp pains stabbing through my back. Dammit. I needed to learn a counter to that.

Smiling in triumph, Logan lunged. I waited till the last second and dodged. One hand slid up his chest and under his chin. I tipped his head back and his feet flew out. I couldn't bring myself to drive him hard into the concrete, so I let go. He managed a breakfall. A grunt of pain said he wasn't unscathed, though.

I dropped to my knees, wrapped an arm around his throat from behind, and locked my legs around his hips. He bucked and arched beneath my arm, fighting the blood-choke. His nails clawed at my arm in increasing desperation. I rolled so my back was to Tom; Logan in front of me.

Now Tom. As soon as I let Logan go.

{Rowan...}

Do it!

Logan went limp in the crook of my elbow and I shoved him aside. Was he unconscious or pretending? I'd killed someone once by misjudging how long to hold that choke. I didn't want to make that mistake with him. He groaned and scrabbled at the smooth concrete floor.

His eyes opened and met mine in bleary confusion. For a moment the real Logan surfaced. His fingertips touched mine and he frowned, his lips forming my name in silent question.

A sharp report shattered the breathless quiet. Something punched me in the back. I coughed and slumped sideways. Logan's eyes widened. Behind me, Michael shouted a denial. Footsteps clattered on the concrete. Someone rolled me onto my back and I stared at the circle of faces overhead.

Logan struggled to his knees and cradled me on his lap, his expression shifting between confusion, anger and fear.

'Don't you die, dammit, Rowan,' he muttered. 'Heal yourself.'

I shook my head, holding hard to the dungeon door. It rattled and trembled with the strength of my father's will to survive and his mandate to protect me at all costs.

'Heal her!' Michael's command came from on high.

'I can't, you idiot! Not a wound this bad,' Logan snapped. 'Only she can. Or Maeve or Jennifer. Wake one of them!'

'There's no point,' I whispered. 'There's not enough time and you know it. I told you I won't be used by any of you as a weapon in your stupid war.' I touched his cheek. 'Let me go, Logan. I won't be Michael's tool.'

'You stupid little fool!' he growled. 'You know Calain will come out and heal you, any second. As he did in Cairns. And in the forest in Chapel Hill.'

I laughed, blood bubbling from my lips. 'No, he won't. Not this time. I've worked out how to stop him.'

It wasn't true, being more of a hope than a plan. But my words held enough confidence that Logan blanched. He opened his mouth, but a male nurse rushed in and shouldered him aside. Logan sat back, covered in my blood, staring at me in horrified disbelief.

I concentrated on staying calm as long as I could; on holding onto the locked dungeon door. When the time was close, and the noise and ruckus around me began to fade, I slipped free of my body and fanned into the *sianfath*. This time I tied a thread of myself to Tom. He stiffened, but didn't speak. His eyes were wide and terrified. Luckily no-one was watching him. He edged from the room, carrying my tiny lifeline with him. A thin hope pinned to a very dubious saviour. He vanished into the corridor and I felt him run towards the cold-storage room. The most likely place for them to take my body.

Strange to think of myself in those terms: merely as a body. But something about being so attenuated into the *sianfath* reduced emotions and physical attachments. I was at one with the world; tempted to let go and relax; to merge with it.

Then my body breathed its last. Calain, held back so far by sheer force of my will, broke free. He roared out of confinement, determined to protect and bring me home again, as he had last time.

This time I was ready for him.

His shade coalesced before me, his dark arms stretching out. His image was hazy, as though he'd forgotten his appearance; who he was. Which was true, in some respects. It hurt to see him like this when so lately I'd seen him alive and vibrant. Of course, that had been over five hundred years before, in real time. My heart ached for all he'd lost; all I'd lost in losing him.

He was the merest memory of a father with nothing left but the edict to protect his child. But he was a dangerous protector. If I couldn't deal with his shade then it was likely to get me killed and I still hadn't worked out how to set him free, as Aeona instructed.

With half an eye on Logan, Michael and Paul, still clustered around my physical form in the room, I clung to Tom and the *sianfath* as Calain's ghost wrenched at me. Pulling at the threads of me, he tried, with increasing desperation, to return me to myself.

It wasn't yet time. I evaded his grasp, anchoring to anything I could, holding on until the final moment.

There. The heart stopped.

The thread binding Logan to me snapped.

TWENTY-EIGHT

Logan laid bloodied palms against his temples and choked a scream of such pain that the insubstantial memory of my heart trembled. He yelled my name in tones of denial, his voice hoarse and broken. Tears coursed down his face and he slumped onto his side, curling into the foetal position next to me, his forehead touching my shoulder.

'What the hell is wrong with him?' Michael nudged Logan with a toe. 'Get up, man. Find the idiot who did this. I want him dealt with. Dammit.' He swore a few more choice words and gestured imperiously to the nurse and a guard. 'Get this body into the storage room. Take blood and tissue samples and we'll get the researchers to start in the morning. I want to know what gene carried that ability she had to suck people dry. Maybe we can find another one that has it.' He jerked a thumb at Logan. 'And get him on his feet. This caterwauling is driving me insane.'

Paul latched onto his father's arm, fury and disgust clear in him. 'What's wrong with you, Dad? Let him be. You've murdered his girlfriend. What do you expect?'

Michael wrenched himself free. 'I didn't kill her. And I expect a little more professionalism from one of my people. He's not even human, so don't waste your sympathy. Nor is she.'

'Not human?' Paul gaped at him.

Shoving past, Michael sent Logan a final, disgusted glare. 'Get out of my way, Paul. I have work to do now. This is a setback that will cost me a lot of time and money. I need to find a replacement for her.' He strode out, leaving Paul standing helplessly over Logan's curled form.

The guards removed my body. I directed my concentration to Calain.

As soon as the life-thread between Logan and I broke, Calain had stopped fighting me. His shadowy form drifted in the *sianfath*, lost and somehow less frightening. Could this be what Aeona meant by setting him free? Would his memories now vanish into the *sianfath* and be lost forever?

For most of my life I'd been afraid of the dark presence in my head; of the inexplicable power and the terrifying capability he wielded. And lately, that had been augmented by the fear of what we could do together. How easily he'd taken me over in Cairns; how close he'd come to destroying thousands of lives. My terror of who he was – and who I was – had hamstrung me; stopped me from saving myself and my family and friends over and over again.

Wouldn't it be best to let him go?

No. Now, faced with the prospect of losing my last connection to my father, I couldn't. He was part of me in more ways than one. I would rather cope with the pain and guard against the potential he had to destroy my world, than let him dissolve into nothing. I could lose everyone I loved and cared about in this place, tonight. I couldn't lose what was left of him, as well.

So this time, I wrapped metaphoric arms around him and carried him with me, reeling in the tie to Tom. I hauled in all the gossamer threads of myself and found my way to where Tom waited, in the cold room, standing over my motionless figure.

As I'd asked him, he stood touching my forehead. But his thin body trembled and tears rolled slow tracks down his cheeks. He swallowed and sniffed, glancing at the door in fear as the sound echoed in the small chamber.

Steeling myself, I pulled energy from the *sianfath*. According to Aeona's book, I'd need at least a normal sidhe's life-energy, thrown all at once into my body, to bring myself back to life. I figured I needed more, given I'd been injured as well. So I drew it in and held it, brilliant and sparkling, entwined within myself and Calain. Now I was light. I was energy and life embodied. Thousands voices whispered the thoughts of thousands of sidhe, past and present, all connected, all part of me.

Then I plunged back, pouring all of me, and all of Calain's lost presence, into the cold flesh lying on the table.

Returning hurt. More than anything I'd ever experienced. Every cell and neural pathway in my body fought me. I burned inside; mind and body afire with the energy, a thousand tiny needles under my skin. But it worked. The gunshot wound closed and Calain retreated behind the block again. My heart restarted.

Gasping, I opened my eyes and found the world darker and colder than before. Tom jumped. He gave a strangled shriek, staring at me.

The energy still fizzed inside me. Too much. I had to get rid of some or it would burn me up. I gripped Tom's arm and poured some into his frail body. I dove deep into his mind and repaired his shields and thought-house, encouraging the *sianfath* to strip away the physical injuries to his brain tissue left by his torture and drugs. I couldn't do a lot about his thought-patterns and self-belief, but perhaps repairing the tissue and nerve damage would help stabilise his brain-chemistry.

With the last of the power, I applied the technique to make myself psychically invisible. Drained, I sagged back onto the table, sniffed and let out a long sigh. Breathing was awesome.

'You're alive!' Tom's whisper was loud in the empty space.

I sat up and patted myself, wrinkling my nose at the bloody shirt's smell and stickiness. 'That was the idea. But I was a bit worried for a few moments there. You did good.' Squeezing his arm, I rolled off the bed and scanned the room.

Three more gurneys were aligned with mine, each with a sheet-draped body lying on it. I'd expected two from my healing of Paul. Who was the third? I lifted each drape and swore as I raised the last one. Guilt and regret closed my throat.

The cloth slithered back. 'I'm sorry, Tom. It's Ian.'

He paled and clutched at the table. 'Did I...? Was it me? I don't remember anything about how we got here.'

I gripped his shoulder. 'No. It was Logan. Eisen activated his Dark gene. Logan doesn't know what he's doing.' At least, I hoped he didn't. I inspected Ian's body and found puncture marks. 'Looks like he was darted as well. He couldn't heal himself. I'm so sorry. This is my fault, Tom. I'll do what I can to set it right.'

He inspected his father's cold, grey countenance and shuddered.

'No. It's not your fault, Rowan.' His jaw hardened and his shoulders lifted. 'You're as much a victim of this shit as I am. This war has been going on for too long. We might not be able to win it here, but we can damned-well win this battle.' He lifted his chin. 'What do we do now? Erin and the others are still out there. How do we get them without alerting Logan?'

'That was the whole point of my dying,' I said. 'It was the only way to break the tie between us. Now Logan won't know what I'm doing. We have a very small window of time and we need to find a way to use it effectively.' I plucked at my wet, cold clothing. 'I'm going to have to change. There's some of these on that shelf.'

Tom blushed and averted his eyes as I shucked the filthy clothing and hid them deep in a rubbish bin. A quick wash at the sink and a drink of cold, metallic-tasting water didn't replace a long, hot bath and a decent meal, but it was better than nothing.

'Right.' I threw back my shoulders. 'Time to see if we can win a battle.'

Armed with nothing more than three scalpels I'd found in the instrument cabinet, I eased the door open and peered out. I was reluctant to use any telepathy or connection to the *sianfath* lest Logan or William sense me. I hadn't gone through that Frankenstein pain to have them alerted to my presence before I'd achieved anything useful. To make sure we weren't recognised by the security cameras, I wrapped a white tshirt over my head like a hood and instructed Tom do the same.

'Do you know which rooms the others are being held in?' I whispered, studying the corridor outside.

Tom, after a moment's thought, nodded. We mapped out a course of action: we would wake Maeve and Jennifer first. We'd need their telekinesis. Then Harry, Anna and Erin. I had hopes Harry would be useful. He was wily old coot and we could use some wily about now.

Logan…well, Logan was a lost cause and I had no idea how to retrieve him, either physically or mentally. Maeve and Erin might. As much as it stuck in my craw to ask them for help, I couldn't see any other way. With all her knowledge of psychology and Erin's understanding of genetics, maybe we could bring him back. But it seemed unlikely and my heart ached at the knowledge I might have to leave him behind.

I checked outside again. Empty. The cold-room stood separate from the double-row of rooms at the other end of the warehouse. In between was a large, open area filled with crates and containers all piled into neat stacks and rows. We'd have to navigate those to get to the rooms, but at least they offered cover.

It must be late. The building had an after-hours feel. Lights were dimmed, and only the hum of airconditioning and the faint ticking of cooling metal and concrete broke the warehouse's cavernous silence.

There were cameras, but there wasn't much I could do about them this time. Any guards I could deal with. We'd have to be quick.

Without lockpicks there was no silent way to open the doors, and no time to waste faffing around, either. We broke the locks. There had to be some advantages to superior strength, after all.

I slipped into Jennifer's room and rummaged in the medicine cabinet until I found the antidote. Injecting her and removing the drip took mere moments, but it felt like an age. Blood thundered in my ears, making it hard to hear any telltale sounds of guards approaching. They must have seen us on the cameras by now.

Unwilling to wait for Jen to wake properly, I threw her over my shoulder and stalked to the next room. Anger mounted as Jennifer groaned and twitched feebly. Who did this sort of thing to a child? What sort of man was Michael Eisen that he thought this justified the ends? I understood his fear of losing Paul, but everyone lost people. It didn't give them the right to torture others in an effort to prevent the inevitable.

I was done. Done with being afraid of Michael and his goons; done with running and hiding. This had to end. Now.

By the time I got to the next door, I was in no mood to even grab the handle. I kicked the door in. It slammed against the wall and the bed's occupant jumped and screamed. I laid Jennifer on the floor, where she blinked vaguely at me. Leaving her, I worked on the straps holding Anna to the bed.

'Sorry, Anna,' I muttered, 'but I've about had enough of this place. It's time to leave.'

'Rowan?' She rubbed her wrists and rose, touching my arm. 'You're alive? But Michael said—'

I laughed shortly. 'The reports of my death were exaggerated – again. C'mon.'

Tom appeared in the doorway, holding Maeve's sagging form, an arm around her waist. His eyes were wild.

'They're coming! What are we going to do? I haven't got Erin or Harry yet.'

'Find out how many.' I surveyed the room. Weapons. There must be something I could use. 'I want Logan ignorant of me being alive for as long as possible.'

Tom's eyes glazed, then widened in horror. 'There are at least forty, coming from all directions, plus Logan and William.'

Beside me, Anna gasped. 'Rowan I—'

'Good,' I said grimly, cutting off her concern.

'What are you going to do?' Tom shifted his weight as Maeve raised her head and squinted at him. 'We can't take them all on.'

'Anna.' I addressed her. 'Get Jennifer and Maeve awake. We need their telekinesis. Tom, go and get Erin and Harry. Get everyone to the storage area near the back door. That's our exit so build a barricade with the crates and deal with anyone who comes in that way.'

'What are you going to do?' Tom repeated, anxiety tightening his voice.

'First I'm going to get us a hostage,' I said through gritted teeth. 'Then I'm going to change this little pawn into a queen of the first order.'

TWENTY-NINE

<Ian? Ian? What's happening? Where are you?>

 ...

Tom dragged the shirt off his head, his face firming into decision. He lowered Maeve into a chair and vanished out the door. Across the hall, another lock splintered. Anna chewed on her bottom lip, her brow furrowing. She opened her mouth then shut it and approached Maeve. She seemed to quite enjoy throwing a glass of water over the sidhe woman.

Within a matter of minutes, my companions had done as I asked and formed a barricade in the open area out of crates, pallets and medical equipment. Jennifer had my scalpels, plus a few more pointy items and was fiercely focussed on the back door. They had stacked several crates against it. Easy enough for a sidhe to move in a hurry, but harder for the men outside. Maeve said nothing and joined her daughter.

I broke into Paul's room and dragged him out of bed. Half-awake and stumbling by my side, he managed a coherent demand for an explanation.

'What the...' He squinted at me as I hauled him over to the others. 'Who the hell are you?'

The t-shirt over my head. I'd forgotten. I pushed it up. 'It's me, Rowan.'

'What? You're dead! I saw you die. How...?'

'Later. Right now I need your help.' I propelled him towards the last gap in the barricade and pointed at the main entrance to the warehouse. 'In about ten seconds forty of your father's men, plus Logan, William and probably your father, are going to storm this building. You're my hostage. I can restrain you if I have to, but I'd rather not. If you're willing to protect us, we might be able to avoid bloodshed. If not, they'll all die.'

'You mean your friends?' He glanced at them.

'No. I mean Michael and all of his men will die.'

'What?' He studied my empty hands. Then he peered through the gap in the crates, at the shivering women, boy-man, teenage girl, and old man hiding there. 'That's ridiculous. What can you possibly do to forty armed soldiers?'

I gave him a bleak smile. 'You don't want to find out, Paul. Your job is to convince your father that I mean it, and that I'll hold you hostage until we're safely out of here.'

His jaw dropped. 'My God. You *do* mean it, don't you? Fine. I'll help. I have no bloody idea what's going on here, but I know my father's not who I thought he was.'

'Good. Because here they come.' I tugged the white shirt over my face again.

Thuds against the blocked door reverberated through the warehouse, followed by shouts. The two other doors burst open and the soldiers rushed in, weapons already raised and pointed. About half carried some sort of semi-automatic rifle. The rest held nine-millimetre handguns. They all wore bulletproof vests. They spread out to form an arc with me and Paul at the centre. I put my arms in the air, watching them.

Jennifer?

~*Y-yes?*~ Even her mental voice sounded scared.

Be ready to deflect bullets. How many do you think you can handle?

~I don't know! Rowan, I can't——~

Yes, you frigging-well can. You're tough, smart and skilled. You've proved that. Time to stop being afraid of who you are, Jen. You are sidhe. Use your gifts. Stop hiding from them.

I felt her hesitate and half-heard the internal debate. I grinned as her fear faded beneath a wall of solid determination. With our thought-window still open so we could communicate, she ignored her mother's questions and moved to the barrier. There she found a spot behind the crates that overlooked the open space.

~Right. I can see about twenty of them.~

Wait. Here. Instead of catching bullets, try this. I sent her a mental image. Her reply giggle was tinged with hysteria.

~That I can do.~

The back door shook again, the steel warehouse wall shaking and thrumming under the impact of something heavy. The crates shuddered. Tom and Harry leaned their weight against them. Erin clung to Anna, trembling. Anna shook her off and hissed at me.

'Rowan! There's something I—'

'Not now,' I snapped back, focussed on the opposite door. Logan, Michael and the big sidhe, William, strode through it.

Michael stalked towards us, glowering.

'Who the hell are you?' He stopped a few feet away, peering at me. 'How did you get in here? Paul? Who is this woman?'

I pulled the white tshirt off my head and smiled at Michael. He blanched, hands raised defensively. Oh yes, Paul had told me his father studied boxing. I'd forgotten. Logan swallowed and whispered my name into the silence that followed.

'How the hell...?' Michael shook himself and straightened, lowering his arms. 'Well, you are full of surprises, aren't you? But it's a good thing you're not dead. Saves me the trouble of finding another one like you.'

I laughed. 'There is no one else like me, Michael.'

He sneered. 'You kids always think that. You're not so special. Everyone's replaceable.'

Beside me, Paul stiffened. 'Even me?' He edged closer to me. Protecting or seeking protection for himself?

'Of course not. What do you think all this has been about?' Michael indicated the warehouse. 'I've spent the last eighteen years building a worldwide business in the medical research and health industry, trying to find a cure for you. And in doing so I realised the potential these sidhe have. Now I'm trying to secure your future, and the world's. Come here.'

I laid a casual hand on Paul's arm. Michael's eyes widened and his lips formed a silent denial.

Paul threw his shoulders back. 'Let them all go, and I will. Hurt any of them and you'll never see me again, Dad. This is insane and you know it.'

'Wait.' Logan elbowed through the line of men, William close by his side. 'Wait. Let me talk to her, Michael.' One corner of his mouth curled up.

'We can't take the chance she'll drain Paul, or you – and my men,' Michael responded.

Logan's mouth twisted. 'She won't risk it. If she does she won't be able to stay conscious. And she's too scared of her ability to do what it takes, anyway. She's bluffing.'

I lifted my chin, trying not to let my anger and trepidation show. He was so damned smug. So certain of himself. As much as I loved him, it annoyed the heck out of me that he thought he knew me so well.

Michael's doubt showed, but he shrugged his agreement.

Logan and William closed the gap between us. I held my ground and sent a quick thought to Jennifer, telling her to be ready. The back door thudded and shook again. Erin and Anna joined the others in holding the crates in place. The noise from their efforts and the smashing of something hard against the outside steel wall echoed into the silence.

Logan jerked his chin at the barricade. 'They'll break through soon, you know. You can't stand against all of us. Give up and I'll make sure everyone lives.'

'And what a lovely life as lab-rats we would have,' I shot back. 'No. Thanks. How about this, instead? Let us go and I won't kill everyone here, including you.'

His smile held the faintest hint of sadness in its condescension. 'We both know you won't do that.'

'I will if you leave me no choice, Logan.' My mouth dried. The steady scorn in his expression showed the inevitability of his answer. He didn't believe me. He was calling my bluff, which meant I couldn't bluff any longer. As far as I could tell, there *was* no other solution. My only hope was to let Calain out so I could use the *shadow-thought* without loss of consciousness. But could I control him? Could I stop him from destroying everyone, not only Michael's men?

'No.' Logan cocked his head. 'You won't risk Anna and Jennifer.'

'You're wasting your time, Logan,' Michael called. 'I have another solution. William. Take him.' The big sidhe wrapped a muscular forearm around Logan's throat and locked a strangle on. Logan struggled but he was outmatched in size and strength. William released the strangle moments before Logan lost consciousness but held the position, ready to put it back on at a moment's notice. His silicon-mask was eerily blank. Logan coughed, his eyes glazed.

I held myself still, watching Michael, keeping my expression calm.

'Let Paul go, or Logan dies,' Michael said. 'And so do the ten others I still have in the other facility here.' He pointed at the door behind him. 'And if you refuse, I will tell my men to open fire on all of you. They're good shots. They won't hit Paul.'

Paul swore. He switched his despair to me. 'I'm sorry. I don't know what else I can do.'

Certainty solidified in me and with it came a deep, perfect calm. 'I do. Get inside the barrier with the others. This is going to get messy.'

'I can't leave you here to face this.' He grabbed my arm, trying to drag me to the shelter.

I twisted free, still watching Michael. 'Go, Paul.'

Something in my face shocked him for he let go, swallowed hard and backed into the gap in the crates.

I lifted my hands. Michael signalled to his men. They settled their guns and took careful aim at me. My heart thudded against my ribs. I resisted the urge to wipe sweaty palms on my pants. Deep inside me, the darkness pushed against the block. The silence of expectation held the warehouse in its suffocating grip.

Jen. Be ready. Would she be able to handle that many guns? *Maeve, help her.*

'Wait.' William shoved Logan aside and closed the gap between us in two long strides. 'Don't kill her.'

Shit. I'd been counting on Michael letting the soldiers shoot. Hoping to get my hands on Eisen in the confusion Jen would create.

One on one with William was so not the plan.

I brought my hands up to a defensive position. He slapped my arm aside easily and seized me by the throat. His finger and thumb pressed into the arteries as he hoisted me up against the crates. I scrabbled at his thumb, uselessly. I struck at the inside of his elbow, but his muscular arm remained rigid. He avoided my kick at a thigh bundle. I gasped for air, weakening.

The block in my mind was strangely quiescent. I was under attack, yet Calain wasn't helping? Same as last time. Why? Was there something special about this particular sidhe?

Then it clicked. Was it possible? Had I really been so blind?

Yes.

So, I was on my own. I couldn't physically defeat someone of William's size and strength. Not with Logan and forty soldiers waiting as well. Which meant the only solution was to open the block and release Calain. But I needed to stay conscious.

The block would have to come down for good.

Then I would find out who I truly was; who Calain's memories made me. Whether I really could control him. My fear of what he might do with the *shadow-thought* was really a fear of what *I* might do with it. My fear that his darkness was actually my own.

I stroked the thick oaken door that held back the terror.

William's fingers tightened. The real world darkened.

Time had run out.

Following Maeve's work in Cairns, I dissolved the door – converting it first from ages-thick oak into pine, then into cardboard, then to cloth and finally to gossamer spiderweb. I ripped it asunder, shredding forever the block that had kept my gifts and Calain's memories imprisoned for so many years.

His shade swept out, bringing with it the memories of a dozen lifetimes, the pain of a thousand losses and the imperative that had driven him for so long: protect me; protect the *sianfath*.

I opened my arms and embraced it all, reeling beneath the weight of six hundred years of responsibility and expectation.

THIRTY

<Logan! You must stop her! She'll destroy us all!>

Maeve, you're a fool.

<But surely you don't want to die any more than we do?>

Right now, I don't give a damn. I've about had it with all of you. Michael was a potential means to an end. It seems I underestimated his stupidity as well.

<Help me stop her, please?>

You created her. And me for that matter. Now you get to live – or die – with the consequences.

I opened my eyes as the world darkened to sepia. I drove the ball of my foot into William's gut, just below his navel. He grunted and released me, bending forward to clutch at his stomach.

Logan moved in before I could finish William. He struck hard against my forearm. My fingers went numb. Logan fisted my shirt, going for a grapple-hold to take me to the ground. I smacked his arm aside with my numb hand and dug my other fingers into his collarbone. He gasped and dropped to his knees, eyes screwed closed with pain.

'And that's where you should be,' I murmured into his ear. 'On your knees before me.'

I struck his temple with my knee and he tumbled into unconsciousness at my feet.

'Shoot her you idiots!' Michael's rage-filled scream bounced off the high ceiling. There was a rustle of cloth. Weapons aimed at me.

With an almighty clatter of hollow metal, forty gun-clips dropped to the concrete. Forty cocking slides shattered. Forty single bullets jumped free from forty chambers and plinked on the ground. Jennifer's work. Without their weapons, the soldiers were rendered harmless. Almost. Only one thing left to do. Their lives were so bright; so very strong. What I could do with that much power.

I, the sum of all things, the embodiment of the *sianfath* and the *ocair*, the truest blend of Calain and Rowan Gilmore, threw my arms wide and laughed. The world's breadth and power lay within my reach. The other-light's glow tempted me. Now it was simple. *Now* I could do what I was born to, so many hundreds of years ago. *Now* I could truly be the *ocair*.

'Rowan?' A familiar voice called to me in fearfilled tones?

Anna emerged from the barricade, her blue eyes stark. Her fingers fluttered, as though she feared to even touch me.

'I am more than Rowan,' I replied. 'I am what we were destined to be.'

'What are you waiting for?' Michael's voice held desperation as he egged his men on. They hesitated, but a few hardy souls pulled out knives and edged forward, eyeing each other and me.

William had recovered and also approached us, his silicon-mask unreadable, blank.

'No.' Anna ignored them, her attention on me. 'You're still Rowan.' She peered at me. 'But you're him too, aren't you? Calain?'

'Together. Yes. Together we can achieve what he set out to. We can destroy the humans and save our people.' Satisfaction glowed in me; a sense of rightness. This was my reason for existing. Our reason.

'No,' Anna repeated. 'You're not Calain. You're a corrupted copy of him. My Calain would never do that. Not to you, not to humans. Would he?'

She tore the mask from William's face.

The man revealed shook his dark head and rubbed a hand over his jaw. Anna gasped. She paled and backed up. The face was not familiar to me. Broad and square-jawed, with short black hair and a crooked nose. The grey eyes were sidhe, but held no spark of the humour and depth that had characterised Calain Gilmore.

'But I thought...' Anna frowned and moved forward again. 'I thought you were him...Calain. You sound like...' She reached towards him but stopped. 'And you move like him. I don't understand.'

'You're right.' I folded my arms. 'It is him – or what's left of him. Isn't it, Maeve?'

Maeve appeared from inside the stacks of crates, her hands twisting together.

'Yes, it's Calain.' Her voice was low and husky. She avoided Anna's shocked, questioning gaze.

'What?' Michael snatched a dagger from one of his men and waved them all forward. 'This is *not* Calain Gilmore. I've seen his image a thousand times. It's burned into my brain. He slaughtered my parents when I was a boy. I would have killed Calain Gilmore the minute he showed up. There is *no* way that's him. You're lying. This is some sort of trick to try and stop me from killing you.'

'No.' Maeve backed away as he advanced. 'I was working as a psychiatric consultant in the UK twelve years ago. I was called in on an amnesia case. It was Calain. After he went overboard off the ferry in the channel. He was alive but he'd no recollection of who he was and he hardly spoke. I recognised him and saw an opportunity. Ian and I...' She swallowed, one hand fluttering at her throat. 'Paid for plastic surgery and gave him a new identity. I taught him how to withstand brainwashing techniques and gave him medication to control the Dark gene. Then we planted him into a Mors Ferrum cell in Britain. A year ago, he was transferred to your cell. He's been our man all along.'

'No!' Michael's face suffused to dark purple. 'You're just trying to turn him against me. You can't. He's not Calain. He's mine and he'll kill you all at my command.' He glared at William. 'Kill them!'

William-Calain took half a step towards Anna, then stopped, frowning.

Jennifer edged out from behind the crates, her grey eyes huge. Maeve grabbed her wrist but Jennifer twisted free.

'William,' Michael said, his voice low and hard. 'Kill them. Finish it, now.'

I smiled. 'He won't kill his wife and daughter, Eisen. He recognised us, even if he doesn't remember exactly who we are. You've lost.'

On the floor, Logan groaned and struggled to his feet. He took one look at William and Michael, scowled and yanked Jennifer to his side. He dug a knifepoint into her throat, drawing a bead of blood. The back door burst open and more men poured in, brandishing more weapons and yelling commands to drop to the ground.

'Tell them to surrender, or I'll kill her, Rowan,' Logan shouted.

I paused, clarity and calm settling my lips into cool disdain. 'She doesn't need my help and she won't surrender.'

Jennifer's eyes narrowed. Logan gargled as his knife-hand twisted, inexorably, towards his own throat and stayed there. The guns in the hands of the new soldiers burst into dozens of pieces and clattered to the concrete.

'I'm not afraid of you, Logan,' Jennifer muttered through clenched teeth. 'I'm not afraid of *any* of you! And nor is Rowan. Are you?'

I laughed. 'Not at all. They are nothing. Watch.'

I drew the bright life from every soldier in the room and gathered it into myself, holding its glittering, pulsing deliciousness tightly in my body. It filled me, prickled under my skin, tasted of lightning, lifted me into the realms of godliness. Fifty soldiers collapsed like stringless puppets. Fifty skulls smacked the ground in hollow succession. Fifty knives rang on concrete; hearts stopped; breath stopped; life stopped. Now there were fifty bags of unremarkable flesh wrapped in black clothing where moments before there had been living humans. Their energy raged inside me, incandescent.

THIRTY-ONE

<Oh, my God. Rowan, stop!>

You really think she'll listen to you now, Maeve? You're more of a fool than I thought.

<Logan!>

'You too, I think, Logan. And you, Eisen,' I said, watching them with disinterest. 'You've both outlived your usefulness.' I thrust my palm against Logan's chest and released a fraction the energy. It burst against his skin in a flash that threw him back. His body impacted a crate with an audible snap of bone. He slumped to the floor, dead or unconscious, it didn't matter.

Jennifer ran to Logan's side and crouched beside him, calling his name.

I swept the others with a cool sneer. 'And perhaps Maeve...'

'Rowan!' Anna stepped in front of me as I reached to take the essence of Eisen and Maeve from their bodies. 'Stop.'

'Why?' Detached curiosity made me hesitate. I had no compunction about killing them. They impeded me. Their lives were meaningless compared to the greater good. I had a task.

Anna cupped my jaw. She flinched at the arc of power that crackled across her fingers, but still ran her thumbs across my cheekbones, her eyes loving, afraid and sad all at once.

'Your choices make you who you are. Your worst moments define who you are, if you let them – remember? Neither my Rowan, nor Calain, are this person. Don't do this, either of you.'

There was no reason to heed her words. I wasn't her daughter or her husband any longer. I was more than both had ever been. The brilliance burned inside me. I was the pinnacle of all that Calain had aimed for. A weapon with which to finish this war for good.

I could destroy Michael's complex, that was easy; that was a start. I could burn him and all his men in it. I could walk out into the world and start the next step in the evolution of mankind. The part where mother Earth fights back. I would be her soldier. Surely that was worth the sacrifice of Rowan and Calain's uniqueness?

Aeona's words echoed from a time long-past, but time was nothing in the *sianfath,* so who could be sure. Perhaps she watched me, still. *His essence is consuming thee and thou'lt need thy full strength to win thy freedom from the Mors Ferrum. Thou dost not need his strength to augment thine own. Thou art strong enow, I promise. Together thou art too dangerous. Release him.*

I surveyed those left standing. Jennifer, her respect fading into fear. Erin, free of her father and clutching now at her damaged brother for support. Maeve, penitent and humbled, tearful. Logan, corrupted and made less by the path down which I had led him. My mother-wife, willing to risk my lethal wrath to try and save me from myself. Michael, being held back by Paul, hurt and willing to hurt even his own son to try and assuage the hole of loss in his heart. And William – no, Calain, - a broken tool being used by others to achieve their own ends.

A battle raged between Rowan's compassion and Calain's ambition. None of these people were important in the grand scheme of things. The world; the Earth and her integrity, that was vital. The most unique individual wasn't worth the trees they sacrificed to feed themselves. And yet, these people…they expected more of me, of Rowan. They had trusted her with their lives, believed in her ability to right the wrongs done. I had her power. My potential was unlimited.

'My worst moments…' I muttered.

'Don't let them define you,' Anna said. 'Let Calain go, please? Let them all go.'

'No!' Michael latched onto my arm, his eyes burning with hunger. 'No. Think what we could do?' He pointed at his men, dead on the floor around him. 'You are the ultimate weapon. You can change the world for the better, and I'll help you do it. Think of what we could achieve with my connections and wealth, and your powers? Everything you ever wanted, we could make happen.'

I hesitated, unbearably tempted.

'Oh!' Anna knocked his hand from my arm. 'You slimy bastard! How *dare* you?' She threw the neatest straight-punch; from the hip, with all her power as I'd taught. Her fist drove into his diaphragm. Coughing and gasping, Michael collapsed.

Exquisite pain sliced through me and I folded as fire flared in my body. The energy inside me. It was too much to hold any longer. I had to decide; had to be rid of it somehow or it would consume me.

Straightening painfully, I pulled William down to my level. Staring into his frowning grey eyes, I touched his forehead. Energy poured from me into him. Carrying his memories, his self, his life story. I entered his mind and stripped aside that which rendered his shield invisible. For the first time, his thought-house appeared. I should have checked sooner, then I would have realised the truth. His protection took the form of Lothien Castle's medieval section. A poor copy, missing most rooms and all of the more recent extensions. Even in his current state, some part of him remembered his roots, if only in pieces. The barest shell of the old Calain sheltered the merest shadow of a man within it.

Carried by the *sianfath*, I walked through the stone walls as though they were insubstantial air. I constructed the missing pieces, rebuilt him, his past, his life as represented by the castle. I added whole wings and rooms, turrets and halls, leaving out only the dungeon. He didn't need that.

Then I Gifted his life back to him; his memories. Silver-green energy raced through darkened, empty halls and rooms, filling them with the light of his own self and the restorative connection to the world from which he'd sprung. As he left me he stripped away the *fartheria* sentinel. Separated from the *shadow-thought's* darkening influence, he became the true Calain again, brilliant, charismatic and intense.

Ghosts of people laughed and danced around me. Fionn's shade swept past, curtsying and brushing my arm with her glimmering-pale fingers. Aeona's lips pressed to my cheek. A thousand others swirled by, carrying the memory of love and loss into Calain's heart again.

Before me, Calain stood rigid, his face twisted into a rictus of pain and wide-eyed fear. He sank to his knees beneath the onslaught of my Gift. Buried his anguish in his hands with a cry that echoed in the vast space.

I withdrew, pulling back into myself, now emptier, lighter, and weaker, all at once. There was something missing. Something that had weighed on me since I was four; a substantial darkness and power gone, forever.

I was free.

Calain lifted his head, blank distance segueing into puzzlement and thence into a strange combination of regret, pain and joy. His gaze fell on me. He whispered my name, Ruadhán, in a voice of wonder that spoke directly to my childhood. He examined the backs of his hands and touched his cheeks.

'Rowan?' Anna's hesitant question drew my attention. She reached out to me. A spark arced between us. She jumped back.

'Don't touch me,' I said. 'It's not safe yet.' I still carried most of the energy of fifty lives, a blazing torch within my body.

'You have to get rid of it,' Maeve ordered. 'Into the forest. Release it before it destroys us all.'

I laughed weakly. 'Shut up, Maeve. You have no idea what you're talking about.' Stretching myself once again into the *sianfath* I returned the energy to the men from whom I'd stolen it. One by one, they cried out in pain as their hearts restarted and their bodies came back to life. I held enough back to weaken them. They would be no threat to us.

Calain, who was William to them, ordered them to lay down their arms, disperse and leave the building. Michael was in no position to argue, especially when Paul reinforced the order with a threat of losing their jobs if they stayed.

'Logan.' I knelt by his side and checked him. The blow had cracked two ribs and his skull. He was bleeding into the brain. But there was no point in curing his body if I couldn't cure his mind.

'Erin.' I waved her over. She came, collapsing to the floor, still trembling.

'Have you found a way to cure the Dark gene yet?'

'I…' She paused and got herself together. 'I think I know what causes it to express, but just using the *sianfath* healing power won't cure anything. It's in how the DNA is folded. Hard to explain.'

'Show me,' I ordered. Spearing through her shields without waiting, I found the knowledge in her mind and withdrew it.

She protested, clutching at her head. I brushed her hurt aside. I had little time to waste for I could only hold this last remnant of energy a few moments longer before it ate through me and left nothing.

'Jennifer, quickly!' It came out as a gasp.

Jennifer hurried to my side, looking anxiously between me, Erin and Logan.

'I need your help. Can you heal him and unfold his DNA if I give you the power?' I placed Erin's knowledge into Jennifer's mind, through her shields.

She flinched, then nodded. Chewing on her lip, she glanced at Maeve.

'But Mother should—'

'I don't trust Maeve, Jennifer,' I said. 'I trust you and Logan trusts you. You've got this.'

'But you fixed Paul,' she whispered. 'Can't you do this, too? I'm scared I'll do it wrong.'

'Paul was luck,' I said. 'I had no idea what I was doing and it was a lot simpler. I could have killed him just throwing power at it like I did. This needs a telekinetic.' I touched her arm. 'Please, Jennifer? Logan needs you.'

She hesitated and squared her jaw, nodding. 'Alright. Give it to me. But slowly.' We knelt on opposite sides of Logan's body. She placed her palm on his chest. She healed his physical injuries easily, then took a deep breath and scowled in concentration, delving into his DNA.

His arm shot up, fingers clamping onto my throat, digging into the blood vessels. I grabbed and twisted. He snarled as his wrist broke with a sickening crunch of bone. Jennifer shrieked and scrambled back. I swung a leg over Logan's hips and dropped my weight onto him. He bridged beneath me. I hooked my feet around his calves and stretched out until he collapsed back to the concrete.

'Stay down you fool,' I grated. I laid an elbow along his jaw and leaned weight into it. He clawed at my arm.

'We're trying to help. Stop fighting me!'

He growled something incomprehensible and dug into the pressure point at my elbow. I yelped. There was no choice. I drew energy from him. Enough to render him unconscious. It flared within me, augmenting the rest. He sagged, his head lolling, heart barely beating under my arm.

'Jennifer,' I panted. 'Do it now, before he wakes again. I can't hold this any longer.'

Wide-eyed, she slid forward and touched his chest.

I scrambled off him and trickled the silvery power into her. Delicately, she taught his cells, told the *sianfath* what she needed of it. It took an agonising length of time and the world vanished around us as we concentrated. For the longest time nothing happened. Behind us, the others stirred and shuffled, their feet scraping on the concrete. We ignored them.

Then Logan's back arched. He scrabbled at the concrete. His mouth gaped in a silent scream and his throat corded as his whole body convulsed. He twitched and slumped into silence, mouth open, eyes closed. Jennifer cried out. She grabbed his head and called his name. Her shoulders sagged. She turned to me in despair.

'I think it worked but I can't reach his mind. He's just…gone. It might have been too much for him.' Tears glistened on her cheeks. 'I'm sorry, Rowan. I tried.' Climbing to her feet she fled to the shelter of Harry's arms, avoiding her mother.

'No!' I cradled his head. 'He's there. He's lost, like Tom was. I can find him.' Holding him still, I speared through his mental shields, seeking the true mind buried somewhere inside. All I found was shame and fear. His house was dark and empty. Shrouded in darkness and lingering horror. I walked through its walls, seeking him in the shadowed lengths of its corridors.

Logan? Logan?

…Rowan?

Come back. You're free now. It's ok.

I can't. I can't be that person again, Rowan. I'm...afraid.

I know. But the Dark gene is suppressed and won't affect you anymore. As you once said to me: trust me, just a little. Come back.

I hurt you. And Jennifer.

I'm ok. We're both ok. We need you. I need you. Please? I can't do this alone.

...

He sighed and his eyes opened. He stared vaguely at the distant ceiling for a few moments before his attention sharpened on me. His hand cupped my neck.

Behind me, Maeve and Tom both uttered warnings. I ignored them and let him pull me into a kiss as gentle and loving as the first one we'd ever shared, deep in the *sianfath's* thrall.

This was the real Logan again.

THIRTY-TWO

<Calain! Do you see what this means? We could make humans—>

-Maeve, close thy mouth. Have you not learned what comes of your interference with my daughter? You, as much as Eisen, are to blame for this. I'll not soon forget what you did to her, to my wife, or to me.-

My tears dripped onto Logan's skin and I buried my face in his neck, sobbing and laughing at the same time. His arms wrapped around, holding me against his chest. Struggling upright, he hauled me to my feet, one arm still around my waist.

'It's ok, Rowan. Really. I'm alright.' He sounded more like himself now, with a hint of male bewilderment at my reaction.

But the pressure of the last two weeks broke in me and I couldn't stop the tears. Another pair of arms enveloped us, and a third. My parents: both of them. That didn't help. I clung to them, helpless, deep sobs wracking my body. Joy and relief intermingled with horror at myself.

My mother pushed the men aside and lifted my chin. She forced me to meet her stern gaze.

'Rowan, enough now. Get control. We have things still to do here.'

Her tone spoke to every moment of my childhood, every reminder that I needed to self-soothe and manage my emotions lest I hurt someone by accident. Taking a long, slow breath, I wiped away the tears with the back of my hand, like a child. Someone produced a tissue. I accepted with a watery laugh.

Flushing, I avoided eye contact with at anyone. I'd been the strong one for weeks now and I'd fallen apart like a kid in front of everyone I respected, and a few I didn't. How pathetic.

Logan gathered me into his arms again. He rested his forehead against mine. 'It's alright, Rowan. We'll be alright now. You did it. Controlled Calain. Even better: you're both free.'

I shook my head, unable to speak through the suffocating weight of emotions.

Not far away, Calain and Anna had been drawn into in a heated discussion with Maeve over what to do with Michael and his entire facility. Maeve and, surprisingly, Anna were for destroying it all and locking Michael away somewhere. Calain was, even more surprisingly, against such actions. Michael curled a lip in silent scorn, guarded now by Harry and a determined Jennifer, who held a scalpel in clear sight. Paul stood by Michael's side, but conflict showed as he listened to the argument. Erin had disappeared. Tom hung around the edges, interpolating a word here and there that everyone ignored.

Anna was right: we weren't through here, yet. Logan caught me close for one last kiss, then released me to join the fray.

'We can't let Michael loose to keep doing what he's been doing!' Maeve indicated the facilities around us. 'He's too close to exposing us all and he won't ever let Rowan or you go, Calain. You *must* listen to me.'

Anna rounded on her. 'No, we *mustn't.*' She prodded Maeve's chest. 'Because of you, my daughter almost died and almost became a mass-murderer. Because of you my husband was made into some sort of double-agent and left us for *fourteen years*. We do *not* have to listen to you.' She subsided. 'But I do agree that Michael has to answer for his crimes.'

Beside her, Calain examined his small, ferocious wife in undisguised admiration. 'Aye, love.' He stroked her cheek. 'Michael must be brought to rights, but we cannot do it through the regular courts or we shall all be exposed, as Maeve said. And we cannot destroy his work.' He spoke with a peculiar precision of tone and inflexion I'd forgotten – as though he monitored each word and its pronunciation before he said it.

'What? Why not?' Maeve frowned at him. 'What he's learned is a danger to every sidhe. He's Mors Ferrum. So far he's been operating alone on this, but if they get possession of what he knows they'll use it against us. The sidhe would be exposed and wiped out within years or even months.'

'We can't destroy his work.' Erin appeared from the hallway to the rooms, carrying a laptop and tapping at the keyboard. 'Because I think he's found something useful.' She spun the screen around and revealed an indecipherable series of graphs and numbers scrolling down the page.

'We can't read that, Erin,' Logan said.

She shrugged. 'I'm pretty sure he's found the unexpressed gene in humans that used to allow them to sense the *sianfath's* flow. His people haven't realised it yet, though. It's been folded, too, so it's not working in humans any longer.' She directed a speculative gaze to me. 'But if you and Jen can fix the Dark gene expression, then you can unfold this, too.'

Maeve gasped, and Harry echoed her. Calain whistled, frowned at Maeve, then glanced at me. He held out a hand. After a moment's hesitation, I let him draw me against his side. He kissed the top of my head and laid his cheek on it, tucking me under one arm and my mother under the other. I remembered his scent. It spoke to a place in my memories that made my chest hurt. My heart filled to the point where I almost started to cry again.

'Fie!' His voice rumbled through his barrel chest. His embrace tightened and dug into my ribs and I flinched. 'She could unfold the DNA in humans, but...'

'What?' Anna looked at him. 'What would it mean? Would it do something awful to humans?'

'Nay.' He shook his head. ''Twould be a blessing for they'd soon *feel* the damage they do to the *sianfath*. It may not repair everything, but 'twould help them to understand the harm they do the world.'

'So, what, then?' Anna said.

Calain grimaced, his expression full of old pain, sorrow and a quickly-smothered inkling of hope. 'To make it worthwhile she'd have to change every human on the planet, and that would kill her long before the task was complete.' His expression shifted to regret, his mouth pressed thin. His arm tightened around me and mine around him.

Part of me found the security of his protectiveness reassuring after the last few weeks' loneliness and fear. Another part resented his assumption he had the right to make decisions for me after all these years away. Still, I couldn't argue with his experience in this matter. He'd watched Aeona die after the abuse of her power.

'There's something else you should know.' Erin broke into the debate, placing the computer down and tapping again at the keyboard. 'I've hacked into Michael's personal files.'

Michael uttered a protest, subsiding when nine people glared at him.

Erin lifted troubled eyes. 'He's already sent our genome sequence to the Mors head offices. Along with the drugs that suppress us and what he knows of all our abilities – which is quite a lot.' She looked at me. 'Even Rowan's *skath-sheel* and Calain's being the *ocair*. And all our blood samples, including Anna's. That means they'll have enough family-related DNA to find the gene for all the female-line gifts we represent – telekinesis, psychometry, precog and shadow-thought. Michael's last email says he sent it all to their head office today, in a courier parcel.' She scowled at the screen. 'To the attention of a Mr Dyson. That's the leader of Mors Ferrum, isn't it?'

A stunned silence met her pronouncement. Maeve collapsed onto a crate. Anna buried her face in Calain's chest. He released me to wrap both arms around her. Logan stepped up behind and held me. Jennifer whimpered and Harry patted her absently on the shoulder, his attention on me.

'Kill him!' Tom's harsh words fell into the quiet, startling everyone. He snatched a knife left behind by one of the soldiers and stalked towards Michael, fire and blood in him. 'Kill him before he does any more damage to us.'

Michael surged to his feet, chest and chin outthrust, scornful sneer curling his lip. Paul raised his fists in a classic boxing stance and stood beside his father, facing Tom. But in his weakened state he would be no match even for Tom.

Harry jumped between them, palms flat on Paul and Tom's chests.

'Now lads, simmer down.' He kept his voice low and calm, catching Tom's eye. 'There's been enough death in the last few days.' He raised his voice a little when Tom uttered a protest. 'Though I admit to feeling the same way and I can't blame you for wanting to kill this *caltena*. But we may yet have a use for him. So be not too hasty.'

Calain and Tom sucked a quick breath at the *Henath* insult. Jennifer giggled and I had to cover my mouth to prevent a chuckle escaping. The crudity, coming as it did from Harry's dignified mouth, broke the rage-filled tension. He hauled the two men apart, then shoved Michael back to sit on the crate. Tom glared and stalked away to sulk in the shadows.

'What use have we for Eisen, pray?' Calain's polite request fell into the space left by Tom's absence. 'I'd as soon have him locked away somewhere he can cause no more mischief.'

Harry bowed. 'He, my lord, is our access to the Mors Ferrum. With him on our side, we can gain entry into their world and infiltrate their organisation. We need to wipe their knowledge of us before it gets out into the world. We must intercept that parcel before its delivery.'

'Don't be ridiculous,' Michael's scoffing reply interrupted them. 'I'm not going to spy for you, *animals.*' He spat to one side. 'You will all be hunted and exterminated – except for her.' He pointed at me while staring at Calain. 'And you. You will get to watch as I turn her into one of my own private pets. She will work for me, on my terms, until she's too weak. Then she'll spend the rest of her days in my labs, and my bed. *That* I will enjoy.'

A ripple of shock swept through his entire audience. Only Logan's tightened embrace stopped me launching myself at Michael. Before I could break free, Calain spoke. Although his hands fisted at his sides, his voice was calm, polite.

'For an intelligent man in the middle of nine people who each have several reasons to hate him, you're behaving in a remarkably stupid manner. Could it be, mayhap, that you're hoping to goad us into killing you?'

Michael glowered and said nothing.

Calain smiled pityingly. 'I suspected as much. Well, now we have a use for you, I shall take delight in keeping you alive. For 'twill vex you extremely.'

Erin let out a crack of laughter that startled all of us. 'I can tell you why he'll help us.' She grinned at Michael. 'I've accessed his son's blood tests. They sequenced his DNA, but they failed to notice something important.' She sneered. 'Presumably because it never occurred to Michael to check for it in his own son.'

'Oh?' Calain prompted her.

Erin turned her irony on Michael. 'Your precious son is one of us. About twelve percent of his DNA is sidhe – on the Y chromosome. So it's from *your* contribution to his existence. Which means you're one of us, too, as much as it pains me to say it. Choke on that, you jerk.'

Tom let out a hysterical giggle and collapsed, pointing at Michael and laughing until he was left breathless on the floor. The rest of us gaped in shock. Michael himself said nothing, his jaw sharp and his expression sickened.

Calain cleared his throat and put Anna gently to one side. His very size and presence commanded attention and everyone gave it to him. I watched in somewhat resentful admiration as he ordered my team around in preparation for departure. Erin, he sent to gather all the computer data she could find and destroy the rest, including any cloud-drive backups. Tom, he instructed to recover Ian's body. Maeve and Jennifer were to release the other sidhe held hostage. All of Michael's men had now evacuated the complex and there was no danger. Harry, he first greeted properly and with great affection, then he set to restraining Michael in such a way that he could still be transported but would give us no difficulty.

Finally, he came to Paul and paused. Calain heaved a regretful sigh and rubbed at the back of his neck.

'Lad, I'm not quite certain what to do with you.' He indicated Michael. 'It's plain you've had nothing to do with your father's plans, but I cannot be sure where your allegiance lies. What say you?'

Paul cleared his throat and straightened. 'Sir, I...I don't know what a sidhe is, but if it's someone like Rowan, then I'd be proud to claim heritage. After what I've seen and heard tonight, I'll happily disown my father and everything he's done.' He took a step away, putting physical as well as metaphorical distance between himself and his father.

'Paul!' Michael's exclamation held pain and anger as well as disappointment. 'I've done *all* of this for you! How dare you abandon me? I had to do it, or I would have lost you, too.'

Paul eyed him pityingly. 'You never – not even once – asked me what I wanted, Dad. Not once, my whole life. You were so sure my life was more important than everyone else's that you were prepared to kill dozens, even thousands, in my name. Do you think I want that on my conscience? If you'd raised me in full awareness of what you were doing, you could have brainwashed me into agreeing with you. But you kept me in the dark and this is what comes of it. You *do* lose me. For good. I don't want to see you again, ever.'

'But they're monsters.' Michael snatched at Paul's arm. 'You saw what she did to my men. She sucked their lives out.' He pointed at Calain. 'And *he* murdered my parents.'

Paul twisted free. 'Maybe. I only have your word for that. And as for Rowan.' He studied me thoughtfully. 'I saw her bring them back to life as well. And spare yours.' He eyed his father, sick disgust clear in his expression. 'But I'm not sure why after what you've done to her. And I know you forced her to cure me by holding her family and friends hostage. You might be able to justify your actions, Dad, but I can't.'

He showed his back to his father and faced Calain, but there was pain as well as resolution in him. Harry led Michael away, out of sight and earshot.

THIRTY-THREE

Is it true, Calain? What Michael said about you killing his parents?
*   -...I did not set the fire that killed them, no, Ruadhán.-*
Why does that sound like you're leaving something out?

Calain gripped Paul's shoulder. 'I'm sorry, lad. This isn't easy on you, either, I know. What can we do to help?'

Paul shrugged. 'Take our jet and get yourselves to wherever you need to go. If you can ditch it in the ocean somewhere I'll have my father declared missing in the crash and then you can keep him.' His shoulders drooped. 'Don't hurt him? He's still my father.'

'Aye, lad.' Calain drew him into a rough hug. 'But you're by far the more honourable man.'

Paul broke free. 'Did you kill his parents?'

Calain met his eye calmly. 'Nay, lad. 'Twas the Mors Ferrum themselves. Dyson ordered it, I understand. Their house was burned, with them in it.'

Paul blanched. 'But why?'

Calain rubbed the back of his head. 'I don't know all the details, for I'm not privy to Dyson's mind. But the Eisens were trying to leave the organisation. Your grandfather had just discovered his sidhe heritage. I was helping them. Trying to find a place where they and their son could be safe. Michael was a babe of three. Dyson took him and raised him in the belief I had killed his parents. Set him a-hunting me and mine.'

'Oh, my God,' Paul murmured. 'Who would do something like that?'

I glanced at Maeve, who had the grace to blush.

Calain gripped Paul's arm. 'It's a war that's gone on a thousand years and more. One that needs an end if the sidhe are to be safe and save the humans from themselves. For neither human nor sidhe can survive much longer if things continue as they are.'

'Well,' Paul said bitterly, 'I'm out of it. You can count on that.'

'Aye, lad.' Calain smiled at him in sympathy. 'But it may not be so easy. Be wary. Those close to your father will be privy to his allegiance. Watch your back.' He slapped Paul's shoulder. 'Where are my manners? I've yet to thank you for helping my daughter. Please, accept my thanks and go with a good heart. If you ever need to reach us, leave a message at Lothien Castle in Ireland. 'Twill get to me. Here.' He tossed a set of keys to Paul. 'Your father's carkeys.'

Paul caught them and flicked them into the air twice. He raised a questioning brow at me. I freed myself from Logan's embrace and threw my arms around Paul's waist. He returned my hug but sighed when we drew apart.

'Sorry it didn't work out so well – us, I mean.' He shrugged.

I chuckled. 'Hardly your fault. Thank you for helping me get free before. And for standing up against your father. That took guts.'

He grimaced. 'More than you know.' He scratched at the scruffy, three-day growth on his chin. 'I don't know what I'm going to do now, though.'

A light cuff on the arm sent him staggering with a protest.

'Sorry,' I said. 'Finishing high school would be a good start. We've missed a few weeks and you've got a company to run once you're done.'

'Oh, man.' He groaned. 'I hadn't thought of that. Well, there goes my plan of backpacking around Europe in my gap year. Now I don't get one. Crap.' He hesitated, gave a half smile and kissed me on the lips. His cheeks flushed and he glanced at Logan. 'Take care of yourself, Rowan. If you ever get sick of this guy, let me know. And keep my phone number, in case you need anything.'

'I will,' I said. 'And I promise we won't let anything happen to your dad.'

His smile broadened, coloured by wonder. 'You're amazing, Rowan. After all he did to you.'

I hugged him again. 'He was trying to protect you. A father will do a lot to protect their child. Besides, Michael raised you, and you're pretty decent, so he can't be all bad.'

He kissed my cheek, flicked a jaunty salute and strolled away.

'Paul!'

He glanced back, lips curving up.

'Can you stop that parcel Michael sent?'

'Not sure.' He tilted his head. 'If that Erin girl found a tracking number tell her to text it to me. I'll see if I can get his PA to contact the courier in the morning.'

He blew me a kiss before vanishing out the side door, into the thick darkness outside.

Harry returned. 'My lord? Tom, Maeve, Erin and Jennifer, along with all the released captives, await us outside. Tom has found several vehicles and Maeve has modified the memories of the captives to prevent our discovery.' He bowed to Calain. 'My lord, I beg your leave to accompany you on your journey.'

Calain opened his arms wide. 'Harry, dear friend, you don't even know where we're going. Besides, what would those two children do without you now? You've always served the Silverblades. You can't jump ship now.'

Harry's mouth twitched. 'Now, sir, you know I wouldn't be. I'd often wondered, but I wasn't sure until I saw young Ruadhán, here. She's almost the spit of Miss Aeona and I knew then, of a certainty, who you were.' He grimaced. 'But you do have the right of it. Miss Erin and Master Tom are not fit to live alone yet. Perhaps, when they are…?'

Calain embraced the old man. 'Then, yes. You're always welcome in my household, Harald, you know that. Thank you for looking after my daughter.'

With a soft laugh, Harry disengaged. 'No, sir. 'Twas the other way around, I assure you. I hope you are very proud of her, because I am.' He beamed at me and wrapped me in a swift, hard hug. A suspicion of tears lurked in his red-rimmed eyes and he kissed my forehead. 'Be safe, child.' He hurried out the door.

Four of us remained. Calain frowned at Logan, who stiffened.

'So, young Logan Freyson,' Calain drawled, 'what do you have to say for yourself?'

'Enough, Calain.' Anna's smile was sympathetic. 'Don't tease him. You can't come in our lives after fourteen years and act like you're still head of the household.'

Calain's looked down his nose. Anna's chin lifted.

'You left us, Calain. Even before you were found by Maeve and made into her puppet. That's not something we're going to get over in a hurry.' She put an arm around my waist. 'It's been the two of us for a very long time. Rowan is a woman grown. Neither she, nor Logan, have to answer to you for anything they've done. There are more important things to do than intimidating them.'

After a long, tense silence, Calain brightened into rueful acceptance. He bowed to all three of us.

'Accept my apologies. This has been a somewhat...' He scrubbed at the back of his neck in a familiar gesture. '...unsettling day for all of us.'

Logan laughed. 'That's the understatement of the year, sir.' He grasped my fingers, interlacing them so our palms touched. I shielded myself, unable to bear any precogs now. I had a feeling the future was going to be difficult enough without trying to understand it tonight. Bone-deep exhaustion, held at bay by adrenalin and fear, crept into my body.

'Where do you intend to go next?' Logan held me firm against his side as I leaned into him. 'Rowan needs rest and you'll want her and Jen to correct your Dark gene before we go much further.' There was a hint of steel in his voice. 'That's what started her on this path, isn't it? You dumped your memories on her and left because you feared what you might become?'

Now Calain's silence held a hint of menace as he drew himself to his full height and looked down his nose at Logan. There was a long moment of tension, then Calain's gaze flicked to me then slid uneasily away. He sighed.

'Aye. And I'm sorry for all of it, even though it had to be done.' He touched my shoulder, his expression immeasurably sad. 'You've no idea how sorry.'

'I know,' I said. I sagged against Logan, wanting very much to be done with all of this; to be somewhere alone and quiet where I could process everything and work out what to do next. He kissed my temple and held me tighter.

'Hang in there. This will be over soon and we can regroup,' he murmured.

'No, we're not done yet.'

'What do you mean?' Logan turned to me. 'Are you alright? Precog?'

'No. But I know where the Mors Ferrum headquarters is based. Harry's right. We have to get that package and wipe all information about us from their databases.'

'How could you possibly know where they are?' He blinked at me. 'Even Michael didn't. Or, at least, that's what he said.'

'He knows something. Erin found it in his files.' I stared into darkness, in the direction she'd gone with the others. 'I was Reading her as she was reading the laptop. The parcel is addressed to a receiving office in Florence, Italy. It didn't say where the headquarters are, but it's a place to start.'

'And she didn't say anything?' Now it was his turn to frown. 'Why?'

I shrugged. 'She's angry and hurt and scared. She wants to get back at the Mors Ferrum, and at you and me for dragging her into this and getting Ian killed. She's going to want to come with us. And, Maeve will, too.'

He screwed up his nose. 'Yes, I suppose she will.'

'Why?' Calain interrupted. 'I assumed Maeve would prefer to stay out of this. She never had a taste for violence, for all she's had a dozen or more Hunters in her keeping for training. She rarely gets involved in their assignments. I was surprised to see her here. Why would she come to Italy with us?'

I glanced at Anna. 'Because her son is there – your son, Dante. She'll want to make sure I fix his Dark gene.'

'Son!' Calain's jaw dropped. 'She had a son without telling me!'

Anna pressed her lips together.

'A hundred and fifty years ago,' I rushed to add.

'And I think we'll need his help,' Logan added. 'He's in Rome so he probably knows already where the Mors Ferrum's headquarters is. His specialty is covert operations and retrieving captured sidhe. His telepathy is unusual. It's a deep-level group-telepathy that makes communication in his teams infallible and instant.'

Nodding, Calain sighed. 'Very well. We'll cross that bridge when we come to it, though I see we have a lot to talk about.' He raised one brow at Anna, who returned a touch of frost. She did, however, take his hand. He paused and slapped at his pocket.

'I forgot.' He withdrew something from his pocket and held it out to me. 'Yours, I believe. You'll have to show me how to use it. Nice little weapon.'

I plucked free my karambit and weighed it. 'Thanks.'

Calain gave me a hesitant half-smile and headed with Anna towards the exit. I slid the knife into my bra-sheath and watched them leave. Having him back in our lives would take some getting used to.

Logan waited until they were out of earshot, then eyed me with worry creasing his brow.

'Rowan, I don't know how to apologise to you. The things I did, and said. They're unforgivable.' Faint hope lit his expression. 'But when you brought me back. The way you looked at me. Is there a chance we can put this behind us?'

I smiled wearily. 'You're still being an idiot, Logan. I knew it wasn't you.' I grimaced. 'Besides, I'd seen it coming. No surprises. I just didn't know *when*.'

'But it *was* me,' he protested. He paced a few steps away and shoved his fingers through his hair. His eyes were haunted, his face drawn and haggard. 'I mean…I *felt* normal. It all made complete sense at the time. I even still loved you. And when you predicted I'd kill you…Christ. That made me stop and wonder what the hell I was doing.'

Chuckling I wrapped my arms around his neck and kissed his cheek. 'I was hoping that would mess with you a little.'

'When you died…' His voice broke and he caught me roughly in his arms, kissing me hard and urgently. Raising his head at last, he kissed me once more, gently. 'Don't do that again, ever. Now Calain's out of your mind and that block is gone, you should have full control over your gifts. You won't have to put yourself in that sort of danger again. Promise me?'

I held his face and shut out the images trying to blossom in my head.

Not yet. Not yet.

I kissed him. 'I can't promise, Logan. I have a feeling things have just begun to get dangerous.'

He leaned back, frowning. 'What does that mean?'

I studied the warehouse's vast emptiness and dark corners. The metal roof pinged and creaked as evening cooled into night.

'Yes, the block is down and the *fartheria* – the sentinel that corrupted Calain's memories – is gone.'

'So?' Logan stroked my back. 'Isn't that a good thing?'

A crate seemed inviting, so I sat on it, weary beyond belief. 'I still have Calain's memories. I don't know how to get rid of them. All I could do was Gift them to him, and that leaves a copy. And embedded in his memories, are Aeona's.' I pressed my palms against my temples. 'I've got seven hundred plus years of violence and death locked away in a back room.'

Logan sat beside me, worry shadowing him again. 'But without the *fartheria* it shouldn't be a problem, should it?'

I leaned forward and rested my head on my palms. 'I don't know. I've got the memories contained but I don't know whether they can still affect me. But the biggest thing is that I can use the *shadow-thought* fully now. Before, I couldn't use it without unbearable pain, or letting Calain's doppelganger loose on the world. So I used it as little as possible.'

'Oh, my God.' Logan groaned, smacking his forehead. 'You asked Michael why Calain didn't capture you all at Ian's house. I've just worked out why.' When I looked askance at him, he continued. 'Michael knew nothing about Calain being there. Calain must have been sent by Maeve. She was trying to force you to use the *shadow-thought* for her benefit. Hoping a threat to Jen and the others would do it. She'd never seen it in action as a weapon. She probably wanted proof of what you could do.'

With a resigned laugh, I tugged on a stray lock of hair behind my ear. 'She's a piece of work, alright. But she's not what I'm worried about now.'

'So?'

'So now there's nothing to stop me.' I shifted away, cold and alone. 'Nothing but my own morality and ethics. I'm not sure that's enough to keep me on the right track. I know myself. I know what I'll do if someone threatens you, or Anna, or Jen. I'll kill to protect you. Without a second thought. If anything, I'm more dangerous now, than ever.'

Logan paled, hesitated, then closed the gap between us and held me close.

'We'll work it out, Rowan. I promise. You chose the right path tonight, even when you were under corrupt-Calain's influence. To me, that proves who you really are.' He kissed my temple. 'Let's go join the others. We have a lot to talk about.'

I said nothing, letting him lead me out, into the darkness.

I am the Light.

I've released the Shadows that woke in me, but I'm not yet free of them, or of the Mors Ferrum.

And the world isn't free of me.

THE END

Other books by Aiki Flinthart

Discover other titles by Aiki Flinthart at:
www.aikiflinthart.com

The Ruadhán Sidhe Novels
(YA Urban Fantasy)
Shadows Wake (#1)
Shadows Bane (#2)
Shadows Fate (#3)

The 80AD series
(YA Adventure/Fantasy)
80AD Book 1: *The Jewel of Asgard*
80AD Book 2: *The Hammer of Thor*
80AD Book 3: *The Tekhen of Anuket*
80AD Book 4: *The Sudarshana*
80AD Book 5: *The Yu Dragon*

The Kalima Chronicles (YA Adventure/Fantasy)
IRON (#1)
FIRE (#2)
STEEL (#3)

Romance/Adventure stories
Sold!

Short Story Anthologies
Return
Like a Woman

Connect with me on Facebook
Twitter: @aikiflinthart
Instagram: Aikiflinthart

Shadows Fate

Book 3 of the Ruadhán Sidhe Novels

CHAPTER ONE

The engines screamed their defiance to the wind and sky. Our voices joined in as we succumbed to the terror of dying in this plane, scattered in broken pieces on the sparkling Mediterranean. I clutched my seat armrests until the leather tore. The hard plastic underneath broke and crumbled into shards.

-*Hang on everyone. We're going in. Maeve, Jennifer, now would be a good time to slow us.*-

<*We're trying, Calain.*> Maeve's hysteria-edged reply thrust into my head. <*We just don't have enough strength or connection to the* sianfath *to control something this big and heavy.*>

Beside me, Logan turned stoic grey eyes my way. His fingers wrapped over mine, crushing. The plane juddered and bounced in an airpocket. Oxygen masks fell from the ceiling and dangled, swaying. In the cockpit, something popped. Calain swore aloud, struggling with the controls. The acrid scent of electrical-fire smoke wafted through the small cabin. An alarm sounded, strident and piercing.

Jennifer burst into tears. 'I can't do it, Mother. I just can't!'

'You *can* and you *will*,' Maeve snapped.

Only Maeve's sharp profile was visible across the aisle but even I could tell she was lying. She twisted and looked back at me, fearful.

'Shit.' I closed my eyes and tried to calm my heart's hammering.

'Five minutes to impact,' Calain shouted over his shoulder. 'Prithee ladies, focus yourselves or we all may perish here.'

I distanced myself from the chaos around and sought the *sianfath*, the life-connection binding all of us to the natural world. I should be able to act as a conduit and feed its power to Maeve and Jennifer to bolster their telekinesis.

But we were over the ocean, not near the forests so integral to the sidhe's connection to the Earth. While there was life in the ocean, it was too scattered for me to draw on.

Maeve's right. We're too far from the forests. I—

<Go beyond, Rowan, Maeve cut in. *The block in your mind is gone. You have the ability to extend much further than you've done before. You could reach around the whole world if you needed to. The coast isn't far. Draw from there.>*

But you'll need massive amounts of energy. People could die if I'm not careful.

<We will die if you don't try!>

I swore.

<Join with Jennifer and I in the lorntinn, she added. *Being connected in the unity with us will make it easier to control the flow and anticipate our needs.>*

I hesitated. Joining with others in the *lorntinn* meant opening my deepest shields, exposing my heart and fears to Maeve. I didn't trust her enough to do that. It might make things a little easier, but it would also give her too much knowledge she could use to manipulate me, later.

I can do it without the lorntinn, I returned.

Her fingers whitened on the seat arm as the plane jolted again. *<Fine. But remember, you* must *hold back a little power for yourself. Without that regulator organ, releasing all the energy to us could leave you with a shortfall.>*

Shut up and let me concentrate. I shut her out and focussed.

Logan squeezed my hand. I tugged free to better keep him from harm. Blowing a thick breath, I stretched further, past the silent depths of water, west to the coast of Italy. Further than I'd ever tried before, attenuating myself into the *sianfath*, stretching thin the anchor that held me to my body; risking losing myself in the rush to save my family. There, at the edges of my extension, the flare of orange non-light indicating humans. A brilliance, a seductive temptation of concentrated energy, drawing me like a moth.

'Three minutes to impact!' Calain's voice had lost its calm. Beside him, in the copilot's seat, my mother called my name in tones of desperation. The plane's juddering increased as it bounced through the thick ocean air. Calain fought to keep the nose up.

There was no time to seek further. I skimmed the fierce essence of human life from the city. The orange brilliance dimmed. The power of thousands of bodies swelled in mine, pricking beneath my skin, tasting of ozone and clouds. I was energy, life, potential. I could do anything.

'Maeve,' I screamed over the din, 'get ready. I've got more than I can handle so we have to do this fast.'

Two silver-green tendrils poured from me, into Maeve and Jennifer. The sidhe women stiffened in their seats. Maeve gasped and Jennifer let out a terrified scream. The energy roiled around their bodies, finding ways in, filling them until they glowed with it. Wisps of smoke coiled up from their clothing. The smoke detector in the cabin added its ear-piercing alarm to the chaos.

'Control it, Jennifer!' Maeve commanded. 'Or it will burn you, inside and out. Use it to power your telekinesis.'

'It's too much!' her daughter cried. 'I don't know how to—'

'One minute!' Calain's roar cut across her.

Jen! I threw the thought at her, pushing it through her mental shields. *Remember the training we did in Brisbane. This is no different. Your go-to move was to push in front and behind at the same time – to balance. Remember Newton's law? Do the same thing: some down against the ocean, some up against the plane.*

Jen's fear-filled thoughts settled into clarity. She thrust and the plane jolted upward, tilting to one side. For a moment the ocean loomed in my window, white-capped waves just fifty or sixty metres beneath the wingtip. Calain swore and twisted at the controls, trying to compensate for Jen's uneven push.

Maeve's jaw clenched and the plane righted itself. I fed both women more energy. Our descent slowed. Maeve's lips drew back from her teeth in an animal snarl. Sweat beaded on her smooth forehead. Jen whimpered.

The plane lurched and dropped a sickening few feet.

I drew more energy. The city's orange reservoir of life dimmed further, blackening to death in a few specks. I groaned but fed Maeve and Jen, regardless. The plane levelled again, slowing until we moved at no more than the speed of a car; then a walk.

Calain leapt from his seat, bending to exit the cockpit. His head brushed the ceiling as he straightened in the cabin. His broad shoulders filled the door. He tugged at the external door control mechanism.

'Everyone ready? Maeve, release us. We'll only have a few minutes to evacuate once we hit water so keep calm.'

Maeve nodded, the muscles on her neck and forearms corded.

Calain braced himself. 'Go.'

The plane dropped the last few feet onto the water. The crash broke my concentration and I released my connection to the city. Logan reached for me.

'Don't!' I panted. 'There's still too much in me. Get out.'

Maeve groaned and whispered a plea for help. She and Jen both still had too much energy as well. I could hold more. They could only channel it. Without anything to expend it on, the power would backlash and destroy them. It would do the same to me, just a little slower. I pulled it back from their bodies and squirrelled it away inside myself. Maeve slumped in her seat, her ridiculous yellow lifejacket rucked up around her neck.

'Mother!' Jen shook Maeve.

My mother, Anna Gilmore, emerged from the cockpit. I gestured urgently at Calain and the door. He yanked it open and hurled it out. He activated the self-inflating life raft and threw that out, too.

Water lapped at the door, splashing into the cabin.

'Logan,' I said, 'get Maeve and Jen out.'

He hesitated then scrambled out of his seat.

Water sloshed over the door frame as the weight balance changed. Anna gasped and retreated. Calain picked her up and hurled her out. Her scream ended in a splash.

Two seats forward, Erin Fairchild stood and rushed to the door, leaping past Calain without hesitation.

'Hey!' Tied to the seat in front of me, Michael Eisen's efforts to free himself shook the chair. 'What about me? Get me out of here!'

Calain gave him a sardonic look. 'I'd far rather let you drown with your plane, Eisen. But we need you for the moment. Cease your caterwauling and hold still.' He drew a knife from his pocket, flicked it open, and slashed the bonds holding Eisen to his seat. Calain jerked his head at the door.

'Out.'

Michael complied, glaring at Calain as he edged past.

Logan, carrying Maeve over his shoulder, jumped into the ocean. Jen followed, staggering as a wave surged beneath the plane. One wing dug into the water and the craft listed dangerously.

Once she was gone, only Calain stood by the door. 'Come, daughter,' he urged me.

I stood in the aisle, clutching at the seat backs and clinging to the ragged edges of self-control. Power pulsed through my body. Too much to manage and my connection to the *sianfath* was lost so I couldn't feed it back to the city. It had to be released, but how?

'Go,' I managed, through gritted teeth. 'I can't hold the energy any longer. At least I can use it to destroy the plane.'

If search parties found the plane intact the accident would be suspicious and our death announcements even more so. If our activities in Italy were to succeed, I needed to be invisible. Dying was the best way.

Calain stepped towards me, brow furrowing over intense grey eyes.

'Do it from outside. You can't stay in here.' The plane rocked violently and he staggered. 'Hurry!' Water poured into the door and the nose tilted, plunging into the cobalt depths.

'I have to be touching it to feed the energy,' I said. My legs trembled with the effort of holding myself up against the incline. 'Otherwise it'll go into the water and be wasted. You need to get clear.'

'God's blood!' Calain growled. From outside, Anna's voice screamed our names. Calain dived into the water and I was alone.

I staggered towards the door as the cabin creaked and shook around me. Water poured in and the nose tilted further. My feet slipped. I hit the floor and slid, catching at a seat frame in desperation. The metal cut cruelly into my skin. Muscles in my shoulder tore and burned like the power within me.

The plane was almost vertical in the ocean, the front windscreen looking into the abyss, the exit in clear air. Water boiled, rising up through the cabin towards me. I sucked three long, deep breaths and jack-knifed my body, flinging myself towards the door. My fingers caught the edge. Saltwater poured over the lip again, blinding me. I fought the urge to gasp for air and held what I had in my lungs.

The door submerged and the plane hung, suspended by the air bubble trapped in the tail. I wriggled into the clear water, my body heavy with the personal items I carried, strapped to my waist. I grabbed the doorframe again, this time from the outside.

For a moment the plane and I hung in gentle, perfect accord with the icy water, floating. Creaks and groans of twisting metal echoed through the liquid grey-blue. Sunlight shimmered past me in flickering beams that softened the aircraft's sharp lines and vanished into darkness.

My lungs ached. My body and mind burned from within. I couldn't wait any longer. Hopefully the others were out of the water.

Silver-green energy poured through me into the metal. The aircraft's unliving body resisted energy meant for the organic. The aluminium glowed red. Water bubbled. Agonising pain lanced through my hands and air cascaded from my lips. I held on grimly, changing the energy's shape, seeking a way to drive it between atomic bonds. There. The silver-green changed to a dull grey and drove into the metal. The heat spread. Energy flashed through the frame, breaking seams and tearing bolts. The life-force of thousands of humans ripped apart the jet's body with the crackling shriek of rending metal, and broke it into a dozen pieces.

The doorframe tore from my grip and slipped into darkness. With barely enough strength left to move my arms, I struck out for the surface. The sun's shimmering-white disc overhead seemed an impossible distance. Too far. Lethargy weighted my limbs. I'd expended too much energy; forgotten to keep any for my body. I hadn't the strength to get to the surface. My mouth opened. I had to breathe.

End of Chapter 1

Shadows Fate will be released in mid 2018

www.aikiflinthart.com